A commotion in the stre[...] Lair drew Asa's attention. Two men stood face to face, shouting at each other, fists clenched. The small crowd egged them on, taunting and jeering.

"Knives!" The smaller of the men thrust out his chest, jutted his chin belligerently and yelled even louder.

"You picked a good way to die. Winner takes all!" The second man stood a head taller and weighed fifty pounds more. From his clothing, he was a mule skinner. His opponent dressed fashionably enough, but Asa suspected he wasn't anything more than a shopkeeper who had come to Golden Junction to make his fortune. More than one sitting at the poker tables had sold their business in another town to get the buy-in. For them it was an all-or-nothing gamble.

Most ended up with nothing.

"I'll cut you up good!"

The mule skinner thumbed his nose and did what he could to gin up support in the crowd. Neither looked capable of lasting more than a few minutes in a serious poker game.

That meant they had to find other ways to corner all the chips. If Asa understood the challenge, one of them was fixing to die.

He caught his breath when both men dumped their chips on the boardwalk in front of the saloon. The small mountain drew him. A quick estimate made the combined trove worth at least twenty thousand dollars. Asa forced himself to look back at the men willing to kill each other for that much money. It was a princely sum, but to wager your life? Asa shook his head sadly at the fact that anyone had come to such an end.

RALPH COMPTON
NEVER BET AGAINST
THE BULLET

A Ralph Compton Western by
JACKSON LOWRY

BERKLEY
New York

BERKLEY
An imprint of Penguin Random House LLC
penguinrandomhouse.com

Copyright © 2020 by The Estate of Ralph Compton
Penguin Random House supports copyright. Copyright fuels creativity, encourages
diverse voices, promotes free speech, and creates a vibrant culture. Thank you for buying
an authorized edition of this book and for complying with copyright laws by not
reproducing, scanning, or distributing any part of it in any form without permission.
You are supporting writers and allowing Penguin Random House to continue to
publish books for every reader.

BERKLEY and the BERKLEY & B colophon are registered trademarks of
Penguin Random House LLC.

ISBN: 9780593100653

First Edition: June 2020

Printed in the United States of America
1   3   5   7   9   10   8   6   4   2

Cover art by Chris McGrath
Cover design by Steve Meditz
Book design by George Towne

THE IMMORTAL COWBOY

This is respectfully dedicated to the "American Cowboy."
His was the saga sparked by the turmoil that followed the
Civil War, and the passing of more than a century has by no
means diminished the flame.

———◈———

True, the old days and the old ways are but treasured memories, and the old trails have grown dim with the ravages of
time, but the spirit of the cowboy lives on.

———◈———

In my travels—to Texas, Oklahoma, Kansas, Nebraska,
Colorado, Wyoming, New Mexico, and Arizona—I always
find something that reminds me of the Old West. While I am
walking these plains and mountains for the first time, there
is this feeling that a part of me is eternal, that I have known
these old trails before. I believe it is the undying spirit of the
frontier calling me, through the mind's eye, to step back into
time. What is the appeal of the Old West of the American
frontier?

———◈———

It has been epitomized by some as the dark and bloody
period in American history. Its heroes—Crockett, Bowie,
Hickok, Earp—have been reviled and criticized. Yet the
Old West lives on, larger than life.

———◈———

It has become a symbol of freedom, when there was always
another mountain to climb and another river to cross; when
a dispute between two men was settled not with expensive
lawyers, but with fists, knives, or guns. Barbaric? Maybe.
But some things never change. When the cowboy rode into
the pages of American history, he left behind a legacy that
lives within the hearts of us all.

—*Ralph Compton*

CHAPTER ONE

A SA NEWCOMBE TRIED not to look down. A spill
down the rocky precipice meant death. With any
luck, it would be fast, quick, but he doubted it. A body
tumbling to the bottom of the five-hundred-foot ravine
would bounce and tumble and leave the poor wight
broken and bleeding—and not dead. Not right away.

"Until sundown. A man falling down there'd be like
a snake and not die until sundown." He swallowed
hard and closed his eyes. His sure-footed mule plod-
ded along and ignored its rider.

His traveling companion called back to him, "You
ain't gettin' cold feet, are you? There's no way to back
out now. We're committed."

Asa forced himself to open his eyes. It was impossible not to glance over the brink and wonder which of
the jagged, rocky outcroppings his body would hit as it
bounced down to the rapidly flowing river at the bot-

tom of the canyon. He decided all of them would be painted with his blood. He blinked and concentrated on the man ahead of him on the three-foot-wide trail. That was the safest way to travel, even if the short, scruffy stranger he had set out with from the Mosquito Pass railroad depot wasn't anything worth looking at. In spite of the cold, stiff wind blowing around the mountainside, sweat beaded on Asa's forehead.

"We ought to be committed," Asa muttered. "It's a day longer getting to Meridian, but the other trail . . ." His voice died out as the other man drew rein. His mule came to a halt and protested loudly. The animal wanted the trip to be over as much as he did. "What's wrong?"

"Got a small problem ahead. The trail's blocked."

"But you said we can't back up!"

"Cain't. No way to turn around. Not enough space. And mules like these here we're astride don't know how to put theyselves into reverse. Even a horse don't back up so good. Reminds me of the time that—"

"What's wrong with the trail?" A thousand terrible reasons for the man's halt flashed through Asa's head. Rocks tumbling from the top of the towering Colorado peak to block the trail. The trail itself, carved into seemingly inert stone, giving way and tumbling half a thousand feet to dam up the river below. Or a body. Another traveler had died on the trail. There was nowhere to give a Christian burial amid the solid rock. The mountains were immutable and unforgiving.

If another poor soul had perished, Asa considered so many things other than burial on the spot. Tossing the corpse over the side was easiest, but he liked that least. Another alternative was to drape the body over his mule and lead the burdened animal back to Meridian, where a decent burial ceremony could be performed. Should a family be notified? How could he find out about the man's people? There wasn't even a marshal in Meridian now. The mayor was the only "authority," and . . .

The lead mule began to snort and kick. Asa leaned over as much as he dared and saw that a body spooked the otherwise staid mule.

"Can we edge past?"

"Edge past? Mister, you got a death wish for certain sure. Ain't no way to get past a mountain lion."

"A mountain lion?"

"The one what's settin' smack-dab in the middle of the trail, sunnin' hisself and not lookin' like he's got a care in the world. As fat and sassy as he is, he won't think of us as food. Not that he would, anyway. I heard tell they don't like to eat people since we don't taste good. All bitter, like our meat's drenched in kerosene, though how a cat would know that's how we taste without tryin' out a sample first is—"

"A mountain lion!" Asa's ire rose. He had let his imagination run wild. His fear of heights had driven out his common sense. "I thought it was a dead man's body blocking our way."

"Ain't never said a thing like that." The man scratched himself, pushed back his hat and showed a receding hairline and a pate glistening with sweat. That display made Asa feel a tad better. The rumpled old man's emotions played hob with him, too. The way he tugged at his tangled gray-shot beard and his nostrils flared betrayed more than a touch of fear. His mouth ran like a frightened deer because he feared the

cougar, and he might even have shared Asa's dread of
the narrow path so high above a mountain valley.

Asa read people well, and he had ignored all the
signs because of his own fearfulness. If only the medicine in his saddlebags wasn't so important, if a life
didn't hang in the balance, he never would have dared
this risky path back home.

"Whoa, wait. The cat's movin'. He's got his front
legs all straight in front and he's stretchin'. He opened
that mouth of his. You want to see his teeth? Dangest,
sharpest teeth I ever did see. What a yawn!"

In spite of himself, Asa leaned far out to peer around
the old man ahead of him. The trail curved back inward
sharply. He saw the trail some distance farther along
but caught only the barest hint of movement. Tawny
fur, sleek and powerful and dangerous. The quick sight
of the mountain lion vanished as the animal moved
away from the brink. Asa imagined it stretched out so
its powerful body blocked the trail farther along.

"Reckon I can shoot it." The grizzled old man drew
a Colt from his belt. Asa saw the well-used, well-
maintained pistol and how the man's easy familiarity
with it suggested expert marksmanship.

"Don't be a fool. If you wound it, we're goners. It'll
fight. One misstep and your mule plunges over the side
and takes you with it." Asa's brain fog lifted. His usual
sharp mind took on the problem. "We can't stay, we
can't back up and the cat is in our way forward."

"That 'bout sez it all, mister. I got to admit that
you're right about shootin' it. I ain't much of a shot.
What if I missed? And gunshots in these hills have
been known to cause an avalanche." The man pushed

his broad-brimmed gray hat back further as he looked above them to check for a possible rockslide.

Asa dismissed that danger. Too many others were more imminent. Something about the man claiming to be a poor shot began to fester. The man lied just because he could. Asa read his expression. The stranger considered himself something of a gunslick, and yet he had claimed to be inept. That was the kind of trick a man used to lead an opponent astray. Asa wasn't any danger, but the man's reaction was to deceive. He shrugged it off. Some men couldn't help themselves when it came to spinning a yarn. It came as easy as breathing.

Risking life and limb, Asa climbed down from his mule. The animal snorted in resignation and began shifting its weight. As it leaned outward, it almost knocked him from the narrow ledge. He twisted about and got in front. From there he got a better look at the mountain lion sunning itself. Shadows crept slowly toward the cat. When it no longer basked in the warmth, it would move. But Asa grew increasingly edgy about reaching home. He needed to get home to Rebecca to help her and the girls. Looking for a way around the cougar, he sneaked a quick peek over the verge. Shakiness hit him, and he knew he would plunge to his death. Even if there was a ledge or another way around the big cat, he wasn't capable of taking it.

The river below gurgled and rushed along. If he fell, his body would be washed away into oblivion. Asa wobbled. Arms around his mule's neck steadied him until the balky animal let out a liquid snort and pulled free. Pebbles tumbled over the edge of the narrow path and rattled for several seconds. Asa vowed not to follow.

He edged past his travel companion—he had never asked for the man's name in his haste to return to Meridian. The man was a prospector from the look of his clothing. Canvas pants, plaid shirt, floppy hat, battered boots and the Colt tucked into his belt. Anyone spotting the two travelers would have been curious at the contrast. Asa was tall and thin as a rail, and he sported a shock of hair so red, it looked as if it was on fire. His blue eyes missed nothing. Hands with long, nimble fingers betrayed how physical work and Asa Newcombe were strangers. No calluses on those hands, which compounded drugs and mixed concoctions. He wiped his sweaty palms on a frock coat both stylish and inexpensive. His green brocade vest and starched white shirt beneath were soaked with his sweat. A few more swipes of his hands along strong thighs steadied him.

No six-shooter hung at his side or weighed him down as he moved with a sure, quick action that threatened his life. He picked up a small stone and threw it at the mountain lion.

"What're you doin', you danged fool? Wake it up, and it's sure to come for us!" The man tried to turn his mule, but there wasn't room. Asa pushed against the mule's rump and held it in place.

The stone clattered along the trail on the far side of the cat. It stirred but didn't awaken. Asa threw another, larger rock. This careened off the hillside before tumbling away to the river below. The mountain lion came fully, instantly awake. It pushed up to a crouch and snarled.

Before Asa's companion could cry out, the apothecary clamped his hand over the man's mouth.

"Hush. Watch."

Asa released his hold when the man sagged. He didn't miss how a hand rested once more on the Colt's butt thrust into the tight belt.

The mountain lion took a tentative step in the direction of the rock Asa had thrown. It snarled, shook its head and then began stalking along the trail. With a tawny, liquid rush, the cat slipped over the side and disappeared.

"It's still there, below us somewhere. You went and woke it up."

"Ride," Asa ordered. "If it comes back—and I don't think it will since there's nothing here for it—we ought to be long gone."

"Mister, you're crazy as a loon. Waiting it out was the smart thing."

Asa edged along the rocky wall, positioned himself and carefully mounted. The mule had tried bucking him off more than once when he stepped up before. Self-preservation told the mule not to make a misstep that would send it over the edge. That might dislodge its unwanted rider, but it also meant catastrophe. As the mule settled down and began its sure-footed plodding again, Asa patted its neck.

"I'll get you an apple when we reach town. A whole bushel basket!"

The mule turned a large brown eye back accusingly.

"I promise. I always keep my promises."

The mule snorted and picked up the pace, much to Asa's regret. He clung to the reins and alternately clamped his eyes shut and opened them in stark fear. At least, the man on the mule ahead of him held his tongue the rest of the way into Meridian.

Some days Lady Luck smiled. On others, she smirked. Asa Newcombe only wanted to accept the good. And today he got it. A couple hours before sundown, he rode into Meridian with friends and neighbors waving and calling to him.

CHAPTER TWO

⌒

"TAKE THIS TO Mr. Thompson right away." Asa Newcombe sealed the envelope and handed it to the towheaded boy. "Tell him to take half today dissolved in a quart of water and then the rest tomorrow."

"What is it?" Wilson Dutton held up the envelope and thumped it with his thumb. Asa almost snatched it from the twelve-year-old's hands. Not only had he risked his life taking the crazy dangerous trail through Mosquito Pass, but he had paid a small fortune getting the chemicals for the mixture sent by rail from Denver. For once, deadlines had been met, and Big Bud Thompson had a good chance of surviving after his fall.

"It's medicine that will reduce his fever and keep him alive . . . if he ever gets it."

"Usual pay?" The boy didn't budge.

"A dollar if you get it to him within the hour," Asa

said. "Or are you looking to apprentice to the undertaker? Mr. Thompson needs it *now*."

"A dollar," Wilson said, rolling the words over and
over like a fine wine caressing his tongue. "You bet,
Mr. Newcombe!" He took two steps for the door, then
spun around. "I almost forget. My pa wants to talk to
you about the railroad spur."

Asa sighed. The boy's pa was the mayor, and he was
always spinning deals that profited himself more than
the people of Meridian, but this time was different.
Everyone in the North Park area profited from having
the railroad use Meridian as a depot.

"Get a move on. I have another prescription to deliver." Asa shook an amber bottle and got the last of
the powder dissolved in the alcohol.

"I can deliver it, too. For another dollar."

"Scat!" Asa chased the boy out of the apothecary
store and on his way. He stopped at the door to watch,
to be sure the delivery was headed to the right place.
When Wilson took off running in the correct direction,
Asa closed the door behind him and locked it. Most
merchants never bothered with locks. Meridian was a
peaceable place, but he worried that some of the powerful drugs he kept on his shelves might disappear.
Laudanum was the least of the drugs that someone so
inclined could take.

He pulled down his bowler to shield his eyes from
the sun and walked briskly across the street to the hotel. The owner's wife was laid up and needed medicine.
Meridian's doctor had died more than a year ago. No
one had stepped up to fill the void. The town shared a
veterinarian with three other towns and only saw the
man a few times a month. That left Asa with the re-

sponsibility to tend to the citizens—and the animals—
the best he could.

"Hello, Joel," he greeted the room clerk. "I have
Miz Selwin's medicine."

The young man smiled weakly. "She's not doing so
good, Mr. Newcombe. Anything to buck her up'll be
good."

"See that she gets a spoonful of this twice a day and
don't let her get up and walk around. She'll be dizzy
and might fall down."

"We wouldn't want that. Not with Mr. Selwin, uh,
not with him . . ." The clerk's words trailed off.

Asa knew what troubled the youngster. His employer got knee-walking drunk too many times a week
for the hotel to thrive or for his wife to heal up. He'd
have to talk to the mayor about that and see what rem-
edy might be possible.

"You might put the medicine into a glass of milk to
help it go down easier. It's bitter."

"All medicine tastes lousy," Joel said. He held up
the amber glass bottle and tried to look through it.
"You know that Mayor Dutton's looking for you?"

"His son, Wilson, told me. Now that I'm sure Miz
Selwin will get her medicine, I'll get on over to town
hall."

"That fellow from the railroad company's in town.
That's what the gossip says." Joel shook the bottle,
smiled weakly and headed for the back room, where
the Selwins had living quarters. Until the woman got
sick, they had enjoyed a fancy suite upstairs on the
third floor. Climbing the steps had taken an increasing
toll on her until they were forced to move a bed into a
first-floor storage room.

Asa stepped out into the late-afternoon sun and took a deep breath to settle his nerves. He took on too much. Rebecca told him that all the time, and he was coming around to agreeing. The trip to the Mosquito Pass watering depot had forced him to leave Meridian and abandon people who needed his services. He took another breath and set off with long strides toward the town hall. Worst of all, he had left Rebecca for four days. In her delicate condition, those four days seemed more like a week. Their daughters, Theresa and Ruth, helped their ma the best they could, but they were only eight and five. He expected a great deal from them, but they were children and able to do only so much.

He marched up the gravel path in front of the town hall and went through the lobby. He touched the brim of his bowler toward the woman at the desk who acted as Mayor Dutton's secretary. Why the mayor of a town with a population of fewer than five hundred needed such help had come up at meetings. Somehow, Oliver Dutton sounded sincere saying the matter was being examined—and yet nothing ever happened. Asa held down his suspicions about the mayor and his secretary having more than a working relationship. It was none of his business, but that didn't stop him from thinking the gossip held a grain of truth.

"Go right on in, Mr. Newcombe," the woman called.

But Asa had already opened the door to the mayor's office. The scent of the polish for the cherrywood desk and side cabinet almost gagged him. Oliver Dutton wasn't one to leave the windows open for ventilation even on a fine summer day like this.

The mayor sat behind his desk, rocked back in a fancy chair, his fingers intertwined across his protruding belly. A shock of blond hair showed that his son had come by his coloration honestly. Asa wondered if that was the only honesty ever to come from the mayor. If Dutton had a way of doing something crooked, he'd prefer that to straightforward fidelity, even if it required more work. It had to be the risk that excited the politician.

Asa caught the other man seated at the side of the desk from the corner of his eye. He had seen Sidney Eastman several times, poking around town and making a nuisance of himself. The last time, three men had accompanied him, one dragging a surveyor's theodolite around while Eastman scribbled notes in a bound volume and exchanged whispers with the other two. It had seemed very official and very secretive.

"Mr. Newcombe, welcome back. I'm glad you were able to get the medicine for Thompson. My son says he looked worlds better after knocking back that powder you sent him."

"He drank it in a glass of whiskey's my bet," Asa said. "That alone would perk him up." He silently heaved a sigh of relief. The mayor's son had done his job delivering the medicine much faster than he would have thought. He reached into his vest pocket for a silver cartwheel to give to the boy's father to pass along, then stopped. He didn't trust Dutton not to keep the money due his son.

"There was someone else, too. The hotel owner's wife?" Sidney Eastman spoke in a measured tone, words clipped and every syllable precise. He sat in the chair ramrod straight. Asa wondered if the man had been in the army. Something about him screamed, *Officer!*

"Her, yes," Asa said. He almost mentioned the special potion he had fetched back for his own wife, then stopped short. That was a private matter. "What's so important that you had to see me? I haven't been back for an hour, and I'd like to see my wife."

"Ah, yes, Mrs. Newcombe," Eastman said. "She's with child. A boy this time?" The steel-colored eyes fixed on Asa in a way that made him suspicious. He knew far too much about the citizens of Meridian to be just casual interest.

"We have hopes in that direction," Asa said cautiously. "The girls would make a baby brother's life miserable until he got older."

"Let him learn who runs the world early in life." Dutton chuckled at that, shook his head, then pulled himself up to his desk and opened a file box stuffed with papers. He took out a few and spun them around so Asa saw they were maps of the surrounding mountains. "That's what I—we—want to discuss, Asa. You're the town's most prominent citizen. With your backing for this project, well, no one would oppose us if you agreed that it is a fine idea."

Asa studied the maps for a moment.

"That's the trail I took getting back to town. It's a treacherous path." He held up the page. The trail had been marked as if railroad tracks ran the distance from the Mosquito Pass depot all the way into Meridian.

"The Colorado and Wyoming Railroad is considering a narrow gauge line to our fair town."

"A spur line, it's called," Eastman piped up. "We have surveyed the entire route, and Meridian is a perfect location."

Asa caught his breath. For almost a year rumors had ricocheted around town about how Meridian was destined to become a ghost town. With the railroad going through Mosquito Pass, they had been bypassed and cut off from more profitable towns.

"What's here that merits a spur?" He studied Eastman's reaction, but Dutton spoke up.

"Well, this isn't public knowledge. Not yet. But the C and W wants our coal deposits exploited. Meridian can supply needed fuel for their locomotives."

"Yes, you see, Mr. Newcombe, the lighter the load on our engines getting up to the Mosquito Pass summit, the better. We won't need the most powerful engines—or even to gang two together for the steep incline. The Front Range is not a forgiving mistress, no, sir. The Rockies make us fight for every inch we climb. Once at the Mosquito Pass depot, refueling with Meridian coal gives us quite an edge."

"And quite a profit," Dutton cut in. He rubbed his hands together. "To get the coal from our mine overland is impossible."

"That trail is a killer," Asa agreed. "And the other road, while safer, takes a day longer."

"Wagons loaded with coal would take far longer still. A week. That's not an expense the C and W can tolerate. But a spur line from the mine to Mosquito Pass can deliver coal in a single day." Eastman leaned forward and looked sincere. Asa heard the ring of urgency in the railroad man's voice.

"What's your connection to C and W?"

Asa's question caused both Dutton and Eastman to sit up straighter. In Eastman's case, bones in his spine snapped at the effort. As if reporting to his senior officer, he cleared his throat and looked straight ahead before speaking.

"It's not widely known, sir, that I am operating vice president of the railroad. If it came out that I am in Meridian contracting for your coal, others would take offense."

"Others?" Asa's persistence irritated the mayor, but Eastman fielded the question easily.

"Let's say that someone like General Palmer would object. The D and RG Railroad is looking to spread its tracks throughout the Front Range with the intent of creating a monopoly. That, as you well know, is not good for smaller towns. While larger ones prosper, ones like Meridian . . ." His voice trailed off as he shrugged eloquently.

Asa nodded. That made sense. So much around the building of the railroads carried the stench of politics and outright fraud. The Crédit Mobilier was only part of it. That was graft on a national scale. He had heard of lesser bribery and intimidation as the railroads spread all over Colorado territory.

"I see your point. But—" Asa waited for his unasked question to get an answer. Dutton jumped into the conversation.

"Mr. Newcombe—Asa—you are a well-respected citizen. People know you, depend on you. Your opinion means a great deal."

"I don't know anything about railroads."

"But you do know what will happen to Meridian if we don't get the C and W spur line. The mine will ensure Meridian's continued existence for years to come. We can make this town into an important trade center for all of North Park. If we play our cards right, the C and W can move freight over the Front Range to the Mosquito Pass depot and down to a new depot here. Here, in Meridian."

"And the railroad intends to spread out along the western slopes with Meridian as a nexus?" Asa's heart raced at the prospect of such trade. Prosperity meant a home for years to come, unlike so many boomtowns throughout Colorado that exploded in size and died within weeks when gold or silver deposits played out.

"I am not at liberty to make such a promise, but let's say, it is not beyond the realm of possibility. We believe towns such as Leadville and Central City will thrive. But please, do not spread this around. There are unscrupulous men who would jump on any rumor and steal away our—your—chance to make Meridian into a prosperous crossroads." Eastman fixed a gimlet stare on Asa, as if defying him to gainsay his words.

"We don't have the labor to open a mine. I've seen the assay and know the coal is of good quality." Asa didn't volunteer that he had done the assay himself, being the only chemist within a hundred miles. The vein running into the side of the mountain dominating Meridian wasn't of metallurgical quality, such as needed by blacksmiths and other iron workers, but it assayed out as a high-grade bituminous. Not anthracite but commercially viable for stoking a locomotive's hot box.

"With the spur connecting us with Denver, workers will be easily hired," Dutton assured him. "The key to our success is that spur."

"I can certainly support the railroad building the tracks, but again, why are you discussing this with me? I'm not even on the town council, and you are mayor, Mr. Dutton."

"Please, please, call me Oliver. Is that all right, Asa?"

He nodded. His mind raced. Meridian being assured of an important stopover along the C and W line meant so much to him and his family personally. He saw his apothecary business expanding as the population rushed in to run the railroad and mine coal by the ton.

"Yes, all that," Eastman said. "Prosperity for the town and yourself."

Asa sucked in his breath. Something didn't make sense.

"When will the C and W begin laying track?" His question caused the two men to exchange knowing looks. That told him more than anything said up to that moment. "There's a roadblock to your scheme. What is it?"

"Asa, Asa, this isn't a scheme, but you are right about there being a problem. Can you explain, Mr. Eastman?"

The railroad vice president stood and began pacing. He gestured as he stalked around the mayor's office, as if onstage and addressing hundreds of people rather than just Asa Newcombe.

"The road—that's how we call the entire railroad—is expanding rapidly. Too rapidly to keep up with generating revenue adequate enough to repay the loans to our bankers."

"Bankers?" Asa's optimism deflated.

"Both in Denver and back East. We are heavily in debt and cannot borrow another penny."

"Pennies needed to run the spur line," Asa guessed.

"Mayor Dutton was right in calling you in. Your acumen and business sense let you see the problem immediately."

Asa held his tongue and waited for the full story.

Eastman stopped his pacing and faced Asa squarely. He cleared his throat and said, "The C and W will sign a contract to buy Meridian coal if the town pays for the spur line."

"I just came over that trail. Even a narrow-gauge track will be difficult to lay." Asa locked his bright blue eyes with Eastman's metal gray ones and asked the key question. "How much will such a spur cost?"

"I feel that two hundred fifty thousand dollars will be enough to build the road," Eastman said.

"And mining engineers tell me that another hundred thousand dollars will open the coal mine." Dutton leaned forward, hands clasped almost as if praying for the money.

"Nobody in Meridian has that kind of money. If we sold the entire town down to the foundations, we couldn't raise three hundred fifty thousand dollars." Asa saw both men staring at him like wolves eyeing a lamb. "*I* don't have that kind of money!"

"We know, Asa, but there is a way you can raise the money." Dutton looked smug.

"Tell me how." For his life, Asa Newcombe had no idea what he could do to bring forth such a princely sum.

Oliver Dutton told him.

CHAPTER THREE

IT SAVES MERIDIAN," Rebecca Newcombe said. She kept her eyes down on her needlepoint, methodically moving the needle and thread to form a pattern inside the circular frame. Asa had no idea what she was making, but every pillow on the davenport sported a cover done with precision and style. He admired her for so much. Not the least of it came for her artistic sense.

"We wouldn't have to move," Asa agreed. He sprawled in his chair, staring at his boots. "That's a comfort because of your condition."

"I'm strong enough, dear," she said, looking up. Her green eyes gleamed in the early-evening light. Her mussed hair was almost as red as his. Almost. Both their girls had the same coppery tresses. Asa hoped the child who would be along in five months would be a boy. Undoubtedly his new son's hair carried the traits of both mother and father, though Asa knew that wasn't necessarily so. His brother, Sean, who had died at Antietam, had had hair as black as the coal lurking beneath the mountainside not five miles from where he sat. And his father had faded in his memory. All he remembered of him was a thin cloud of gray hair and a bald pate, but his mother's hair had been as brilliantly colored as his own.

He brought himself back to the here and now. His mind wandered because he lacked the determination to accept what Mayor Dutton had asked of him. Memories soothed. At least some memories of his family.

He turned grim. They were long dead.

"Asa, are you thinking about your pa again? You have that look on your face."

"What look?" he snapped at her, though he hadn't intend to be so sharp. Memories of his father always affected him this way. It pained him that his wife recognized it so easily. That meant he thought far too much of Donal Newcombe and—

"Asa, please. You're upsetting yourself, and that bothers me." She laid her hand on her slightly bulging belly. She manipulated him, and he disliked that. But it told him how seriously she took the matter.

"If the railroad comes to Meridian, the town will grow and prosper. There wouldn't be any reason for us to leave." He scowled as plans for moving to Denver raced through his mind again, as they had so many times before. The family had to move soon, or Rebecca would be forced to travel along the dangerous trail to the Mosquito Pass depot in cold weather. This high in the Front Range brought winter for most of the year. Only a couple more months without snow stretched ahead.

"What has Mr. Dutton asked of you? You don't quite spit his name every time you mention it."

"The railroad requires the town to pay for the track. That means more than a quarter of a million dollars."

"So much!" Rebecca's eyes widened. "There's not enough in town for such a huge sum. Can't the railroad pay for their own tracks?"

"There're benefits. If Meridian pays for the rail, we own it. We get fees every time a train goes over the track. More than this, a coal mine ensures that a regular schedule is kept. But Dutton knows we cannot possibly raise so much money. So does Eastman."

"You don't like him, do you?"

"He is a cold one. Hard to read. Thoughts run through his skull that I cannot fathom."

"You sound as if you're sitting across from him in a poker game." She saw his expression then and muttered, "Oh! They know your background."

"I don't know how they found out I was a gambler before coming to Meridian—before we moved to Denver, even. It's been almost ten years since I sat down at a poker table to place a bet."

"You gave up gambling, but you never promised me you'd stop. You wouldn't be breaking your word if you got into a faro game or dealt some poker." She went back to carefully guiding her needle through the cloth. From what he saw from across the room, Rebecca threaded out a bright yellow wildflower amid greenery already stitched in. She might intend to sell this minor artwork at the church social at the end of the month. Even a few cents helped the family budget.

"Who'd run the store while I'm gone?" Asa floundered for reasons not to do as Dutton wanted.

"What will happen to the store if Meridian becomes a ghost town? We'll lose everything without a miracle."

"I hardly think this will be a miracle. It sounds to me like a confidence game."

"Don't sulk, dear. It doesn't become you." Rebecca drew a few more stitches, then said, "You told me opening an apothecary shop let you make a difference, and that is especially true now in a town like Meridian that doesn't have a doctor."

"I do what I can."

"You've saved lives. Mr. Thompson is on his way to recovery."

"Miz Selwin's not doing so good."

"You aren't God. You don't hold the power of life and death in your hands."

"I know that, but what if I *can* save the town? Dutton wants me to ante up and get into this huge poker game that's coming up. I've never heard of Big Ed Edwards and hardly know where Golden Junction is. It must be another of those boomtowns whose time has passed by."

"So this Big Ed Edwards tries to save his town with a huge game. Can't you do the same for Meridian? What do you have to lose?"

"Dutton has robbed the town coffers and borrowed from everyone he can browbeat to get me the five-thousand-dollar entry price. That's what I have to lose. I can lose everyone's money, and that'll mean *I* will be responsible for destroying the town."

"It is not certain that Meridian dies if you don't win. If your odds of winning are one in a thousand, that's one chance Meridian doesn't have otherwise." She knotted the thread and bit it off. Rebecca held up the finished embroidery. "There. That will make a nice addition to the church rummage sale."

Arguing with his wife got him nowhere. Worse, he saw her point. There was absolutely no chance for Meridian if he didn't enter the winner-take-all poker game against—what? From the sound of it, Big Ed Edwards drew gamblers from all over Colorado. Dutton claimed there was a top prize of upward of a half-million dollars. For all the high-stakes poker games Asa had been in, never had that much money been on the line.

The biggest game of his life had been his last. More than a hundred thousand dollars rode on the turn of a single card. The game had ended badly.

"My pa died," he whispered.

"I know, dear."

He almost snapped at her. She didn't know what it was like seeing his pa stretched out on the riverboat's deck, his fancy blue brocade vest turning red with blood gushing out from his bullet-holed heart. Blood spattering the headlight diamond and the man's face draining of all color. The pot had been lost, and Asa Newcombe had lost even more when his father died.

He stared at the picture of his family on a table across the room. His wife. His two daughters. Everything fell into place like gear wheels and cogs in a finely wrought pocket watch. He had been the best gambler along the entire Mississippi, and that included his father. Giving up the turn of the card and the click of dice had been his decision to change his life, and that picture of Rebecca and the girls was how it had changed.

If he didn't try to win the money needed to lay the track into Meridian, he had to close his apothecary shop immediately and move the family. And if Meridian declined even more, that left him and his family in a town barely able to endure another fierce winter. He held the fate of Meridian and his own family in his hands.

He stared at them. Long, slender, strong fingers. Quick movement. Dexterous. Asa looked up. Rebecca handed him a box of cards.

"I play solitaire when the girls take their naps." She sighed. "I haven't had much time, and Theresa won't take a nap anymore. She's too old."

He slid his thumbnail along the top, opened the box and slid the pasteboards out onto a side table. A quick move fanned them out. He scooped them up and shuffled a few times.

"Look at you, still a natural, Asa. How does it feel, slipping your fingers across the playing cards?"

Two quick shuffles, the cards fanned out, a cut and moves so fast, his fingers blurred. The cards dealt into two stacks, one for Rebecca and the other for him.

"Which hand do you want? You can swap if you want."

"Should I change?"

His expression turned to stone. Not a muscle twitched. He had looked like this for years along the river, never betraying anything.

"I'll switch." She pushed her cards across and picked up the hand he had dealt himself. Rebecca turned the cards over. "Four queens. That's good, isn't it?"

"It should win the pot. Most of the time." He turned over a hand with four kings. "It's not likely, though, with me dealing."

"You cheated!"

"I'll be up against men who are even better card mechanics," he said. "I'm out of practice."

"You don't have to cheat to win."

"No, I don't. There aren't many gamblers who know odds better than I do."

She touched his hand lightly and left the room without another word. Asa stewed in his own juices. Knowing how to cheat at cards proved useful catching those who did. With a high-stakes game like this, the hands without attempts at stacking the deck or dealing seconds would be few and far between. How well he saw what went on reflected on how much he won.

He settled back in his chair, tented his fingers and rested his chin on the tips. Nothing said he had to remain until the last hand. Win enough—so much!—to pay for the spur line and get the coal mine started, then leave. Most gamblers always went for the final win, and most gamblers lost huge pots. Money meant less than the glory, the thrill, the feeling of being the best. He had sat across the table from enough men he wanted to humiliate. Many he had. The ones he hadn't humiliated often enough left him with nothing but holes in his pockets. But win or lose, there had always been the lure of the next game.

"One game only. One game and I retire again and get back to being an apothecary."

He shoved to his feet and went to a bay window. A padded lid had provided a nice spot to sit in the warm winter afternoon sun during years gone past. He lifted the lid and stared at the contents of the box underneath. If he intended to gamble for so much money, he had to look the part. He pulled out a long black frock coat with silk lapels and laid it aside. A shirt so white, it hurt his eyes to look at, even in the dim light of a coal oil lamp. Fancy pants with black silk ribbons down the sides, a vest with enough pockets for chips and twenty-dollar gold pieces and an expensive pocket watch left over from his last three-day-long game on a riverboat docked at New Orleans. He stared at it and the bullet hole clean through the middle. With a trembling hand, he slid the watch back into a vest pocket.

"And the rest of what I'll need."

He picked up a heavy polished walnut box and carefully placed it on the table behind him. A slow, deep breath settled his nerves. He opened the box. It had been a while since he had oiled the Colt Peacemaker, but he would before he left for Golden Junction and the biggest poker match in the history of the territory.

Asa touched the cold steel, and memories flooded back. None of them were good. He found the holster and strapped it on. The Peacemaker dropped into the holster. A small shrug of his shoulders, then he slapped leather. The six-shooter slid into his hand with old, familiar, expert ease. He found himself pointing the gun at his own reflection in the bay window. That warned him of what to expect in the coming days.

He silently returned the pistol and holster to the box.

CHAPTER FOUR

ᒐ

"Come on out, Asa, and tell the crowd what you're going to do." Oliver Dutton took Asa by the arm and tugged until he took a step in the direction the mayor wanted.

He hesitated to leave his shop. The people gathered in the street began to chant his name.

"Please, this isn't something I want to do. I have work." He wondered what would happen if he backed out of his promise to play in the big poker game. Looking past the mayor at the adoring people in front of the small shop told him he might get lynched. For all that, getting strung up might have been better than going through with the harebrained scheme and losing the money his neighbors had donated.

"Time's a-wastin'!" Dutton got behind him and bulldozed him onto the boardwalk. A cheer went up. "They love you for saving Meridian. Say something, Asa."

"I don't know what to tell them."

"It won't matter. You have them on your side."

Asa stepped forward. Even with the warm sun against his face, it shouldn't have caused sweat to bead like it did. He raised his hand to quiet the crowd. Instead, they cheered even louder. Dutton pushed against him and kept him from retreating into the apothecary shop.

"You're crazy to trust me like this," Asa said. This provoked laughter. "It's been ten years since I even dealt a hand."

"Good thing, too. We need you in the apothecary and not in the saloon at the faro table." Whoever said this caused a new ripple of laughter. "What are the odds, Asa? What are the odds you'll bring back the bacon?"

Telling them he was more likely to lose their money than win struck him as wrong. Even if it was the gospel truth, it wasn't what they wanted to hear. There hadn't been much hope in Meridian before the promise of that narrow-gauge railroad spur. Asa saw the difference all around him. Crushing that hope would have been a crime.

He still wondered if the smart thing to do wasn't to pull up stakes right now and leave for Denver before the early-autumn snow began flying. No matter how much money people in town put up, his gamble was life and death. If he joined the poker game in Golden Junction, there wouldn't be enough time to move Rebecca and the girls.

"How much have you collected, Mr. Reese?" Oliver Dutton gripped Asa's arm and held him in place as he addressed a well-dressed man in front of the crowd.

"My bank's holding almost four thousand dollars, Mr. Mayor! We're looking to get the rest of the entry money by the end of the week."

"Just in time," Dutton said. "The big game starts in less than two weeks. How long will it take to clean out the rest of those varmints, Asa? A day? Two? You'll be in the saddle getting there and returning to us longer than the game. Right, Asa?" Dutton laughed. The crowd joined him.

Asa felt blood rush to his face, turning his pale skin almost as red as his hair. He wanted to tell them it wasn't like that. The C and W Railroad wasn't going to lay tracks most of the way to Meridian. Eastman had been adamant about that point. All or nothing. Win or lose. There wasn't any other outcome.

"You've seen he's rarin' to go. Wave to them, Asa. Then you get on back to work. We need your headache powders all mixed up before you leave." Dutton grabbed Asa's arm and held his hand high.

The cheer deafened Asa. Dutton released him and hurried off without another word. Asa stumbled back into his shop, only to hear someone call his name. He turned.

"Hello, Padre. What can I do for you?"

The priest sidled up and spoke in a conspiratorial tone.

"I'm so glad to speak privately with you, Mr. Newcombe. Here. Here's almost five hundred dollars." The priest shoved a box into Asa's hands. "It's the church building money."

"You were going to replace the roof—the part that fell in last month. You have to finish the repair before winter."

"We can seal off that part of the church, if we have to go to that extreme. Saving the town is more important. Without parishioners, there's no need for a roof."

"Give this to Mr. Reese. He's keeping track of all the money." Asa felt sick to his stomach.

"I . . . I don't trust him. He . . . I don't trust him."

Asa studied the priest closely. Wendell Reese was Catholic, and Father Magruder took his confession. Something the banker had confessed must have brought on this distrust.

"I understand," Asa said.

The priest smiled wanly and said, "You should have been a minister. You see truth better than most men of the cloth, Asa." Father Magruder hesitated, then finished, "This is a skill you learned from gambling, I am sure. You must know what's in a man's mind."

"In his heart," Asa contradicted.

Father Magruder's head bobbed, and then he hurried off. He looked over his shoulder at Asa for a moment, then disappeared in the direction of his church.

Asa went into his shop and spread the contents of the box onto his counter. A quick count, a recount, and he shook his head. The priest had given him more than six hundred dollars. He had no idea what he should do. Reese was keeping the rest of the townspeople's money in his vault. If he didn't turn over this money, the five-thousand-dollar ante might not be collected. Did that give Asa an excuse not to go to Golden Junction?

"You're too honest, Asa. You'll turn it over."

He spun guiltily. He felt even worse when his wife came into the shop. She had a way of reading his mind. If any other gambler had ever developed Rebecca's skill, Asa would have lost every poker hand.

"You take it to the bank," he said. "I've got a mountain of work to do."

"Before you leave?"

"There's more being gambled than the town's money. What if the C and W can't get the track run here before the worst of the winter storms? I don't know a thing about building a railroad."

"Nobody in Meridian does," she said. "So everyone is gambling. Was Mr. Eastman telling the truth?"

"I only heard the mayor telling what had been promised. Eastman lit out mighty fast when I showed up."

"You did the assay on the ore. The coal is there to be mined, isn't it?"

He nodded. He gathered the padre's money, counted it a third time, and put it in the box. Rebecca tucked it under her arm.

"There are so many things that can go wrong. Not enough money's collected for me to get into the game. I can lose. It's been a long time since I laid a bet. It's a skill that has to be honed by experience, by constant practice."

"You'll be fine, dear."

"And the tracks might not get laid when Dutton expects. What if the C and W won't pay enough for the coal to make mining profitable? We need to get a couple hundred miners to work there, too. That's a lot. Meridian would more than double in size."

"I hear of all the failed gold mines up and down the western slope of the Front Range," she said. "How many miners are willing to get a regular paycheck instead of starving as they hunt for something that's never quite there?"

Asa wasn't going to debate the point with her. Prospectors were different from miners. The lure of a big strike kept the prospectors moving on, starving, dying. He understood them because being a gambler wasn't that much different. Gambling was an addiction as much as laudanum or opium, but he recognized an even bigger lure. The potential of winning gave a thrill unlike anything else he had ever experienced. It was as if anticipation for that pot of gold at the end of the rainbow mattered more than the gold itself.

"I must go. I don't want the children getting into mischief." Rebecca looked nervous at being entrusted with so much money.

"I should take you to the bank." Asa looked at the box with the money. There wasn't enough crime in Meridian to merit hiring a marshal after the old one had left, but seldom had this much money been floating around town.

"You just want to strap on the six-shooter again. Oh, go on. You can catch up with me. I really must hurry." Rebecca looked around, saw no one, and then gave him a quick peck on the cheek. She smoothed her skirts and took the box in both hands.

With that, she left the shop. Asa made sure the chemicals and drugs were properly placed in cabinets, then opened a drawer in a wall cabinet. His holster and six-shooter rested there, calling to him as strongly as the lure of once more being in a poker game. He recognized old feelings. He should never have taken the pistol out of its case and brought the gun and the holster here.

He opened the gate and rotated the cylinder to be sure the six-gun was loaded. A fancy spin rolled the weapon around and returned it to the holster.

Feeling out of place since no one else in sight wore iron, he hurried down the main street to the crossing street where Reese's bank dominated the cul-de-sac.

Rebecca was just going into the bank. He lengthened his stride, then slowed and went to the boardwalk
in front of the tobacconist's store.

"I didn't expect to see you in town," he said. "We
came all the way from the Mosquito Pass depot, and I
never caught your name."

The bearded man who had ridden ahead of him
along the narrow trail sat in a chair outside the shop,
puffing away on a fat cigar. He blew smoke rings with
practiced ease. Only when he had puffed out an inter-
locking pair did he turn his attention to Asa.

"Business kept me here."

"What business is that? Meridian's not the most
prosperous town in Colorado."

"You fixin' to go into that bank at the end of the
street?"

"Why do you ask?" Asa's hackles rose. The man's
demeanor put a burr under his saddle and turned him
suspicious.

"No reason. Just that I took a shine to you out on
the trail, and you look like a man who can use some
good advice." The grizzled man stubbed out his cigar
and tucked the butt into his pocket. He stood and
waited. But for what?

"I have business there."

"Best go do it, then."

Asa frowned. He went to the bank entrance and
paused. Rebecca sat at Wendell Reese's desk, the padre's money spread out between them. She tapped one
pile after another, as if explaining to the banker how
much actually was being deposited. As Asa stepped in,
a gunshot from the direction of the tobacco store
sounded.

He glanced over his shoulder. His onetime traveling companion had vanished. Who fired the shot was a poser. No one else took notice of the shot, so he shrugged it off.

"Asa, come on over. Your lovely wife's brought enough money to give us the full five thousand." Reese motioned. Asa stepped closer and then froze. The thunder of horses outside was completely out of the ordinary for a sleepy Meridian afternoon.

Five men with bandannas pulled up to hide their faces jumped down from their horses. The instant their boots hit the ground, their hands went for their six-shooters.

"Robbery!" Asa shouted. "They're robbing the bank!"

Two long strides covered the distance to the banker. One arm swept up his wife and spun her around so she could hide behind the heavy desk.

"Asa, don't!"

His wife's cry went unheeded. A single fluid movement filled his fist with the Peacemaker's butt. He fanned off two rounds as the first bank robber burst into the lobby. The outlaw yelped, tried to take a step and fell forward. His six-gun clattered to the wood floor. Asa already aimed at the next owlhoot rushing in. This shot was well aimed. His lead hit the man in the middle of his chest. The masked man sank to the floor as if his bones had turned to jelly.

Then all hell broke loose. The three remaining robbers had had time to figure out where the resistance was coming from, and they loosed a fusillade that filled the entire room with white smoke. Asa had seen what was coming and dragged Rebecca down to the floor. As an afterthought, he reached up and grabbed Reese's collar. He yanked so hard on the bank presi-

dent that the celluloid collar popped off. But the effort
achieved what he intended. Reese's feet slid from
under him, and he crouched low behind the desk.

Asa peeked up over the desk and got off another
shot at a robber. He missed in the smoke and confusion. A new hailstorm tore through the air and splin-
tered the desk. Not daring to look, he hunkered down
with one arm around Rebecca. She trembled against
him. All he could think of was their unborn child.

This set him into action. He pushed her toward
Wendell Reese and dived from behind the desk. After
three more shots, his Peacemaker came up empty.

The shots weren't effective, other than to give extra
speed to the retreating robbers.

He saw that one teller had a six-gun, and he had emptied it. The other rested a sawed-off shotgun on the counter. From his pasty face and thousand-yard stare, he had
frozen with fright. After checking to make sure Rebecca
was unharmed, Asa got to his feet slowly, making sure
the tellers recognized him, and walked over to them.

The one with the shotgun required the most attention. Asa slipped the weapon away from a trembling
grip, then thrust out his hand.

"Well done." He held his hand out until the shock
passed enough for the teller to weakly shake. The other
teller was in better shape. His fingers shook as he reloaded his six-gun, and Asa saw no reason to engage him.
Let the bank employees take over. That was their job.

He was only the town apothecary. Asa stared at the
Peacemaker in his hand. Faint curls of gun smoke rose
from the barrel. He was only the town apothecary—
and its gunman, too. That was a job he had never expected to be heaped on him.

"Asa, are you all right?" Rebecca clung to him. He held her until she stopped quaking. Or was he the one shaking? Asa found it impossible to tell.

He wanted to reload like the teller had already done, but he had only the bullets in his cylinder. Before he left for Golden Junction, he'd need more ammo. Lots more.

"Asa, you saved our hides. There's never been a robbery in this town before. Why'd they want to rob me now?"

Asa knew the banker wasn't thinking straight. The padre's money was still piled on his desk and in the vault rested more than four thousand dollars more. They had struck, thinking to collect all the money he was supposed to use to enter the big game.

"Package up the money and have it ready. I'm on the trail to Golden Junction at first light."

Only then did Reese understand the motive for the robbery happening when it did.

CHAPTER FIVE

"THE GIRLS ARE still asleep," Rebecca Newcombe said. She clung to her husband's arm. For two cents he would give up on the crazy idea of winning enough money to save Meridian and stay with his family.

"I looked in on them." He gripped the gelding's reins tightly, then forced himself to relax. The sooner he got to Golden Junction and saw how the game ran, the quicker he came home. If the entire trip didn't take more than a week and he lost the town's money, he still had a chance of packing up and moving his wife and children back to Denver before the weather turned.

He'd have to leave, he suspected. His neighbors had all bought into the mayor's fairy tale of Asa being the best gambler in all of Colorado and how he would win the money needed to save Meridian. Anything less would be seen as failure. Or betrayal. Asa might be lucky to escape Meridian if he didn't win enough money.

"Good luck." She clung to him. Tears turned his shirt damp.

"I'll win enough to get the spur line built."

Rebecca looked up at him. He kissed her, then hastily mounted. If he didn't ride off now, his nerves would break, and nothing anyone said or did would make him go. Asa rode slowly down the road leading into town. He turned and waved to Rebecca. In spite of him thinking they were still asleep, Theresa and Ruth both pressed their noses against the dining room window. He watched as long as he could stand it, then put his heels to the horse's flanks and galloped off toward the bank.

Dawn cast a wan light on the bank's front doors, where Wendell Reese and the mayor were standing. Reese held saddlebags, and Dutton had a rifle barrel resting in the crook of his left arm. Asa smiled ruefully. The mayor should have been on guard the day before. His portly figure and hangdog look, along with the rifle, would have been enough to stop the robbers. They would have fallen off their horses laughing.

Asa drew rein and touched the brim of his sil belly Stetson. His usual workaday garb had been put away in favor of trail clothing and a long duster. His gambler's getup taken from the cedar chest was carefully packed in his saddlebags. He had put on a little weight. The fancy vest gripped down around his torso a mite more than it should have, but the black frock coat and snowy white shirt with the sapphire studs looked as good as the day he had won them in a game of highlow. Luck had been with him then, and he had won every stitch of the other gambler's clothes. Back in those days, he had never even considered letting the man keep his trousers. He hadn't known the odds, and

Asa made sure he paid the price. And everyone would again learn who was best at the poker table when he donned the clothes and strode into a gambling hall. Presence meant as much as skill in some games, and Asa knew how to *look* like a winner.

Memory failed him about what had happened to the trousers, but the boots now fit like soft leather gloves. He had spent an extra hour polishing them, making certain the knives sheathed just below the tops came free easily. He had another knife sheathed along the inside of his left arm and had a derringer tucked away in a vest pocket across from his watch. The Peacemaker hung at his right hip. He had made certain he carried several boxes of spare ammo. The gunfight with the outlaws trying to rob the bank had turned him cautious. And ready.

"You're all duded up, Asa, with that hat and those boots." Dutton's voice cracked with strain. "You do look the part."

"If that's what it takes, more power to you," said Reese. "But Oliver's right. You cut a fine figure. You'll do us proud." He wrapped both arms around the saddlebags. Asa wondered if he was going to surrender the money. After all, Reese was a banker and hated to part with so much as a bent penny.

"Any trace of the robbers?" Asa knew the answer before Dutton replied.

"A posse went after them, but they gave our men the slip. There's a good chance you killed one, what with the trails of blood they left in their wake. A couple others were wounded. Looks like you shot them up pretty bad." Dutton grew uncomfortable with the sorry report. "Wendell, give him the money. Let him hit the trail."

"We should have men riding with him. To protect the money."

Asa knew what Reese really meant. "I won't run off and steal the money. You've got my family you can hold hostage." He didn't add that he was more likely to lose the entire five thousand dollars in the first hand he played than he was to steal it.

"Don't go suggesting Asa's a crook, Wendell. Give him the money." When the banker hesitated, Dutton yanked the saddlebags free and handed them up to Asa. "Do us proud, Asa. The town's counting on you. All he meant was that road agents might take advantage of you, that's all. He didn't mean you were going to steal the money. Did you, Mr. Reese?" Dutton glared at the banker, who looked defiant. Giving up the money was harder than pulling teeth for him.

Asa slung the saddlebags over the back of his saddle and tied them down. A quick shift in the saddle settled the Peacemaker riding at his hip. To his surprise, Dutton handed up the Winchester.

"The firepower does you more good than me."

"I hope I don't have to use it." Asa slid the rifle into the saddle sheath. He realized that the robbers weren't likely to give up after failing to steal the money from the bank. Sniping a lone rider was easier and safer. With the rifle, he made that less safe for them. All he had to do was avoid getting ambushed.

The road to Golden Junction stretched close to a hundred miles before him. A touch to the brim of his Stetson once more and he wheeled his horse about and trotted from Meridian. He rode down the main street, a long shadow cast in front of him. The townspeople stirred and readied themselves for another day. He was a mile out of town before the restaurant opened to take in customers for breakfast. Two miles separated him from the bank when Reese let in his first patrons. And five miles stretched behind him when the last business to open greeted its first client.

Asa wished he was back in Meridian to open his apothecary shop and greet the first customers of the day.

No!" ASA NEWCOMBE sat bolt upright, hand clutching his six-gun. Sweat ran down his forehead, and for a terrifying instant, he thought he was blind. A quick swipe took away the sweat and gave him a chance to realize it was the middle of the night. A nightmare had stalked his sleep and left nothing more than a phantom.

He lowered his Peacemaker and lay back, staring up into the starry sky. His breathing returned to normal and his racing heart slowed, but sleep was a stranger now. Reliving the moment in the bank when he had fanned off the rounds into the robber had been more vivid than reality. Every instant had etched itself in his memory. The feel of the gun bucking in his grip. The way the outlaw fell forward, Asa's lead tearing apart his guts. The smell of money and blood and fear. Sounds of confusion and panic from outside.

And how the robber looked like his pa.

Their faces flowed and merged and Asa lifted the gun and fired and—

"Stop it!" he cried aloud into the night. A distant wolf answered, undoubtedly telling him to be quiet. He whispered to himself, "Stop reliving it. There's nothing you can do to change what's happened." He blinked a few times and rolled onto his side so the silent, dark trees rose to fill his vision. Intently staring into the unmoving woods lulled him back to sleep. When he woke again, the sun worked its way through tall mountain peaks.

He considered breakfast, but his belly churned and roiled too much for him to keep anything down. Even the thought of coffee sickened him. After tending to his horse and making sure the gelding had its fill of water from a nearby stream, he mounted and got back onto the trail. A day's ride would take him to a main road, and travel from then on into Golden Junction would be quicker. But for this day, he had to pioneer his own route.

By noon hunger had worked its way into his belly. His stomach growled loud enough to disturb his horse.

"There, there," he said, leaning forward to pat the horse's neck. "We can take a break."

The horse began crow-hopping. A few more aggrieved snorts warned Asa that the sounds of his obvious hunger weren't what spooked the horse. He let the horse whirl about so he could get a good look at his back trail. While he saw nothing out of the ordinary, he sensed that someone was following him. Their keeping out of sight warned him their motives were less than honorable.

He got his horse under control and headed off to his left, reaching the top of a rise. For more than five minutes, he sat as still as a statue. Then he saw them. Two riders on his trail rushed to take cover when they realized how exposed they were. The brief glimpse told him nothing of their identity, but the only others likely to be heading in this direction from Meridian had tried to rob the bank. Since they had failed, the best way of making their inept thievery pay off was to waylay the man carrying the five thousand dollars they wanted.

Asa half drew the rifle when a flash of reflected sunlight came from the woods. A shot in that direction had to flush the pair, but he was in no position for a protracted fight. Better to hide than to shoot it out. If he shot, they had no reason to creep up on him. The fight would be to the death.

His best chance was to leave the trail and head higher into the mountains, hoping to lose them in the winding canyons and thicker forests of pine and juniper. The horse kept up a steady gait for almost fifteen minutes before flagging. The slope turned steeply upward. At this altitude, simply walking took a man's breath unless he was accustomed to trekking up and down sloping mountains. Asa regretted not getting out more, but there had always been another prescription to mix for a customer. He spent ten hours a day preparing powders and potions and left his shop too tired to do much else.

Even when he had worked as a professional gambler, he had been in better shape.

"Younger, too," he muttered under his breath. But keeping fit had been essential because too many times a quick escape had been necessary when a game went sideways on him. Not every Western town appreciated gamblers or their ways.

He cut along a ridge rather than letting his horse slide down the slope on the far side. The towering peaks in the Front Range warned him to be careful where he fled. Without firsthand knowledge of the land, he could find himself caught struggling up an incline. His back would be exposed if he tried to scale the steeper hills.

A smile crept across his lips when he saw a chance to leave the pair behind him wondering where he had vanished. Three canyons branched deeper into the mountains. Each fed the stream that cut down through the rock. They would expect him to follow the water upstream to hide his tracks. All three canyons afforded that excuse.

He spit on the back of his left hand and slapped his right down hard. The spittle sailed off toward the right-hand canyon. The canyon angled sharply within a few hundred yards and would screen him from prying eyes after the bend. Even better, it headed, more or less, toward the southwest—where he wanted to go. With any luck, the canyon opened back into the vast space west of the Front Range and gave him an easy ride into Golden Junction.

By choosing the direction randomly as he had, any bias he might have put into a decision vanished. He urged his horse into the water and splashed his way to the sharp bend in the canyon. As he traveled along the stream, the canyon walls rose abruptly on either side. The day hadn't been all that warm. Heat trapped from the sun boiled off the sheer rock faces and made him sweat. His horse tried to slow. He kept it moving another hundred yards before giving it a chance to rest and drink from the crystal clear flow.

He listened hard for any sound of pursuit. If there were only two outlaws, they had a decision to make when they came to the trio of canyon mouths. If each took a canyon, they still had a one-in-three chance of not choosing the right path. If they stuck together, as Asa suspected they would, they would cut their chance of finding him even more.

Rather than ride and tire his horse more, he walked along the rocky riverbank, leading his mount. The heat became oppressive. Not a puff of wind blew down the canyon. As he walked, he hunted the sides for a trail to the rim. In places where such a trail might have existed, he saw only rockfalls. He began fretting about getting caught in an avalanche.

He picked up the pace and began to worry as the canyon made one sharp turn after another.

After rounding a particularly acute bend, he stopped and stared. A spectacular waterfall fed the river from several hundred feet above. Nowhere did he see a trail up to the top of the waterfall. Worse, he had blundered into a box canyon.

"Trapped. I rode into a trap." He let his horse rest while he investigated the end of the canyon, hoping to find a hidden way out. Finding nothing, he dared the waterfall and dashed through to stand on a moss-slippery rock behind the sheet of falling water. If his luck changed, there would be a tunnel cut through the mountainside.

A ton of dynamite wouldn't do more than scratch this tough granite. Even if it had been sandstone, tunneling through miles of it was out of the question.

He endured another shower and pulled his horse away from a patch of juicy grass. The steep canyon walls brought sundown faster than the trail he had ridden earlier. The heat helped dry him off as he wended his way back, letting the horse pick its own path in the gathering darkness. A misstep now meant a broken leg. Being on foot meant an even chancier confrontation with the outlaws tracking him.

The sun was setting in the far west by the time he came to the canyon mouth. While trying another canyon to throw them off his trail might work, such a tactic gave poor odds. Pick one and he had a fifty-fifty chance of running into the outlaws. And nothing said he came out any better than the box canyon he had just escaped. Better to edge back in the direction he had come, find the trail to Golden Junction and head there directly.

All he had to do was avoid the pair of owlhoots after him.

Asa pulled down his hat brim to shield his eyes from the low sun as he rode into it. The sound of a horse nickering was his first clue his plan had failed. The gelding's ears flicked back and forth, and its eyes rolled. Something had upset the animal.

The bullet ripping past his head was the final clue things had gone to hell in a handbasket. Both outlaws cut off his escape. Worst of all, they had the sun to their backs and were almost invisible to him.

Asa drew his six-gun and fired blindly. It was all he could do if he wanted to stay alive.

CHAPTER SIX

HE WAS A goner if he didn't get the sun out of his eyes. Asa dropped low and pressed in close to his gelding's neck and kicked hard to get the most speed out of the horse. He cut off at an angle and got the worst of the blinding rays out of his face. But the hot lead tearing past ripped closer and closer. When his horse stumbled and went to its knees, Asa flew head over heels and landed flat on his back.

Staring up at the twilight sky was a hint of what awaited him. He'd be in a shallow grave staring up, and then everything would turn black. Dead. He would be dead if he didn't bestir his bones and get to cover.

He started to roll to his right, then reversed and used the momentum to carry him over and over down a low slope. Rocks cut at him and more than one bramble bush stuck thistles into his face. The pain served as a warning. He heaved harder, rolled faster and ended up at the bottom of a ravine. Most of the water had diverted to a lower streambed, but he still got a fair amount of mud on his coat.

"Hey, mister, why don't you just give up? All we want's the money." The words from above and out of sight past the ravine lip came muffled but still menacing.

"What money?" He used the banter to stall and reload. They weren't stupid men. They had to know any money he carried had to be in the saddlebags. His horse must have survived the fall and run off.

The road agents need only run down his horse and they'd have what they wanted. There wasn't any cause for them to kill him.

"I just want to ride on. I don't have any money."

"Now, mister, we know that's a bald-faced lie. The folks in that town back yonder, they gave you a big parcel crammed with money. Five thousand dollars, it was. Ain't that right, Otto?"

"We know it was. They had cake sales and church socials to raise it. Rumor had it that the priest handed over all his parish money. That's a lot of plate passing, I'd say."

Asa crept along the ravine. Staying in one spot let the men bracket him. He gripped the Peacemaker and marveled at how natural it felt in his hand once again. It had been ten years. Then he had strapped it on and killed a bank robber the same day. If he didn't double that head count right now, his corpse would end up stripped and left for the coyotes. The men after him weren't the kind to let anything go to waste. The money was mostly what they sought, but his fine leather boots and fancy sapphire studs and Colt would be plucked from him. And his Stetson. It had cost close to fifty dollars back in the day. They'd be sure to take the hat.

He picked up a fallen branch, worked it upright between two rocks and tossed his hat onto the top. The Stetson rocked back and forth, caught in a faint vespers wind blowing down the slopes of the Front Range.

Moving as quietly as he could, he positioned himself against the ravine bank and looked up. His best chance now was to wait.

"Now, mister, you just insulted us. We ain't fallin' for no hat stuck atop a stick. We're smarter than that. Ain't we, Otto?"

A pebble tumbled past Asa. He looked up and saw the dark silhouette of a head poke over the bank. He took careful aim and made sure he wasn't falling for the trick that had not fooled the outlaws. This was one of them. He fired.

A small grunt sounded. A hat fell into the ravine, followed by a six-shooter. The outlaw—it must have been Otto—slowly slid over the verge like a snake. When his body got far enough, he tumbled to crash onto the rocky floor. He lay still. Even if Asa hadn't drilled him, the fall would have done him in from the way his head twisted about at a crazy angle.

Asa slipped his Peacemaker back into his holster, cautiously reached out and snagged the outlaw's six-gun. He grabbed the front of the man's shirt and dragged him closer to take all the ammo in his belt. The six-shooter felt unbalanced in his hand. Asa mentally corrected for this. If he shot, he wanted to be dead on-target.

"Otto? You get him?"

"Yeah." Asa muffled his voice and hoped he fooled

the other outlaw, at least long enough to get in a shot at him. "Bottom ravine. Fell."

"You're such a clumsy oaf. I don't know what I'm going to do with you."

Asa started to climb up the steep embankment, then froze. His instincts warned him he was walking into a trap, that he had not fooled his ambusher one iota.

"Shot. Caught a bullet." Though he kept up the act, he knew right away that his deception had failed.

The outlaw burst out from his cover, turned and opened fire all the way to the bottom of the ravine. Asa flattened against the ravine embankment and burrowed in the best he could as bullets tore up the dirt around him. With a twist that wrenched his ribs, he got around and opened fire on the indistinct figure. Darkness hid much of the ravine. The only way Asa had of knowing where his assailant was hiding came from muzzle flashes. The first few had dazzled him, but he heard crunching gravel.

He tracked the sound, then whirled around and fired in the opposite direction. A sharp yelp of pain rewarded him. The outlaw had been tossing stones to lure him into giving away his position. Asa tried to end the fight then and there, but his six-shooter came up empty.

Although the other man was invisible, Asa knew he had a similar problem. The metallic click of a hammer falling on a spent cartridge told the tale. They both had to reload.

Only Asa had an ace in the hole. He dropped the captured six-gun and whipped out his Peacemaker. He bracketed the area he suspected of harboring the gunman. Another grunt of pain signaled how accurate he had been.

"Just gimme the money. You can go on your way," the outlaw called.

Asa was long past bartering his life for the money. This was a duel to the death. Not the time to be faint of heart. After emptying his Peacemaker, he waited for a lull on the outlaw's part. Rather than reloading his own gun, Asa threw caution to the wind and ran flat out for the spot across the ravine where the outlaw had to be hiding. As his long legs devoured the distance, he stretched out his left arm, flexed his muscles and released the mechanism sheathing the stiletto. It whipped out into his hand as he vaulted over a tumble of rocks. His gamble paid off. The outlaw stared up in surprise, his six-shooter gate open and cartridges spilled out on the ground as he reloaded.

Then he died.

Asa started to slash in the other direction across the man's neck but stopped. His heart hammered. He felt a wildness that he had forgotten he could experience. He dropped to his knees and peered at the dead man, his throat slashed from ear to ear. Panting a few more times settled himself down. He drove the knife blade into the dirt and pulled it out. A second thrust cleaned it enough for him to fasten it back into the spring device on his arm.

He rolled around and stared back in the direction of the other dead road agent. Two men had died by his hand. And the bank robber back in Meridian made three. For so many years, his life had been peaceful, the only trouble being an argument between his children or not getting a decent supply of chemicals for his shop.

He cursed Dutton for talking him into this fool's errand. He had hardly gotten on the trail to Golden Junction and he had killed three men already. When his nerves calmed enough, he got to his feet and walked slowly across the ravine. Flies already buzzed around the body of the first outlaw. He considered taking the time to give both dead men a decent burial.

"What do I owe them? They tried to kill me."

Still, letting the coyotes and wolves dine on their flesh wasn't the Christian thing to do. He found a break in the embankment and scrambled up to hunt for his horse. He put his fingers to his lips to whistle, then stopped. Something felt wrong. Just as he had known the second outlaw hadn't been fooled by his mumbled replies, he knew letting out a whistle would be dangerous, if not deadly.

He reloaded, checked his knives, then began hiking toward a wooded area. The gelding had bolted in that direction. The brambles and thick undergrowth would slow any creature. If his horse had gotten tangled in the thicket, it would slow and eventually forget why it was frightened. He slipped into the woods and experienced real darkness. With even starlight cut off, he had to go on carefully.

The sounds reaching him came from deeper in the woods. He drew his pistol as he worked through the bushes. To his ears, he sounded like a wild stampede. But his horse's neighing drowned out his advance.

For a few seconds, he saw only his horse. Then a shadowy figure moved around and worked to untie the saddlebags holding the five thousand dollars.

There had been a third road agent. This one had left his partners to plunder the cash intended to save Meridian. Asa took aim, then hesitated. In the dark, he was more likely to hit his horse than the outlaw.

Fortune favored the bold. His pa had told him that so many times it was etched into his very soul. Walking slowly toward the outlaw, he made no effort to hide. His horse caught his scent and tried to rear.

"Whoa, stay down. None of that kicking at the air, boy." The road agent tried to calm the horse, but the gelding was having none of it. He jerked and kicked and shied away.

Asa kept walking, his Peacemaker pointed in the direction of man and beast.

When he came within ten feet, the outlaw saw him.

"Danged if you ain't part cat. How many of them nine lives have you used up? Must be most all of them."

"I never expected to see you again." Asa pointed his six-shooter directly at the man who had accompanied him from the Mosquito Pass depot to Meridian—the one who had to have been the gang's lookout at the tobacco store.

"Reckon I can say the same. Let's me and you split the money. Since you're here and my two worthless buddies ain't, you must have ventilated them. I heard some gunfire. That was you killin' 'em?"

"I cut one's throat."

The outlaw laughed. "I hope it was Otto. He never knew when to shut his yap."

"I can't let you take a dime of that money."

"You don't think you have a ghost of a chance to win in that consarned poker game, now, do you? The best gamblers in the territory are going to play. Word is that there might be a million dollars or more on the final table. Now, that's so much money, I have no idea what it would look like. I ain't one of them there millionaire railroad tycoons or gold mine owners. That's why this money's so attractive. I can understand a few thousand dollars and can appreciate how I'd spend it."

"Whores? Firewater?"

"Them's a pair of mighty fine ideas. I didn't think a man like you would understand, but I see how wrong I was. Come with me. We split the money, we get ourselves a couple whores and enough popskull to get crazy knee-walkin' drunk and—"

The entire time the outlaw had been talking, he worked at the rawhide strips holding the saddlebags to the saddle. When he got the bags free, he slung them toward Asa and went for his six-shooter. Asa had watched his every move and listened with half an ear to the spiel. The man wasn't fool enough to think he'd talk Asa Newcombe into wanton sexual debauchery and getting blind drunk.

Asa fired. The man grunted and then returned fire. The horse reared between them, making the fight more difficult. The outlaw dropped to his knees and scooped up the saddlebags, firing as fast as he could. The dark shielded both of them. Bullets flew wildly. One whined past Asa's ear, but he never felt the bite of hot lead. His pistol came up empty. His pa had told him to never retreat, never surrender. He rushed on. As he stepped forward, he reached down and drew a knife from the top of his right boot.

The two collided and went rolling over and over. The horse continued to paw the air and swing deadly hooves just inches above them. Asa ignored his horse and strove to drive his knife into an exposed gut. He felt the blade sink deep just under a left rib. He twisted it and then lost his grip. A heavy hand pushed against his face and shoved him back.

The other knife in his left boot came out. He held it easily, moving it in small circles.

"I declare, you can use both hands. Any gambler able to do that has an advantage." The man had looked old with the gray hair and long beard, but he moved like a snake. His vitality proved more than Asa could handle.

Asa felt his left wrist caught in a powerful grip. He drove his knee upward into his enemy's belly. The grip on his wrist vanished. So did the knife.

"Fisticuffs. That's what it comes down to. Winner take all." The outlaw punched hard and doubled Asa over. The man was a head shorter and on the bow-legged side, but he moved with a bounce in his step. In spite of the wound Asa had delivered to the man's belly, the fight was proving to be one-sided—against Asa.

The spring-loaded knife along his left arm slammed into his hand, and he drove the tip forward. Dampness exploded over his fingers and soaked his coat sleeve.

The outlaw gasped, turned and kicked like a mule. His boot knocked Asa backward. Asa's heel caught a rock, and he sat heavily. He grimly clung to his knife, the knife that had already taken one life. But his opponent was nowhere near. He rolled to the side, came to his feet and dropped into a knife fighter's crouch. He heard cursing and thrashing through brush, growing more distant by the second. Finally only night sounds remained, crickets and his horse pawing at the ground.

Asa wiped off his knife again, reset it along his arm, then reloaded his Peacemaker. Only then did he hunt for the saddlebags, which he found easily, if somewhat clumsily, by tripping over them. It took longer for him to retrieve his other two knives. He swung into the saddle and retreated through the forest until he came out near the ravine.

The outlaw had hightailed it. He had two nasty wounds, but Asa had no idea if either was fatal. From the inventive cursing as the short outlaw had run away, he wasn't likely to keel over from the knife cuts. Even taking that into account, Asa should have tracked him down and finished him. He'd have done the same for a wounded deer. Then he thought of the bodies in the ravine below and how close he had come to being dead, too. A tug on the reins turned the horse around; then he reconsidered. It took a few minutes to find a spot along the ravine where the side had collapsed, allowing the horse to slip and slide down.

Asa found digging in the ravine bottom difficult and finally put the two bodies together in a shallow depression, then stacked rocks on top of the pair. He said a short prayer, then mounted and patted his horse's neck.

"That's more than they deserved." He checked to be sure the saddlebags were firmly tied down, his Peacemaker rode easy at his hip, and he had wiped as much gore and dirt from his duster as he could.

Although dog-tired, he wanted to put as much distance between him and the site of the killings as possible. More than this, the third man roamed the night. Even if he was seriously wounded, all he had to do was lie in wait to ambush an unwary rider. Asa fit the bill perfectly. The horse was as tired as he was but showed heart and kept walking.

By the time dawn outlined the mountains to the east, he found the road to Golden Junction.

And he found something more that made him grab for his six-shooter, draw and cock it.

CHAPTER SEVEN

THE DAWN WIND sluggishly blew past Asa Newcombe, tugged at his bloodied duster and pushed
his Stetson up on his forehead. The sun was to his left,
so he had a clear sight of the rider squarely in the sights
of his six-shooter.

"You look like you were pulled through a knothole
backward," the man said. He tugged on his horse's
reins and came closer. Impeccably dressed, he might
have just stepped out of a haberdashery rather than enduring the dusty road for what had to have been miles
and miles. A long, thin waxed mustache danced as he
smiled. That smile was as cruel as Asa remembered.

"Give me a reason not to pull the trigger," he said.
His voice cracked. He needed a long drink of water
from his canteen. The truth was, after all he had been
through since riding from Meridian, he needed something a lot more powerful.

"Because I am your savior, Asa. That's why you won't shoot me down. Here." The man reached back and rummaged about in a large burlap bag slung over his horse's rump. Turning back, he held out a bottle of whiskey. Asa knew it was the finest money could buy, just like the man's fancy morning coat and his bright red silk vest with a matching cravat held in place by a headlight diamond the size of a man's thumbnail. The tall top hat wobbled a bit in the breeze. As the man reached up to steady it, his coat pulled open, revealing a double shoulder rig. He wore six-shooters under each armpit. In a cross-draw holster at his left hip hung a bigger six-gun. If the man moved too fast, he'd clank from all his hideout guns.

And this was just the obvious arsenal.

Asa reckoned he saw at least two sheathed knives. That meant he missed that many more.

"Here, Asa, take a long drink. You look as if you need it more than I do." The man's smile turned even more vicious. "Is that blood? Mud? You been wrestling hogs again?"

Asa's finger tightened on the trigger. It had been fully ten years since he had run afoul of Laramie Frank Gillette. He had hoped never to see the man again, but if Gillette was ever destined to intrude on his life again, this was the obvious place. Let a hint of a big pot waft on the breeze, and Laramie Frank's nostrils would expand and he'd follow the scent to the ends of the earth.

"You scared them all off with that clown suit." Asa weighed his chances of getting away with murder if he drew back another fraction of an inch on the trigger. If going to Golden Junction set him on a killing spree, adding Laramie Frank Gillette to the list of deceased appealed to him a lot more than it should have for a law-abiding family man.

His finger relaxed, and he placed the gun into his holster with exaggerated care. He edged closer and reached out for the whiskey. Gillette drew back at the last instant so Asa's fingers only brushed the rounded bottle. Actually grasping it proved impossible.

"You owe me, Asa. You have to pay up before I give you a taste of this fine whiskey. It's mighty good booze, too." Gillette licked his lips and made a smacking sound. "How much was it you owe me?"

"The price of a bullet," Asa snapped. He regretted not filling the gambler full of holes. He wheeled his horse around and started toward Golden Junction.

"Wait up. Don't go away mad. We can negotiate like gentlemen, as hard as that must be for you. It was a hundred dollars, but if you give me fifty, I'll let you have a sip." Gillette held the bottle up and pretended to drink. "A big discount on a debt honestly owed—and you get something to slake your thirst. You do still drink, don't you, Asa? It'd be a pity to give up one of life's finest pleasures."

Gillette trotted alongside Asa, who did his best to ignore him. He had a mission, and Gillette wasn't part of it.

"The *Dixie Queen*, wasn't it? Where we parted company."

"You know it was. Be quiet, or I'll—"

"Or what, Asa? Silence me like you did—"

Asa balled his fist and swung it around like a mallet. He missed landing squarely it in the middle of Gillette's face. His fingers swept past the heavily waxed mustache, causing it to fray. The power of his missed blow caused him to lose balance. He would have tumbled from the saddle if Gillette hadn't reached out and grabbed his shoulder. The gambler's strong hand held him long enough for him to recover his seat. He fumed and would have taken a second swing at Gillette if the gambler hadn't drifted a couple yards away.

The smirk irritated Asa more than making a fool of himself by missing his punch.

"Is that a wedding band on your finger? I do declare, it is. You, of all people, married. The way you used to cut such a wide swath among the ladies along the river, I thought you'd never settle down with just one. Or that you could. What was it that the lovely whore in New Orleans gave you? I thought that made your manhood fall off after a month or two."

"You want to settle scores here and now, Gillette?"

"Oh, please, call me Laramie. All my friends do. And we're going to be great friends, Asa. Until we face each other across a green felt table again. Then it's every man for himself. Just like before, on the river."

Asa saw red and reached for his Peacemaker, but he was tired and slow. Gillette shrugged his shoulder, whipped out one of the Smith and Wesson .38s from under his arm and had it aimed in an unsettling rock-solid grip before Asa could get a steady hold of his own gun.

"For a plugged nickel, I'd kill you here and now. I'd take your ante money and feel like a king when I used it to take everyone else's money. But shooting you isn't going to give me the pleasure that beating you at poker will. Or faro. Name your game, and I'll clean you out."

"You'd be better off murdering me. If we get into a game, face-to-face, you'd never stand a chance. You didn't ten years ago, and you don't now."

"You won't have your pa this time to help you cheat me."

Asa flushed but held back a sharp retort. The barrel of that .38 looked big enough to stick his head in and look around.

Gillette started to say something, then returned his six-gun to his holster. He twirled his mustache back into a needle point and put his heels to his horse, galloping away without even a hint of another cutting taunt. Asa rested his hand on the Winchester's stock. A rifle shot was possible for another minute until Gillette topped a rise in the road and disappeared down the far side. Asa sagged, exhausted by all that had happened to him that day.

The fight with the road agents had been draining. But somehow the killing hadn't left its scar on his soul the way gunning down the bank robber had. Once he started shooting men, it got easier. That bothered him, but not as much as running into Frank Gillette after all these years. Some memories lingered; others he fought to forget. Gillette stirred the embers of his fiercest memories of gambling along the Mississippi. Not many of those memories were pleasant, especially the last time he had laid down a hand on a riverboat.

A small straight, trey through seven. It had been enough to win a thousand-dollar pot. Raking in the money had ignited bad feelings and . . .

He slumped in the saddle. His energy drained like water through a hole in the bottom of a rain barrel. He had reached the point where going on wasn't possible. With some reluctance but resigned to physical and mental exhaustion, he gave the horse its head and let it take him to a stream a quarter mile off the road.

Asa fell from horseback, sat heavily and stared at the gurgling stream. Supreme effort got him to his feet. He stripped off his bloodied duster and the clothes beneath it. After kicking off his fine leather boots, now sadly in need of polishing again, he finished undressing and waded into the stream. The icy water brought him instantly awake. He shivered as he washed away the last traces of the outlaws' blood. He lurched back to the bank, unsaddled his horse, hobbled it and then set about washing his clothes. By the time he finished, the sun had poked well above the Front Range and given him a chance to hang his wet, clean clothing on a tree limb to dry. When he got a fire going, he fixed a small meal. He lacked an appetite but forced himself to eat. He had not had eaten since breakfast in Meridian the day before.

The plate and cup rinsed off, he dressed. The effort that took convinced him he needed at least a few hours of sleep. It bothered him that the outlaw who had accompanied him from the Mosquito Pass depot, the same one who had been lookout for the bank robbery, had gotten away, but he was sure the man had been badly injured. By now he might have bled to death from either of the knife wounds Asa delivered so savagely.

Asa still moved his camp away from the stream and into a secluded spot where he might sleep safely. He stretched out, head on his saddle and the saddlebags under his shoulder. He stared out into the woods, his eyes wide open. Then his lids drooped, and he fell into a heavy sleep.

He came awake with a start, six-shooter in hand. It took him a few seconds for his sleep-numbed brain to realize his horse was missing.

"The hobbles. I forgot the hobbles!"

He rose to his feet. He took two quick steps and stumbled on the hobbles. They had been unfastened. Someone had stolen his horse.

He glanced back. The saddlebags with the five thousand dollars had been untouched because he had been asleep atop them. Looking around, he found the tracks leading away. He stalked off, intent on the trail. From ahead he heard horses whinny. He ran through the brush and caught sight of Frank Gillette leading his horse off.

The gambler made a mocking gesture and called, "You got three days to get to Golden Junction before they close off the town. You're a loser, Newcombe, a loser!"

Asa shot high. His second round tore through a tree limb, and then Gillette galloped off, taking the gelding with him

Furious, Asa almost followed on foot. His fiery temper cooled a mite, and he remembered his gear was back in his camp. His saddle— and his saddlebags. Retracing his path, he cursed under his breath the entire way. He expected to find everything gone, but what he feared was not to be.

"Is this going to be my luck?" He sat cross legged and opened the saddlebags. The money was packed into one side of the saddlebags. His fancy duds were in the other.

There was nothing else to do but heave the saddle to his shoulder and get back to the road. It would have been a couple days' travel to Golden Junction on horseback. On foot it stretched to a week. As he hiked, Gillette's taunt came back to bedevil him. Close the town off? If he didn't get to Golden Junction before the games started, they wouldn't let him in?

That might be for the best. He wouldn't lose the ante money raised in Meridian. But that also doomed the town. Without the money to build the railroad spur, Meridian had no chance of surviving. It would be nothing more than another town that had outlived its usefulness. Before the railroad had gone through Mosquito Pass, Meridian had been on the road from Denver to Leadville. The railroad had ruined the town, and now the chance for the railroad to save it was in jeopardy if he didn't win at least enough to get tracks laid.

Starting the coal mine was another matter. The tracks had to reach Meridian first before miners would come to town. So many parts had to fit together. As he stumbled along, he considered his entire errand to be only a cog in a finely made watch. Every gear had to mesh, every cog and escapement swing just right, the stem and the hands and everything—all had to be perfect or Meridian would become a ghost town.

The thought of a watch made him press his fingers into his vest and trace the outline of the watch there. His father's watch. All he had inherited from Donal Newcombe other than nightmares.

He lengthened his stride, as if he could leave behind those bad memories. By noon he knew he was never going to reach Golden Junction on foot. His legs ached, and his feet had begun to swell. Swinging the saddle around, he dropped it near a tall bush beside the road and sat to rest. Time wore on him, but wasting a few minutes meant very little. He sipped water, chewed on a buffalo-jerky strip and stared down the road toward Golden Junction. As he thought about getting to the big game, a small dust cloud appeared ahead and grew larger.

Asa climbed to his feet when he saw a man riding a mule and leading four more, all laden with diamond-hitched loads. He waited for the rider to get closer before waving at him and calling out.

The man astride the lead mule moved his hand to a holstered six-gun. Asa didn't blame him, considering how he had lost his horse—and all the road agents trying to steal his ante money.

"Howdy," the man greeted. He squinted a bit as he looked Asa up and down. "Your horse die under you?"

"It was stolen," Asa said, "and that leaves me in quite a pickle. I have to get to Golden Junction."

The rider looked back over his shoulder, nodded and then spit a gob of chewing tobacco. "Just left there. Those people have done gone loco." He eyed Asa a bit more. "Are you goin' there for Big Ed Edwards' crazy card game?"

"There's a deadline for getting into town and signing up." Asa hesitated, then boldly asked, "How much for one of your mules?"

"How much? You ain't got enough money, do you?" The man's look turned into cunning appraisal. "Heard tell the buy-in runs a gent five thousand dollars."

"I'm going in a bit light," Asa said, knowing where

the negotiation led if he admitted to that much money on his person.

"You expect to sweet-talk your way in?" The man scratched his chin, spit again and wiped his lips with his sleeve. "I doubt you can do that. Big Ed's a hard-hearted, no-account, thievin'—"

"Twenty dollars."

"Twenty! I got a shipment to deliver. Why, any of my pack mules is worth, oh, five hundred dollars."

The dickering went on until Asa paid over an outrageous hundred dollars. His poke reduced, he knew he'd have to really talk fast to get in, if the ante amount was strictly followed.

"You can hide the load on my mule," Asa said, "and come back for it."

"I'll split it up on the other three. They're strong cusses."

"That's smart," Asa said, helping drop the mule's load so he could put his saddle on. "You can never tell who might come along and, even if you hid it well, steal what you left."

"I used to follow the Oregon Trail, picking up furniture and belongings. Made a good living off selling what them folks had to leave behind." He bit off another inch of chaw, worked on it a few seconds, spit and said, "You treat Ole Abigail good, now, you hear? She's my favorite."

"She ought to be. She just made you a hundred dollars."

This caused the mule skinner to laugh. He spit a final time and continued on his way, letting Asa deal with the mule on his own.

"So, Old Abigail, we're a team now. It's not the first time I've had to ride a mule, so I know how to do it.

Sorry I don't have an apple for you." Asa spent close to a half hour letting the mule get used to him.

The time spent paid off. Abigail set off for Golden Junction at a brisk pace, giving Asa hope of reaching the town before it was closed off for the game.

CHAPTER EIGHT

THE STEADY STREAM of wagons and riders pouring out of Golden Junction worried Asa Newcombe. He called to one man struggling with a three-horse team. The fourth yoke hung empty. The lack of a horse there caused the other three to pull at an angle. He wanted to tell the driver to unhitch one horse and tie it to the rear of the wagon. Two horses had enough strength to pull the wagon, hardly laden from the way it bounced and careened about. The man was in too big a rush to take the time to follow any advice.

"What's the hurry?" Asa shouted.

"Getting out of that crazy place before they shut it down."

"What do you mean?"

"The whole town's gonna be sealed off for the poker game. There's money to be made from all the gamblers rushing in, but I never in all my born days seen so many gunfighters. There's gonna be blood flowin' in the streets, mark my words. Besides, Golden Junction's best days are behind it. The whole place is dyin'. A ghost town waitin' to happen."

As Asa rode past, he saw the man's load consisted of household goods. That told him a great deal. Merchants might prosper from the newcomers, but ordinary citizens saw nothing to be gained from staying where mayhem was given free rein.

"Good luck," Asa called as the man drove past.

The driver gave him a quick look. "You already have luck on your side, mister. They're gonna close the town before you can get there. That's as heaven-sent as anything to happen to you in that cursed town."

"Wait! What do you mean? The game's not starting until tomorrow!"

"Poker tomorrow, last gamblers in at sundown today." The driver snapped the reins and got his mismatched team pulling away.

Asa wasted no time urging his mule to full speed. The stalwart creature put its head down and obliged. A mile down the road, Asa topped a rise and looked down on Golden Junction. The mining town huddled in a shallow bowl, hills surrounding it on three sides. Mine shafts had been bored into every available section of rock, the tailings dribbling from the mine mouths like stony black drool. He was not knowledgeable enough to tell at a glance how profitable the mines had been.

Had been. Asa wasn't an expert, but not a one of the mines he saw above the town had been worked in some time. That explained why the poker game had been proposed. An inflow of gamblers spending as they sat

at the green-felt-covered tables provided what might be
Golden Junction's last gasp.

Halfway between him and the town's perimeter, some
activity showed. Barbed wire fencing had been run
across the road. A single gate cut in the fence was flanked
by a guard tower. Atop the tower two men moved about
listlessly. It was too far for Asa to tell, but he guessed
they were armed with rifles.

"Giddyup," he urged, putting his heels to the mule's
flanks. Old Abigail snorted and started down the hill,
not quite trotting but as close as a mule could get.
Nearer, he saw three guards moving to shut and lock
the gate.

He shouted and waved. The tower guards spotted him.
He had ridden close enough to see they were armed.
They leveled their weapons at him, ready to fire.

"Don't latch the gate. I want in. I'm here for the game!"

The guards continued to move the crude gate. He
heard a shout from a crowd in the town. The single
word—"Fire!"—echoed along the road.

Asa bent low and got to the gate as a cannon belched.
White smoke filled the roadway beyond. He kicked out
and shoved hard against the gate, momentarily stopping it from closing. Then he burst through to the town
side of the fence.

"You get out! You sneaked in after the deadline!" A
burly guard stalked over to where Asa sat astride the
mule. "You gotta leave. The cannon's done been fired!"

"I made it before you shut the gate. I'm here to play
poker, and nothing's going to stop me." Asa turned
slightly and rested his hand on the butt of his Peacemaker. The guard stopped and held up his hand. The
other guards trained their rifles on Asa.

"Leave. I got orders. No more in after the cannon."

"Is your boss willing to lose another five thousand dollars? That's the ante, isn't it? I've got the buy-in money."

"I got orders."

Asa tensed, ready to pull his six-gun. He hadn't come this far, endured so much, to be chased off. His choler caused the guard to hesitate. The man turned and held a quick conference with the two sentinels flanking him. They argued for a few seconds. A decision was reached.

Asa approved of it. They didn't want to exchange gunfire any more than he did.

"Go on to the bank. It's on Main Street. You can't miss it. Check in there."

"Thanks," Asa said warily. He waited until the three men lowered their rifles. Then he stared at the two men atop the tower. They hadn't heard the exchange, but seeing their boss wave him through caused them to lower their rifles, too.

Asa rode slowly the rest of the way into Golden Junction, but he felt as if he had a target painted on his back. By the time he got to the first saloon, the Silver Bucket, he relaxed a little. Asa shook himself. He wasn't relaxing. He was getting excited in ways he remembered from ten years ago. The saloon doors were swung wide open and bad piano music rolled into the street, followed by cigar smoke and the sharp tang of spilled beer. Men cursed and shouted and laughed inside as they drank.

This used to be his world. It felt odd returning to it. And, he admitted uneasily, good. He belonged here more than he did behind the counter of an apothecary

store mixing patent medicines for people with head-
aches and the clap.

The sun warmed his back as he rode along, heading
for the bank. The guard had been right. It wasn't possible to miss it. The two-story redbrick building had
cost a pretty penny to build. Groaning from stiff muscles, Asa dismounted and secured Abigail to an iron
ring at the side of the bank. Dozens of men milled
around outside, and a short line waited impatiently to
get into the lobby. He sized up the men. They all had a
hard look to them. None carried himself like a gambler. More guards, he decided. As he went to the end
of the line, he frowned. Guards, yes, but why so many?
There was an army company of them that he had seen
out at the fence and around the bank.

He edged forward, saddlebags slung over his shoulder. Asa kept his hand hovering near his six-gun. Being robbed this close to being accepted into the game
wasn't going to happen. If anyone crossed him now,
they'd better be ready to trade a few ounces of lead. He
was tired and at the end of his rope. More than this, he
was on edge and excited.

One by one the men ahead of him forked over their
cash and were given a cloth bag. This puzzled him until he got to the teller's cage. The teller had two men
standing behind him, shotguns resting in the crooks of
their arms. He mentally increased the number in Big
Ed Edwards' army by two.

"You're the last one," the teller said. "Let's see the
color of your money."

Asa silently took out the stake given him by the
people of Meridian. The teller carefully counted, fin-

ished, frowned and then counted again. He looked up, shaking his head.

"What's wrong?" Asa felt a tightness in his belly.

"You're short by a hundred dollars. Five thousand is the minimum. You can put in more, but you haven't enough as it stands."

Asa tensed. The mule had cost a hundred.

"I bought a mule. I'll throw in the mule and that'll make the full amount."

"Nope, sorry. Can't take anything but scrip or specie. Those are the rules."

"You're saying I can't get into the game?"

"I didn't make the rules. You pony up a hundred bucks right now and you're in. Otherwise . . ." The teller pointed to the door.

Asa began searching his pockets. Nothing he had was acceptable. He placed his father's watch on the counter. The teller glanced at it and shook his head. Asa found a few coins.

"If you can't make the nut, get out. I want to start some serious drinking over at the Oriental Tiger Lair."

"A saloon," Asa muttered. "What if I get into a game and win the money, then—"

"When I walk out and lock the bank door, the game's set. It's now or never."

Asa had no idea what to do. He leaned forward, hands on the counter. He heard someone coming up behind him.

"That's a mighty fine watch. I'd be willing to pay, oh, ninety-five dollars for it."

Asa spun, hand going to his Peacemaker. He heard the men with shotguns cocking their weapons. If he drew on Laramie Frank Gillette, they'd blow his head off. He faced the man squarely.

"You heard. I need a hundred dollars."

"That *is* your papa's watch, isn't it?" Gillette reached around and pushed it around on the counter, using the tip of his index finger, as if the watch would burn his flesh. "Yep, that's it, all right. Somebody done shot a hole smack through the middle. And look at that. The time's stopped at one fifteen on the dot. Unless I miss my guess, that'd be one fifteen in the a.m. What a shame how that bullet really tore up the clockwork."

"You stole my horse. Pay me a hundred for the horse, and we're even."

"I didn't steal a horse. I found one on the road to town and brought it with me. It's a fine gelding, too." Gillette sneered. His mustache twitched. Asa started to unload a haymaker. Let the guards gun him down. He'd have an instant of satisfaction, mashing Gillette's nose into bloody pulp.

"I didn't steal any horse," Gillette hurried on, seeing the fury on Asa's face, "but I surely would like that watch. As a souvenir of my days on the river."

"Will you two get out? The bank's closed." The teller tapped his fingers on the counter.

"A hundred for my pa's watch?" Asa hardly croaked out the words. Emotion strangled him.

"Here it is." Gillette wiggled his fingers, and as if by magic, a hundred-dollar bill appeared between his fingers.

Asa moved faster than Gillette, snatching the bill. He dropped it on the counter.

"Five thousand," the teller said tiredly. "Here you

are." He pushed a cloth bag across the counter. Asa hefted it.

"Thank you. I'll give it a good home." Gillette held up the watch and peered through the hole drilled in it. He winked, tossed the watch into the air, caught it and left the bank, laughing.

Asa used every bit of self-control not to shoot down the gambler.

He stopped the teller to ask, "What's in the bag?"

"Chips. Those are all you need. When one person wins all the chips, the game's over. No money in any game. Just chips."

"You're keeping the money in the vault?" He looked past the two shotgun guards.

"That's the idea. We got nigh on a million and a half dollars waiting for the winner. I hope it doesn't take long. I want to clear out of town." The teller left.

Asa opened the bag and saw a double handful of chips, white, red, blue and black. Counting quickly, he figured out how the chips equaled the five-thousand-dollar ante he had forked over in the bank. He tucked away the cloth bag in his coat pocket, then mounted the mule and began exploring the town.

Other than an electric feel like that in the air before a lightning strike, Golden Junction seemed no different from any other boomtown. As Asa rode, though, he saw how most of the stores were closed. Many were boarded over. Golden Junction was already on its way to becoming a ghost town. The few remaining stores catered to the gamblers who had come to take part in the winner-take-all poker game.

Asa circled the bank and saw how heavily guarded

it was. Not only were armed men on the roof; several patrolled like army sentries on the ground. Not far away tethered horses showed the guards anticipated chasing down robbers.

"So much money," Asa muttered, staring at the barred windows and the brick walls. If only he were a ghost that could reach through solid walls and iron bars, taking the money Meridian needed would be easy as pie. When two guards began tracking him on his circuit of the bank, he knew he was drawing unwanted attention. Robbing the bank wasn't on his mind, but the guards thought so.

He rode back down Main Street and saw the small-stakes gambles going on. The bets were tiny compared to those made in the saloons where faro and poker ruled. Through open doors he saw chuck-a-luck and other dice games. The familiar whir and click of a roulette ball spinning and dropping set his heart racing. For ten years he hadn't placed a single bet. Now the old urges returned. He came alive in ways working in an apothecary store stifled.

Seeing a four-story building down a side street, he turned in that direction. The hotel towered over every shop around it. He stopped in front, then kicked at the mule to move on. Staying in the Everest Hotel wasn't for him. Whether it had always been a brothel or just turned into one to accommodate the influx of gamblers didn't matter. He wanted a bed, not a bed with a paid companion.

As he continued on his way, half-naked ladies of the night leaned from upper-story windows and called to him. Asa ignored them and had insults heaped on him. The words meant nothing. He knew what he was. He was a family man, with a loving wife, two young girls and another child on the way.

"That's why I'm here," he told himself. "For Rebecca and the girls. And a son. I'll have a son this time." Not moving them from Meridian before the winter set in was the gamble he took, why he had come to Golden Junction.

He rode to the end of the street. A barbed wire fence stretched across it, blocking any further travel. Asa rode close enough to kick at a post. It wobbled. The fence was recent and not well constructed. Perversely, he kicked harder and knocked the post loose. Before a final kick upended the post, he felt a chill run up and down his spine.

The sound of a rifle jacking a round into the chamber echoed through the still night. It came to him this wasn't an echo. At least four rifles were ready to fire. He looked over his shoulder and saw the rifles were all aimed at him.

Without being ordered to, he lifted his hands.

CHAPTER NINE

"YOU TRYIN' TO let in latecomers?" The man directly in front of Asa drew a bead. "We got orders to shoot anybody tryin' that."

"I just wanted to find a place to make camp for the night. The rooms in town are a bit pricey for me."

"Live with it," the guard said. "You're lucky we don't shoot you right here."

"Yeah," piped up another. "The only reason we don't is that we'd have to dig a grave for you. The boss don't want no bodies layin' around town."

"That's good to know," Asa said. "You mean, Big Ed Edwards?"

"None other than." The leader turned and showed his right arm. "This here shows who's in charge."

Asa saw the red armband emblazoned with a king from a deck of Bulldog Squeezers Cards. Looking at the other three guards, Asa realized that each had an armband but with a different playing card. The higher the card, the more authority, he guessed. The leader had a king. The loudmouth beside him sported a five of clubs. The other two kept their ranks hidden, but from their toadying behavior, he took them to be even lower than the five. He had run afoul of an officer, a sergeant and two privates in Big Ed's Golden Junction private army.

"We keep things legit," the king of clubs said. "And we got the power to shoot anybody breakin' the rules."

"What might these rules be?" Asa saw how the guards let their rifles droop off target. He wasn't in any real danger from them.

"The boss will tell everybody in about a half hour. Get yourself on over to the Silver Bucket, where he'll greet you and explain how somebody's gonna get real rich."

"A million dollars, that's what the bankers are saying," piped up the five of clubs. "I want to see that stack of money."

"I heard tell it was more. Makes me wish I had buy-in money. I'd be filthy rich and—" The wistful guard fell silent when the king of clubs whacked the back of his head with an open hand.

Asa wanted to let them work out their disagreements by themselves.

"I'll make my way on over to the saloon. You have any recommendations for a place to sleep, since you don't want me pitching camp here?"

The king grunted and motioned with his rifle. Asa didn't press him for an answer. He rode slowly, aware of the four men arguing over who had to reset the fence post. He took a street running parallel to Main Street and saw a half dozen small games of chance already in progress, ranging from mumblety-peg to dice. A hubbub farther along the street drew him to a large lot festooned with dilapidated army tents. Simply stopping to stare at the encampment brought out a weaselly man with darting eyes and nervous hand gestures.

"You huntin' fer a place to sleep? Look no more. This is the place you want. Ten dollars a night."

"Ten!" Asa was outraged at the price. A hotel shouldn't even charge that much—though the Everest likely did because of the additional bed warmer.

"You get a tent and a pallet. There's plenny o' room for your tack. We even got a guard to watch over the tent town to keep sneak thieves away. You don't want some miscreant makin' off with your property whilst you're busy winnin' the main prize."

"I certainly don't want a miscreant stealing from me," Asa said sarcastically. The proprietor ignored the tone.

"Better hurry. The town's all fillin' up quick. You just holler, and I'll get you situated." The entrepreneur hurried off to another rider looking over the field of tents with some distrust, leaving Asa by himself.

He dismounted and considered how he might improve his situation. At ten dollars a night, it would drain his stake slowly. Finding food and other services had to cost even more. Five thousand seemed like a pitiful poke the longer he stayed in Golden Junction.

"Hey, mister. You."

Asa jerked away when someone tugged on his sleeve. This man must have struggled to reach town. He wore tattered clothing that betrayed him as a prospector. Canvas trousers, a red-and-black plaid shirt, a floppy-brimmed black felt hat and boots so scuffed, they were almost white showed him as being down on his luck.

"You one of the local citizens?" Asa asked.

"Naw, I came here to win the big pot. But I'm a frugal cayuse. The same as you. I heard you dickering with Breckinridge."

"The purveyor of these fine dwellings?" Asa again failed to contain his scorn.

"Ten dollars is a lot for me. I'm used to unrolling my blanket under the stars for nothing. What do you say about splitting a tent? Each of us chipping in five a night?"

Asa saw how quickly the tents were being rented. Sleeping on the street wasn't likely to be tolerated by the militia Big Ed Edwards had patrolling Golden Junction.

"I'm Asa Newcombe." He thrust out his hand.

"Call me Desert Pete. I spent so much time down south in the Sonoran Desert, I got to the point where I didn't even have enough spit to lay claim to a last name."

"You must have done all right for yourself if you can buy into the game."

"More than all right, Asa, more than all right. Now, let's get ourselves settled before Breckinridge ups the price."

It took another fifteen minutes of negotiating. Desert Pete had hit the nail on the head. Breckinridge tried to charge fifteen for the tent since two of them were sharing. Asa got the feeling that while the man's greed was obvious, he enjoyed dickering more than taking the extra money. They settled on twelve dollars a night for the two of them.

"All I've got are the chips." Asa patted himself down, hunting for any money.

"That's good enough. When it gets closer to the end of the game, face value on them's likely to be more. Whoever wins has to corner all them chips." Breckinridge grinned. His teeth looked like black granite tombstones. His eyes glowed as both men counted out two nights' stay.

For another five dollars, Asa stabled his mule.

"Let's wander a mite, Asa. Just to get the lay of the land."

Asa wasn't interested in Desert Pete as a partner. Certainly not when the real gambling began. Still, having someone at his back who wouldn't stab him at the first chance was prudent until he understood how best to win the money and hightail it.

They walked down the middle of Main Street. As they did, Desert Pete stomped his foot hard, then did a curious dance. He looked around, scratched his crotch and hurried to catch up since Asa tried to put distance between himself and such crazy behavior.

"There's something strange about Golden Junction," Desert Pete said. "You ever been to Tombstone?"

Asa shook his head. He was more interested in the Silver Bucket Saloon than a lecture on all the places where Desert Pete had dug in the ground. He started up the steps to the saloon and paused. Two men were pitching pennies, only they used five-dollar chips. In the brief time he watched, one man lost almost a hundred dollars. Rather than explain to him how the winner had cheated, he pushed past and into the Silver Bucket. The saloon was immense and packed with men shoulder to shoulder.

A man banged away at a piano. Asa tried to make out the tune and failed. It was only additional noise adding to the uproar inside. Men sat at tables, already gambling. The nearest table held eight men playing stud poker. Asa watched carefully, seeing if any of the gamblers cheated. Two worked together. They'd end up fleecing the other six and then split the take.

He hesitated to watch the faro dealer at a table just inside the door. Asa decided to get such thoughts out of his head now and play for keeps later. The woman dealing wore a scoop-neck red silk dress that descended so low, the tops of her breasts bulged up and threatened to spill out. The players mechanically moved their money around the table, paying little attention to what had been played and the odds of winning. They bet more heavily when the dark-haired woman bent over the table to pay off winning bets and to sweep up the losing chips.

"She's quite a looker, eh?" Desert Pete pressed close. "When I win the big pot, her and me's going to paint the town red."

"Golden Junction?"

"Naw, San Francisco. Or maybe New York City. With money like that, a trip around the world's not out of reach. Why not have a filly as purty as her help me spend it?"

Dreams. Asa saw that more than the lure of a huge pot had brought the gamblers together.

Desert Pete reached around him and dropped a black chip—a hundred-dollar bet—onto the faro table. He lost. With a hard elbow, he worked his way closer to the table. Asa let him try to impress the dealer with his largesse. Asa had no doubt that she'd be a willing travel companion, should the miner win big. From the way Desert Pete dropped his second bet onto the table, Asa knew there was almost no chance for him to come out on top.

Asa fought off the press of the crowd to get to the long Brunswick bar. Like all of them made by that company, it had fancy woodwork and a large mirror behind the barkeep.

"Beer," he shouted.

The smallish man in the canvas apron drew a beer and set it in front of Asa. He mouthed something.

"What's that?"

"Five," the barkeep shouted. "Five dollars!"

Asa almost walked away. A five-dollar beer meant whiskey would go for three or four times as much. The merchants were making out like bandits, and the tournament hadn't even officially begun. He dropped a red chip with some regret. Between lodging, livery and a single beer, he was running through his stake at what seemed to him a frantic rate. Sipping slowly, he vowed to make this his last drink. It never paid to get drunk during a game. If the others at the table did, so much the better. Their grasp on the odds faded with every shot of whiskey and made winning that much easier.

Still, the beer went down cool. Getting to Golden Junction had been a trial. He owed himself this one drink before he got down to business.

He looked around when an expectant murmur passed through the crowd. Standing on tiptoe, he saw a well-dressed man climb up onto the stage along the far side of the saloon. He was gray-haired and stout and carried himself as if he owned everything in sight. When he cleared his throat and introduced himself, the truth of the matter came out. The man did own it all.

"Gents, welcome to the biggest game in the whole danged West! There's never been anything like the Golden Junction Gaming Extravaganza. For those poor, blighted souls who don't know me, I'm Big Ed Edwards, the creator of the game of the century!"

A cheer that caused a ringing in Asa's ears went up. He finished his beer. Swallowing cleared his hearing.

"Y'all know the rules, but I want to make certain there's no dispute. You are here to get rich, not get into trouble." He gestured. The guard wearing the king of clubs armband stepped out from the wings, brandishing his rifle. "This here's Lou Gallant, head of my security force. It's a militia, and it's intended to keep you honest. No thieving allowed, or Mr. Gallant will deliver justice swift and deadly. Go on, get yourself a drink, Lou, so I can finish telling these fine gentlemen the rest of what they're in for."

Edwards cleared his throat and struck a pose like an orator ready to pontificate for the rest of the day.

"You've swapped for chips in place of your greenbacks and gold pieces. Those are safe and secure in my bank, waiting for the winner to collect it all. That might be in a day or a week. It won't matter how long it takes. Play continues until one of you lucky gents has all the chips in the players' pokes. You don't have to tote your winnings around. You can stash any of your chips in the bank and draw them out whenever you like. They're the same as money as long as the contest goes on."

Asa heard one man nearby mumble, "The price of

everything's sky-high. There's not gonna be any call to put our spare chips in his bank—there won't *be* any spare chips."

Asa didn't doubt prices would go up the longer the games ran. Big Ed Edwards stood to make a fortune, especially since the winnings would come from the herd of players and not from his own pocket.

"The rules are simple enough. You decide what games to play. I don't much care. We'll cater to your druthers, be it any brand of poker, dice, faro, roulette, rummy or even the heathen game of fan-tan. We aim to please!"

A roar went up.

"There's not much more to say, other than Golden Junction is hereby sealed tighter than a banker's wallet. Nobody gets in, nobody gets out—until the last card is turned and a winner is announced."

Asa caught his breath. Winning just the money needed for Meridian's enterprises and then leaving thereafter weren't going to be possible. He either lost all the money given him by the town, or he won the whole damned thing.

"Mr. Gallant has orders to shoot to kill, and I assure you, he's a fine marksman."

"A hundred dollars he kills somebody before morning!" The bet came from someone behind Asa. In a few seconds, a dozen others were taking one side or the other on the bet.

"That's the spirit. Race horses up and down Main Street or play high-low or invent your own games. Bet on which flea jumps off a hot griddle first. Whoever wins all the chips becomes a millionaire! Now, get going. Drinks are on the house the rest of the night. And gamble!"

Another deafening cheer went up. The crowd surged and swayed and pressed all around Asa. A dozen tables already had men working toward winning all the chips. He got to a wall and edged along it, sidling to the door. Stepping into the cold night air shocked him awake. In spite of everything that he had done—and that had been done to him—that day, he was alert.

He almost turned and went back into the saloon. A few hands of poker would get him back into the spirit. Then he froze. Two men approached him in the middle of the street.

"Hold this." One man shoved a cloth bag into Asa's hands. He rattled it. The chips swapped for the buy-in weighed down the sack.

"Yeah, you'll do." A second man thrust his chips bag into Asa's hands.

"What do you want me to do?"

"Hold them until there's a winner."

Asa started to speak, then clamped his mouth shut. The men squared off in the street. He gasped when they slapped leather. Both of their six-shooters discharged at the same instant. The muzzle flashes momentarily blinded Asa. When the dancing yellow and blue dots faded, one man was sprawled on his back. The other clutched his side. The crowd watching stayed mute for a moment, then cheered when the wounded man lifted his six-gun and began firing into the air.

He hobbled over and yanked both cloth bags of chips from Asa's hands.

He held those up as he had his gun. The crowd went wild. They hoisted the man onto their shoulders and carted him off down the street, hooting and hollering. Asa saw how the militiamen flanked the crowd. In a minute he stood alone outside the Silver Bucket Saloon, just him and the body in the street.

Asa started to walk over to see how the loser of the bet had fared, but the sick churn in his gut told him. The winner was wounded. The loser was dead. Two of Lou Gallant's men came from inside the saloon and carried off the body.

The Golden Junction undertaker was going to be cheated out of his fee unless the winner paid for the funeral.

Steps heavy, Asa went back to the tent he was sharing with Desert Pete and flopped down under his blanket. He stood to lose more than the money from Meridian if he wasn't cagey. Sleep crept up on him and filled his dreams with leering faces, flashing guns and cascades of poker chips falling from the sky.

CHAPTER TEN

THE LOUD NOISE woke him. Asa rolled onto his back and, eyes still closed, tried to identify the curious sound. He sat up, bumped into the sloping tent and dropped back. Everything flooded back to him as he stared into the sunlit canvas flap.

He started to poke his tentmate, then decided it wasn't worth it. Desert Pete shuddered with every exhalation, causing the horrible noise. Asa gathered his gear, made sure he had the cloth bag holding his poker chips, then slid from the tent, stood and stretched. The sun poked up over the Front Range and promised a fine late-summer day. It took a bit of hunting, but he found the barbershop. It didn't surprise him that there weren't any customers. He paid a dollar chip for a bath with hot water and dressed in his fancy duds.

Asa preened in front of a mirror, brushed off his Stetson and noticed a bullet hole shot through the brim that hadn't been there before. He aligned his tie and sapphire studs on his shirt, buttoned his vest and paused as he touched the empty watch pocket. Laramie Frank Gillette had the watch that belonged there. Asa's hand brushed the butt of his Peacemaker. Before he left Golden Junction, his pa's watch would rest in the vest pocket again.

"You look like a real cardsharp, mister," the barber said. "You thinkin' on scarin' the others with your fancy dress and manner? It won't work. They're all just like you."

"They're not just like me," Asa declared. "They're not going to win." He smiled, touched the brim of his hat and left. The street had been abandoned when he went into the barbershop. Now men crowded to get into the saloons and begin gambling.

He sauntered back to the tent city and tucked his dirty trail clothes into his saddlebags. Rummaging about woke the snoring prospector. Desert Pete yawned mightily and wiggled like a snake from the tent. Asa watched as he did his curious dance, stomping about, taking a few steps and repeating the jig.

"Foot gone to sleep?"

"I spent too many years boring into mountains not to notice strange things when it comes to rocks." Desert Pete stomped again, shook his head in dismay at something that didn't strike him as quite right with the ground, then gave Asa a long look. "You're sure duded up. You look like one of them."

Asa settled his clothing, knowing the barber had been wrong. How he presented himself to the other gamblers mattered. If he convinced them he was a professional gambler, they would treat him differently. If they showed the slightest bit of caution in the way they bet, he had an advantage. From what he had seen, most of the wealth seekers drawn by Big Ed Edwards to his game were amateurs. The professional gamblers—like Gillette—would never be cowed. For men like him, Asa had other tactics to separate them from their chips.

"I look like one of them because I *am* one of them."

"How come you're not pushing your way into a game, then? You don't seem to be in any hurry."

"Card playing is like going into battle. You don't just rush in and bet all willy-nilly. You need to have a plan and follow it."

"So what's your plan, General?"

Asa laughed. He hadn't considered it before, but he felt like a general in charge of an entire army. His men were chips, and every bet was a skirmish.

"Since the one who wins the last hand walks away with everything, I intend to let most of them eliminate one another. The more I play, the more likely I am to have a run of bad luck."

"Let the opposition take themselves out, then swoop in for the kill? That's not bad. You saw the fight last night? One gent's already doubled his stake because he has a quick gun."

"I saw," Asa said. "That makes the winner harder to beat since he has twice the ante of anyone else."

Desert Pete shook his head. "That's not perzactly true. Five thousand was the minimum buy-in. More than a few have more in their poke."

Asa hadn't realized that. It meant some players had the backup to outlast a stretch of bad luck.

"Thanks for telling me. That's valuable information. I know another . . . entrant . . . who likely has more than the minimum." If anyone had come loaded for bear, it'd be Gillette. Better to let the others snipe at Gillette and nibble away at his stake before taking him on.

The risk he took was that Gillette was a competent gambler and might end up with a large stake when he and Asa faced each other. Asa remembered how that had gone before. This time Gillette would lose every last chip.

He wandered out onto Main Street, seeing smaller bets being placed all around. Two men played paper-rock-scissors for a hundred dollars' worth of chips. Others crouched in the dirt, rolling dice as if they were illicitly gambling on an army post and were afraid the duty sergeant would catch them. Asa poked his head into the Oriental Tiger Lair Drinking Emporium. Every table was crowded. Four faro tables did brisk business. A roulette wheel clanked and squeaked. The disrepair didn't stop a half dozen players from laying bets.

Asa continued his scouting around town. A couple times he saw Desert Pete hopping and then dropping to hands and knees, acting like a dog sniffing about. The man had spent too much time in the sun, and it had affected his brain. Still, he had bought his way into Golden Junction. Heatstroke cooking his good sense was possible, but he had ponied up a small fortune to be able to dance and stomp. Asa almost called out to the prospector, but Desert Pete had become intent on rattling a door to an abandoned shop. He pulled nails free and slid into the building.

Asa let him be so he could continue with his own study of the opposition. A half hour later, he was getting the itch to find a poker game and enter into the flow of the town. A woman coming from the general store caught his eye. He had to smile. Lovely and trim, she was trying to carry far too many packages. As she stepped down from the boardwalk, the top package escaped, causing the rest to fall like dominoes.

She heaved a sigh and muttered to herself. Trying to pick up the fallen packages, she fumbled and dropped them again. Asa crossed the street and scooped up two of the boxes.

"Let me help, if you will."

She reared back and eyed him. A slow smile came to her thin rouged lips. Her blue eyes sparkled and she held out her gloved hand, indicating he should proceed. Asa gathered the packages and waited to hand them to her. She made no move to take them.

"If you would help me with them, I'd be most appreciative."

Asa had nothing better to do at the moment, and the powerful pull of shuffling cards and clicking chips faded. "It would be my pleasure."

"You are a gentleman among so many . . . who aren't." She made a face as she took in men spilling from a nearby saloon, shoving and cursing.

She set out, opened a parasol to protect her fair skin from the summer sun and set a pace that put her a half step ahead. Asa appreciated the view as her bustle swayed.

"What do you think of Golden Junction so far?" Her voice was soft and carried a sensuous tone that began to worry him.

"I appreciate the scenery," he said. "And the opportunities here."

"Do you now?" She turned and batted her eyes at

him. Her long dark lashes gave her what Asa had heard called bedroom eyes.

"Please don't get the wrong idea. I'm married." He turned his left hand so she caught the gold glint off his wedding band.

"How unfortunate," she said. Before he protested, she grinned and added, "For me. Up there. Please put the packages on the porch."

He looked up and saw they had arrived at the Everest Hotel. Soiled doves waved from the upper windows. It was impossible to miss how some of the Cyprians pointed at him and the lady and began whispering.

"Would you join me on the veranda for a drink?" She paused and added, "Nonalcoholic, of course."

"Of course." He piled the packages up by the door.

"Jeremiah! The boxes. And fetch us a couple glasses of lemonade."

The liveried servant scooped up the packages and said, "At once, Miss Lorraine."

She settled down on a long sofa and patted the spot beside her. Asa hesitated.

"I won't besmirch your honor, sir. You do seem to be very married."

Asa sat. He appreciated the clean lines of her face, the long, graceful neck, the swell of her breasts under the immaculate white blouse and the soft perfume scent from her carefully coiffed dark hair.

"Thank you, Jeremiah." She handed Asa a glass of lemonade taken off the servant's tray. Their fingers touched for a brief instant. She smiled almost sadly. "Because you are on a diet doesn't mean you can't look at the menu."

"There are certainly many delicious things on that

menu, but I'll have to take a pass on them," Asa said. He felt taken back ten years to when he rode up and down the Mississippi on the riverboats. Romancing the ladies was as much a part of his life as the turn of the cards. But that was in the past, before he'd met Rebecca.

"You are so polite and witty. That's such a difference from most men in Golden Junction."

Asa sipped the lemonade. It was stronger than most whiskey. He fought to keep from making a face.

"I apologize for not having sugar. Such things in Golden Junction are . . . rare these days. I have put in an order for some, but delivery is a problem."

"Why do you stay? Most of the stores are closed."

"After the mines played out, many of the men left and took their money with them. Golden Junction is a shadow of its former self. Though business is down, Big Ed convinced me to stay until after his crazy scheme." She smiled brightly. "I'm glad I stayed. I wouldn't have met you if I had left a week ago." She held out her gloved hand. "I am Lorraine Overton. And, yes, I own this hotel and employ the young ladies in the upper-floor rooms."

"Right now they are gossiping about you—us." Asa downed the drink in a gulp. His lips began to pucker from the sour lemonade.

"Chin-wagging is quite important. The one with the most secret information gains a certain notoriety."

"You say Edwards talked you into staying."

"Oh, really, sir. Don't waltz around it. He paid me a decent sum to remain until after his poker game. The men get bored with doing nothing but gaming, after all."

"That's not my experience. Until they win a pile, the game is most important."

"I hope you are right. And, yes, I consider this huge poker game to be something of a fraud. Big Ed seldom does anything honestly if he can find a way to do it with a crooked twist. He enjoys that more than having money, I think."

"Sealing everyone in town riles me," Asa said. "That gives him an advantage, but I'm not sure how or to do what."

"He owns the richest of the mines—the ones that produced quite a lot of gold. His Merry Mary Mine assayed out at four ounces a ton. By the time it played out, he owned the town. The bank, the saloons, most of the businesses."

"But not the Everest?"

"You are most inquisitive, sir. I'd sell it for a song and a dance and move on. When the game is over, I intend to." Miss Lorraine licked her lips, put down her glass and sat primly, her hands folded in her lap. She looked at him coyly. "Spending time with me is not a gamble."

She was well schooled and the perfect courtesan. Asa had seldom seen many in his roaming days along the river, from Saint Louis down to New Orleans, to match her in style or classic beauty.

"Your invitation is appreciated, but I must regretfully decline." He held up his wedding band again.

"There is no reason for any to know but us. I assure you, your time will not be wasted."

"I'd know." He laughed and craned around to look at the upper stories of the hotel. "And at least six of your girls would also know."

Miss Lorraine sighed heavily. Every movement of hers was a thing of grace and beauty. A pang of regret passed quickly, though. "If exuberance at winning overwhelms your sense of duty, please come back."

"Not duty, Miss Lorraine, not duty. And I have yet to place a bet."

"Smart and faithful. Where were you before I came to Golden Junction?" She sounded as if she meant the question seriously.

He stood, bowed slightly, tipped his hat and left before she wore him down. He had never been unfaithful to Rebecca, and he was not going to start now, even with a woman as charming as Lorraine Overton, however pleasurable that would have been. Keeping his vow to be faithful meant as much as his love for Rebecca. If a man broke his word, he had nothing.

The ladies upstairs waved and shouted lewd suggestions. He waved, then turned toward the Silver Bucket. Spending the morning scouting the town, talking with Miss Lorraine and seeing how eager others were to gamble caused him to feel the itch. His fingers twitched, and his heart beat faster at the thought of sitting at a poker table.

He pushed open the double doors and looked around the saloon. It was time to win the money that would keep Meridian from the fate facing Golden Junction.

CHAPTER ELEVEN

H E SOAKED IN the atmosphere through his pores. Asa closed his eyes, listened to the click of dice and the soft whisper of cards being dealt. To him this was the patter of rain on a rooftop and the soft wind blowing through pines. He sucked in a deep breath and coughed. It had been too long since he had been cooped up in a room filled with this much smoke, though. In his apothecary shop, he forbade anyone smoking. Other than the shop and his home, he didn't get around much in Meridian.

But this! He remembered every detail from working the suckers on riverboats.

"Howdy, partner."

He glanced to his right. Three crowded faro tables showed where a considerable amount of the action in this saloon centered. The game was easy, the odds were easy and the winning was easy if you were the house. But his tentmate stood in front of the table. A single glance warned Asa that Desert Pete's bet was a loser.

"You play faro much?" He stood beside the old prospector.

"Enough. I got this lucky feeling about the table."

Asa looked over the man dealing. He was well dressed, if anything better than Asa, straight as a ramrod and about a sturdy five ten, and his demeanor commanded the table. There was no question that he ran the bank and that he'd take no guff off anyone, in spite of the ever-present smile. As he reached out to pull in the lost bets—including the one Desert Pete had dropped—Asa saw the scars on the man's wrist. He had been a slave. His dark eyes locked with Asa's, as if daring him to place a bet.

"The four," he told Desert Pete. "Give it a try."

"You want to double up on that bet, sir?" The dealer's voice was soft. He taunted Asa into action.

Asa silently dropped a black chip on top of Desert Pete's ten-dollar bet. The dealer smiled slightly and nodded. The soda card came up from the shoe and was pushed aside. The banker's card went to the right of the box, followed by the player's card to the left. The banker flipped his card.

"Eight, the loser." A dexterous move turned the player's card. The man's eyebrows rose. "Four, the winner. You gents are lucky." He slid even money over, ten to Desert Pete and a hundred to Asa. "You want to stick around a few more hands and bet the turn? I'll give you five-to-one odds."

"Not four to one?" Asa's eyebrows went up at this. He realized that he mimicked the banker and laughed.

He had fallen into old habits. In a game, mirroring his opponent's gestures always gave him a slight edge. "You're feeling mighty generous."

When the deck got down to a final three cards, betting on the numerical order gave the higher odds.

"What should I bet on, mister?" Desert Pete tugged at his sleeve. "You got Lady Luck riding on your shoulder. This is the first bet I won all morning long."

The banker said, "Give him the benefit of your expertise. You're on a winning streak."

"One bet's not a streak."

"A philosopher as well as a gambler." The banker smiled broadly and thrust out his hand. The frilly lace cuff bobbed about, hiding the scars. "The name's Washington Reynolds, but my friends call me Wash."

"Asa Newcombe, and nobody ever calls me Red."

Wash laughed, deep and vibrant. "I'll remember that, Asa. You interested in working the box with me?"

He considered the offer. Two at the faro table sped up the betting. With so many gamblers anxious to win the big pot, he and Wash might turn a couple thousand dollars an hour.

"Let me give you an answer in a while. I want to look over the rest of the competition." He felt as if a magnet was pulling him from the faro when he saw Laramie Frank Gillette strut into the saloon. The man made a beeline for an empty chair at a green-baize-covered table. He dropped a stack of chips onto the table and took a hand being dealt, as if he had been in the game all night long.

"Don't take too long." Wash grinned even more broadly. "I don't expect it to take me more'n another hour to clean out everybody in Golden Junction and win the big pot."

Asa touched the brim of his hat in acknowledgment and brushed off Desert Pete's wail about staying to help him bet. If the prospector bet on gut feelings rather than on odds, Wash Reynolds would be five thousand closer to his goal in nothing flat.

That'd leave it to Asa to win the money away from another cagey gambler.

He slid back and forth through the crowd. Most bet on trivial games, the flip of a coin or how many beer glasses they could stack before they all fell over. Asa saw the barkeeps egging their customers on. They raked in the chips. He realized another reason for substituting the chips for actual money was how few of the men understood the cost of what they did. A man touched a twenty-dollar gold piece with something approaching reverence. Parting with it required certain determination. But a red chip? Or even a hundred-dollar black chip? They weren't real money, and very few of the men had experience thinking of them as such.

A few paces to the side of the table where Gillette had come to roost provided Asa the perfect view of the gambler's hands and how he shuffled and dealt. The first few hands went off with only a few chips changing hands. Then Gillette flipped through the deck, as if looking for a marked deck. Asa moved a step closer when Gillette turned over one card after another, then scooped them up and riffled through again.

"What's it you see, partner?"

Asa jumped. He was concentrating so hard on what

Gillette was doing that he had neglected to see Desert Pete come up.

"I lost a thousand to that black fellow. I have to admit, he made it painless. And quick. He wasn't cheating, was he?"

"No," Asa answered, distracted. Gillette riffled through the deck again and once more dropped a half dozen cards faceup before squaring the deck, shuffling and dealing. "But he is."

"How?"

"That's the house's deck, and it's not marked. But when the cards are cut, the patterns along the edges are off by a fraction of an inch. He's memorizing the patterns and knows what half the cards are by now."

"So they are marked?"

"A defect in how they're printed and cut. Edge sorting, it's called. There were rumors that Gillette used ace sequencing when he played blackjack, but that's easier than what he's doing now."

"So them folks across from him are guessing what everyone else has, but—what's his name?—Laramie Frank Gillette knows what's he up against?"

"He'll fold a losing hand. Maybe not every time, but enough to preserve his stake."

Asa and Desert Pete watched a few minutes. It went as predicted.

"Big Ed Edwards ought to do something about it. He's the honcho running this party." Pete picked at his teeth with a broken thumbnail as he opined.

Asa laughed and shook his head.

"I don't want him to. Let somebody else complain, if they even notice how they're being snookered."

Desert Pete scowled, then chuckled.

"You're a devious one, aren't you? If you know how he's cheating, you can do it, too, when you face off. You reckon it's going to come down to the two of you—isn't that it?"

"Something like that, but I don't cheat. I don't have to."

Asa considered that face-off. Gillette had more tricks than edge sorting to rely on. If he tried it in a game, Asa could do the same, too. Better to ask for a new deck after every few hands. Memorizing the misprints on the cards without seeing their faces repeatedly was almost impossible and leveled the playing field—the playing table.

He left Desert Pete and found a game where he faced three professionals and four others with no sense of how to gamble. Working carefully, he won small pots. One by one the unskilled players dropped out. From the expression on the final one to leave, he had lost all his chips. One day and out.

"Cut," came the sharp command. The deck ended up in front of him. Asa used a multiple cut that bought him a frown from the dealer. The man tried to replace the cut deck the way it had been passed to Asa, but a quick grab of the man's wrist prevented it.

"Keep the cut honest," Asa ordered.

He saw the play of emotion on the man's face. One question had to be asking this annoying newcomer to the table to join the cheat against the other players. Then the face turned impassive, and a slow deal began. As far as Asa saw, it was legitimate. No dealing seconds or off the bottom. He glanced at his hand, pushed in five hundred dollars and sat back to see what the result of such a large bet would be. The players had upped by fives and maybe tens. Such a huge opening bet had to drive out most of the players.

Asa forced himself to remain deadpan when all the others met his bet.

The play came around again. Asa stood on his hand. By the time it came for a showdown, the pot held more than fifteen thousand dollars.

"Let's see what you've got," Asa said. The others at the table edged a little closer. For Asa, and the others, this hand set the standard against all other betting.

"You should have drawn. You can't beat this." The dealer laid down a full house, tens full of jacks. He reached for the pot.

Asa stopped him by dropping his cards on the dealer's grasping hands.

For a moment, no one moved. Then the dealer jerked back as if the cards burned him.

"Straight flush. A low one, but still a winner." Asa's cards were diamonds, five through nine.

"You were dealt that? How'd you stack the deck?"

"You dealt. All I did was cut—and made sure you kept the cut." Asa moved his elbow enough to push back his fancy coattails so he could grab for his Peacemaker, should the need arise. He tried to read his angry opponent. If he guessed wrong, lead would fly.

"You cheated. You had to. Nobody is dealt a hand like that without cheating." The dealer pushed back from the table. Asa guessed he had a derringer in a spring-loaded arm rig from the way he moved so stiffly.

"Let me buy you a drink. The price Big Ed charges, it'll cost me most of the winnings." Asa waited to see if the small joke had a calming effect.

"I watched you both real close," piped up another player. "He beat you fair and square."

"Might be the two are in cahoots. A fake fight would make the rest of us think it was all on the up-and-up." The player directly across from Asa poked them both, egging them on.

"Are you planning on betting on which of us survives?" Asa never took his eyes off the dealer, but his question broke the man's anger—or redirected it.

"Mathias, you thinking on eliminating me by pushing me into a gunfight?"

Asa pushed back another few inches from the table. The tide had turned. The dealer and Mathias now glared at each other. Before they joined forces against him, Asa raked the chips into his hat and hastily left. He had hardly reached the door when the two began throwing punches. As he stepped into the street, gunfire began.

Which way would he have bet? On the dealer or his adversary?

Asa shook himself. Wagering over a man's life was wrong.

He started across the street but was stopped by a man who looked down in the mouth.

"Please, mister, I lost all my stake. I'll starve if I don't have any money."

"You won't starve. The game'll be over soon enough before that happens."

"From the look of that mountain of chips, you're gonna win." The man tensed and moved as if he readied for a quick draw.

Asa shifted the hat holding his chips to his right hand and thrust out his left. The spring mechanism along his left forearm kicked the stiletto into his grip.

He held the sharp edge against the man's neck. They held the tableau for a heartbeat. The beggar backed away, hands open and empty in front of his chest.

"I didn't mean anything. I didn't."

"Here," Asa said, tossing the man a blue chip.

It came as no surprise that the man looked at it, mumbled thanks and rushed into the Silver Bucket. It would end up being lost in a few minutes. Asa hoped Wash Reynolds ended up with it in his stack.

He reloaded his spring knife and went to the bank. He had a stack of chips to put into his account so he wouldn't have to ward off others like the man he'd just met.

CHAPTER TWELVE

ASA NEWCOMBE SLOWED as he neared the bank. His sharp eyes fixed on a man sitting in the shadows, his hat pulled down to shade his eyes. Something about him put Asa on edge. When the man stirred, he showed dried blood on the side of his shirt. Whatever injury he had taken had caused him to bleed like a stuck pig. As the man turned, Asa went for his six-gun. He stopped in middraw when one of Big Ed Edwards' militia went to the man and spoke. The militiaman waved his arms around like a windmill, then called out.

The man wearing the king of clubs armband, Lou Gallant, sauntered over, crowded close and towered over the seated man. The three talked a few seconds, then the man with the bloodied shirt stood.

Asa had seen him before. Too many times. They had shared the trail from the Mosquito Pass depot to Meridian and crossed paths there before the abortive bank robbery, and the last time had been out on the trail leading to Golden Junction. Asa had wondered how badly he had injured the man in the fight that had seen the man's partners killed. Asa had wounded him twice, but not fatally.

Now Big Ed's militia would take care of him.

He moved to a spot across the street to watch, to be sure this time. Asa went cold inside when Gallant shook the smaller man's hand. The outlaw slapped the militiaman on the back and walked away, each shaky step signifying that Asa had done more than scratch him. Every move echoed pain. A few inches one way or the other and Asa would have ended the man's foul life.

The two militiamen left behind talked; then Gallant pointed down the street. His underling hurried off. Whatever the meeting had been about, they all parted on good terms. Asa walked slowly toward the bank, wondering if he should tell Edwards that his chief of security was consorting with a known bank robber. He went into the bank and looked around. A half dozen guards watched him like a hawk.

Whatever Gallant and the others were up to, Asa doubted it involved all these men. He went to the teller who had swapped his money for chips the day before.

"I'd like to bank ten thousand in chips." Keeping back three thousand was adequate for most games he'd enter later.

"Ten? Done." The teller scribbled out a receipt and pushed it across to Asa as he counted the chips.

"Wait a minute. You put down ninety-five hundred."

"There's a service fee for banking your winnings."

"I won't pay it." Asa pushed the receipt back. If he had intended to warn the bank about a possible bank robber running loose in Golden Junction, the good deed died on his lips. They were as big a thief as anyone sticking up the bank using a six-shooter.

"That's up to you."

"Wait. I want cash for the chips. I want to cash in."

The teller looked left and right. Both guards moved closer. Asa tried to ignore them, but it became hard when both moved their rifles around and trained them on him. The fastest gunman in the West could never have shot his way out of the cross fire they would have him in if he started anything.

"Can't do that. Nobody gets the money until the final payout, when there's a winner. Then he gets the entire amount."

"I want to cash out early."

The teller puffed up a mite and looked down his nose at Asa. The guards edged closer and made no bones about putting him into their sights. A quick glance showed the guards in the overhead garrets had also reacted. He was the target for no fewer than four guards now.

"No." The teller's declaration came hard and harsh.

"Cash me in or—"

"Or nothing. We're not going to have a problem with you, are we?" The voice came from the doorway behind him. Asa glanced over his shoulder. Lou Gallant entered.

"No problem." Asa scooped up his chips. The teller made a show of tearing the receipt in half, then in quarters and letting the pieces flutter to the counter.

"You might reconsider. It's getting vicious out there, and some of the owlhoots participating have the look of evil in their eyes."

Asa faced Gallant. His temper flared. He barely controlled the outburst accusing Gallant of conspiring to rob the bank. What words had been exchanged? Gallant might not know the bank robber's history. But Asa doubted that.

He shoved all the chips into the cloth bag that had carried his initial five thousand. It bulged. If he had won any more, he'd have needed a second bag. Not saying another word, he pushed past Gallant and went outside. His heart hammered. Big Ed Edwards had stacked the deck. Once in this game, there were only two ways out. Most would lose. One would win. No one left early.

If Asa had a lick of sense, he'd get on his mule and ride out of town. Better yet, he'd take his gelding back from that horse thief Gillette. Then he'd leave. Instead, he went in the direction taken by the robber, not sure what he'd do if he found him. His fingers danced lightly over the butt of his six-gun. Settling the score had to be done eventually, but at the moment, he was more interested in finding out what the outlaw was up to.

Him and Lou Gallant and the other militiaman.

Keeping a sharp lookout, he went up the street until he came to the edge of town. The barbed wire fence had been restored, and just inside walked a militiaman with a red armband showing he was the ten of clubs. Not equal in rank to Lou Gallant but probably higher than a low-ranking soldier.

Asa watched the armed guard on his sentry route and experienced a sudden loss of nerve. A lie to the mayor and the citizens of Meridian explained away the lack of money. While their hopes had been high for him, he doubted many actually thought he'd return with the railroad money. There was still time to pack up his family and get to Denver before the first snow—and before Rebecca delivered their third child.

All this crossed his mind. Asa's luck ran true. His brief hesitation as he ruminated over possible excuses prevented a guard he hadn't seen trailing the ten of clubs from gunning him down. This militiaman wore a deuce of clubs armband and carried a sawed-off shotgun as well as two pistols at his hips slung in cross-draw holsters. It was as if each guard packed more iron than the preceding one.

He spun and returned to town, this time going through the town square, where a small crowd was assembled. Carpenters sawed and hammered thick slabs of wood to make a platform.

Asa asked an onlooker, "What're they building? It's too big to be a gallows."

"It's a ring for a fight. There's going to be one at sundown. Or maybe tomorrow, whenever they get fighters. You want to lay a bet?" The man looked eagerly at Asa. "I'll give you better odds than any of the other punters."

"I don't even know who's fighting."

"What's the difference?"

Asa laughed harshly and walked away. Bets were being made, and no one even knew who the fighters were. A red sash hung on one post, and the opposite corner had a yellow. For all anyone knew, the fighters wearing those sashes hadn't been decided yet. The betting frenzy had seized everyone in town.

If Asa couldn't cash out and he was trapped in the town by armed guards, he had to win the big pot. Doing that meant smart card play. Betting on fisticuffs was a sure way to lose money. The only way a fight wouldn't be fixed was if it ended when one fighter died. That made it in earnest for the boxers.

He walked a little faster from the town square as he wondered if the fight was going to be to the death. From the deaths he had already seen, he didn't discount the notion.

The Silver Bucket beckoned. He went in and cast an eye around. In the short time he'd been gone, the numbers had thinned. The men who thought they would sit down and win in a hurry had done the opposite. The professional gamblers methodically cleaned them out. Asa knew the others had no reason to cheat. Not yet. Simply knowing the odds won more hands than bottom dealing. At least so far.

"Asa, come on over." Wash Reynolds motioned him over to the faro table. "Nobody else wanted to run the bank, so this looks to be my exclusive table."

"You need help to fleece them? Is that it?" Asa laughed at the idea. Even with a simple game like faro, the amateurs got wiped out in a hurry. This was a game favored by drunken miners and cowboys who wanted to ogle the usually lovely female dealer rather than win. The more they lost, the more they thought the dealer liked them. Big Ed Edwards' contest had displaced the lady dealer he had seen earlier. Asa wondered if Miss Lorraine's house of ill repute had gained in the number of soiled doves, women displaced from the gambling dens and faro tables.

"There's a lull. Men gotta eat." Wash spoke with contempt at such weakness.

"You don't?" Asa watched his reaction. Wash studied him as closely.

"Neither do you. I went close to forty-eight hours in a poker game over in Abilene last year. Never so much as stood up. When the game was over, my legs collapsed under me when I tried to leave."

"If you won, there'd be plenty of ladies to help you."

"There were. Come on around and work the box. We can split the take. And the ladies, after we make a fortune." Wash shuffled the cards, cut them with one hand, folded them into piles and manipulated the pasteboards to show Asa how dexterous he was.

Asa tried not to be too obvious as he considered the other gambler. He'd have to face off with Wash sooner or later. They both held the same ideas, and he needed to get an idea about the man's tolerance for risk, how he bet, everything he could about his betting and bluffing. Working alongside Wash for a few hours seemed an ideal way to learn without risking any of his stake.

"Deal. I'll handle the box." Asa came around, did a quick count on how much Wash had on the table, then matched it. "We split fifty-fifty when we fold the table."

"Agreed."

Wash began his spiel when a knot of men came up. Among them only one was a serious gambler. Asa and Wash worked the crowd, cleaned out some, paid off others and finally called it quits around two in the morning.

"It seems a shame to let all of them get away without contributing," Wash said, glancing at the still crowded saloon.

"There's always tomorrow. Or, rather, later today. We don't have to clean them all out in a single day, unless you're in a hurry."

A flicker of emotion lit the man's dark eyes.

"I want out of Golden Junction as quick as I can go. There's something wrong about this place."

Asa considered telling him about the militiamen and the bank robber. For some reason, he kept silent. A quick count of the chips Wash shoved in his direction showed they had each made back their stake. Five thousand each for a few hours of being the bank at a faro table.

"Not bad," Asa said. "I enjoy faro, but I'm itching to get into a poker game."

"Like you did before? I saw how you cleaned out a couple of those greenhorns."

"Good night." Asa slapped Wash on the shoulder, shook his hand and left. His every move had been scrutinized. It was good being among professionals. As he stepped into the cold night lit by a blanket of stars above, he remembered all the things about the gambling life he had enjoyed. And only now did he know how much he had missed it.

He made sure his Peacemaker rode easy at his hip, then set off for the tent city. He made his way through the rows, found his and Desert Pete's tent and crawled in. The prospector hadn't returned. That surprised him. The way Pete bet, he should have been wiped out by now. Asa settled his stuffed bag of chips under his shoulder, scooted about to get comfortable and drifted off to sleep.

He came awake with a start. He had just had an anxiety dream of the bank robber he had stabbed and Lou Gallant and a gang of others taunting him, poking him, stealing from him. It hardly qualified as a nightmare, but it had been unpleasant. Rolling onto his back, he stared at the canvas above him.

Then he sat bolt upright. The bag where he had stashed his chips lay where he had put it, but the end had been cut open. His winnings—all his winnings—were gone.

Panicky, he crawled from the tent and looked around. Sunrise threatened but Golden Junction remained in darkness and would for another half hour. Asa circled the tent, studying the ground for tracks. His eyes darted all about, frantically searching for a clue as to the thief. So many men came and went that even his own tracks were obliterated as surely as if a buffalo herd had thundered through. Figuring which belonged to the sneak thief wasn't possible. He looked around, hoping to catch someone fleeing or looking guilty.

He might as well have been in a ghost town. Nobody stirred.

Panic turning to anger, he prowled through the tent city. His rage burned down to the embers of frustration when the impossibility of catching the crook hit him like a punch to the gut. He left the lines of tents and found one of the militiamen asleep in a chair on the boardwalk in front of a bakery. The fragrant smell of baking bread made his mouth water, but he had more immediate concerns. He kicked hard, caught the chair leg under the sleeping man and dumped him hard to the boards.

"Wha!" The guard went for his six-gun. Asa stepped on his wrist. The man looked up in fear. His wide eyes fixed on the fuming Asa. "Don't kill me!"

"I was robbed." Asa released the hand under his boot. The man wore a four of clubs armband—barely more than a private. "Who's in charge?"

"Mr. Edwards. H-he's the one you got t-to t-talk to."

The guard pointed down the street in the direction of the bank. Asa started to ask if the guard had any idea who had robbed him, then stalked off, fuming mad. Asa had never liked people who assumed a redhead had a fiery temper, but right now they would have been right. He went to the bank, expecting to kick in the front door to vent some of his anger. To his surprise, the door was open, and a half dozen people had crowded into the lobby.

"Where's Edwards?" He made no attempt to be polite. The time for that was past.

"What can I do for you, son?" Big Ed Edwards came around the end of a railing dividing the lobby from a half dozen desks. Behind the desks, the vault was securely closed.

"I was robbed. I was sleeping in a tent over by the town plaza, and somebody stole all my winnings."

"Now, that's a crying shame. What do you want me to do about it?"

"Your militia's everywhere. That's as close to a marshal and deputies as I've seen here. Catch the thief. Get my chips back."

Edwards laughed so hard, he had to put his hands onto his belly to keep it from bouncing painfully. He wiped tears from his eyes and looked at his two tellers. Both men had their hands under the counter. Asa knew they were ready to drag out their six-shooters and open fire at the slightest provocation. He was so mad, he didn't care. The half dozen others in the lobby all rested their hands on their own weapons.

"That's about the funniest thing I've heard in a spell. Son—"

"I'm not your son." Asa's tone caused Edwards to sober up. Steel came into the man's eyes and words.

"The militia keeps the peace. They're not here to enforce any laws. In fact, right now in Golden Junction, there aren't any laws. Just rules. Of poker. Or whatever game you're playing. That's it. Son."

Asa took a deep breath. It didn't calm him one whit. If anything, Edwards' attitude had made him even angrier. "You won't even try to find the sneak thief?"

"You should have banked your chips in the vault. They'd've been safe there."

"For a percentage."

"Next time, you shouldn't be so stingy. Pay the fee."

"I lost everything."

"That's going to be true of all but one gambler. The lure of such a big payoff is what got you here. Every last one of you thinks he'll be the winner. You just happened to lose quicker than most."

Asa started to argue, then whirled about and stormed from the bank before he did something he'd regret. He was outgunned in the bank. Worst of all, Big Ed Edwards was right. He should have bitten the bullet and paid the percentage to keep his winnings in the bank vault. He'd have been robbed but nowhere near as much as he had lost to the sneak thief.

He closed his eyes and turned his face to the rising sun, basking in its warmth. He had no idea what he was going to do now, but he had to think of something.

CHAPTER THIRTEEN

A SA NEWCOMBE STOMPED back to the tent city. He stopped at the edge when he saw a pile of gear—his. The tent master, Breckinridge, grunted and cursed as he dragged another man's gear from the middle of the tent city and dumped it beside Asa's.

"What are you doing? You don't have any right to touch my tack."

Breckinridge squinted and looked as if he wanted to spit on Asa's belongings. He scratched himself, kicked at a burlap bag holding something that moved sluggishly and finally said, "Twenty. Rent's up to twenty a night for the tent, you and that poxy miner you're sharing it with."

"That's highway robbery!"

"Find someplace else, then, if you don't like my price."

Asa looked around and saw many of the tents had been knocked down and hastily folded. The more men who lost their buy-ins, the more that got booted from the camp.

"I can pay," Asa said. He felt his face turning as red as his hair. Holding back his ire proved increasingly difficult.

"Then pony up, gambler man." Breckinridge held out his dirty palm. "No? Thought so. Heard tell you were flat broke after somebody stole your poke last night."

"How'd you know that?" Suspicion flared. Asa thought he had found the sneak thief.

"This is a small town—and I got friends." Breckinridge motioned. The militiaman Asa had spoken to came over, a rifle cradled in the crook of his left arm. He had the look of a man spoiling for a fight.

Asa was willing to give it to him.

"You find Mr. Edwards?" The guard moved so he'd have a better shot at Asa without also hitting Breckinridge.

Before he could address this threat, Asa saw the tent master reaching behind his back. He came out with a hideout gun that had been thrust into his belt at the small of his back.

"Don't go makin' trouble. You don't even have money left for a decent funeral."

Having nothing to gain and his life to lose, Asa shouldered his saddle and carried the rest of his gear in his arms. He staggered a little under the load as he went to the livery. The stable boy fed the animals crowded into the stalls, some having two horses.

"I'm leaving my tack here. Any extra cost for that?" Asa waited for the reply. The boy kept working, head down and mumbling. "Thanks."

He hurried out before he found out what the boy

had actually said. It was bad enough losing the stack of chips. Having his mule and saddle taken meant a long walk home. If he had to use shank's mare to return, that would be doubly humiliating. Not only would he have lost the town's money; he'd have lost his mount as well. Enduring the town's wrath was easy compared to the disapproval of his children. Their lives would be miserable, and they'd have to take abuse from their schoolmates.

Asa wandered, not sure where his feet were taking him. He stopped and stared at the ring constructed in the town plaza. Two men would wrap the colored sashes around their waists and whale away at each other until one died or no longer answered the bell. He had heard tell that some of the bare-knuckle fights lasted a hundred rounds or more. A knockdown ended a round. He balled his fists and imagined himself in the ring.

What would that pay, squaring off against another fighter? He had seen some men in town who looked more like grizzly bears than humans. Fighting any of them would make for a short bout. If he bet money he didn't have and lost, he'd likely get strung up. Or the bettors cheated out of their winnings would pay the winner to continue pounding until nothing remained alive.

Asa ran his fingers over his cheek. He wasn't vain but knew he was far from ugly. Women gave him second glances. He suspected Miss Lorraine had been drawn to his good looks. Having his face mashed into bloody pulp would accomplish nothing. If he'd had any experience in prizefighting, he would have volunteered to enter the ring. Because he lacked such a background, he needed other ways of making a few dollars.

Without realizing it, he wandered around the town, past the Everest, where he touched the brim of his hat to Miss Lorraine, sitting on the porch sipping her bitter lemonade, and hurried on, pretending he hadn't seen her motion him over.

When he reached the Silver Bucket, he paused. If Desert Pete had a few chips left, he could offer to turn them into a new fortune—for a cut of the action. The old prospector had cottoned to him enough to loan him some chips. Asa went into the smoke-filled saloon and looked around.

Wash Reynolds continued to run the bank at the faro table. Asa went over and asked, "Have you seen Desert Pete anywhere?"

"He came in a couple hours back, all covered in dirt like he'd been rolling around out in the street. I haven't seen hide nor hair of him since."

"Someone rob him?" Asa tried to keep the catch out of his voice. Wash heard the concern.

"He didn't look too happy, but let me ask that question of you."

Asa tried to hold back the torrential outpouring of anger and words and failed. He told the other gambler of his sorry situation.

"Fifty percent," Wash said.

"What's that? I don't understand."

"I'll loan you a thousand dollars, but you have to pay me back fifteen hundred. Anything beyond that's yours." His long fingers stroked the sides of twin stacks of chips. A quick twist shuffled the markers together, reversed them and returned them to the initial chimneys of chips. He spread them out on the table and gestured for Asa to take them.

Asa was experienced enough to count them at a glance. One thousand dollars. He chewed on his lower lip and reached out. He stopped short of taking the chips. He pressed his palm down and leaned forward. "I might lose it all. What then?"

"Then you owe me fifteen hundred dollars, payable when you get it. It won't matter if that's a day or a year. You'll owe me."

In his head, Asa did all the calculations of things that could wrong, of the lucky bets and the doomed ones.

"I'll put my store up against this. It's worth far more than a thousand dollars. Or the inventory is."

Wash shrugged. "What do I care about a shop in a town I've never been to? Are you taking the chips or not?"

Asa thrust out his hand. It was Wash's turn to hesitate. Then he shook.

"Get out there and make me richer," Wash said. A quick move slid the chips in Asa's direction. "I can use the jump on you when we sit down to the final hand."

Asa took the chips and worked his way through the still shoulder-to-shoulder crowd in the saloon. He spent a few minutes studying the players at each poker table and finally decided on one where each gambler had the look of a professional. The way they dressed—much like the way he did now—and acted convinced him this table was hard but promised the best payoff. The men were used to big bets and big bluffs. All he had to do was last long enough to figure out what every twitch and tic meant.

He put his thousand in chips down. The others all had ten times that in front of them. The dealer signaled for him to ante up. A hundred dollars. These were the high stakes he sought.

Asa concentrated on the game flow. Cards spun about and landed in front of players, in front of him. He sneaked a quick peak at the corners and worked off this to be sure no one behind him passed along his hand to others. It took a few hands for him to figure out the alliances at the table. Three of the gamblers worked together. After the others were cleaned out, they would split the take among them. Two acted as shills for the third, pushing up the bidding and making appropriate remarks. Once he understood this and deciphered some of the signs, he began winning small pots from them.

Two others dropped out, leaving Asa to the mercy of the three who bet in cahoots. He accepted small losses, but his few wins were insignificant. He knew they were waiting for the kill. When he got a decent hand, they would jump in and get him to bet heavily. Whichever of the trio remained knew what his partners held in their hands, and this gave him a good notion as to what Asa held.

"I'll stand pat," he said. The hand was a winner in most games. He wasn't sure with his opposition.

"Looks like our friend has a full house. Otherwise, he'd be dipping his toe into the water and taking a card or two."

The signals flashed around the table. None of the trio had that good a hand. But neither did Asa.

"You aren't looking at my hand, are you?" Asa joked to see what reaction he got. They worried he did have a full house, and that beat anything any of them held.

"I think he's bluffing," said the man to Asa's right. "But I fold."

This produced a few guffaws, and the play circled again until it came to a showdown between Asa and the gambler across the table.

"What's it going to be, my lad? You have that big hand, or are you bluffing?"

Asa pushed in all his chips. He had more than doubled the loan from Wash so far. A quick count showed he bet close to four thousand dollars.

"Find out. Call me."

The man got antsy. He fingered his chips and glanced at his cards, then rubbed his mouth.

"If I raise, you have to match that. You don't have any more chips on the table."

Asa saw his ploy. Put in a bid high enough to force his opponent to fold because he had nothing in reserve. Asa touched his coat pocket and smiled slightly. He turned impassive, but the man had seen the move and took it to mean Asa had plenty to back up any raise.

"I fold." The man threw in his hand. "What do you have? What's your full house?"

Asa raked in the pot. He was back to almost ten thousand, and that was after he repaid Wash. After three handfuls of chips, he had stuffed his coat pocket.

"Thanks, gentlemen. It's been instructive."

"Wait! What did you have?" The man reached across the table to turn over Asa's hand.

Asa leaned forward and pinned his wrist to the table.

"You had to pay for the privilege. We'll likely meet again. There's no need for you to know my secrets."

"There you are! I been looking high and low for you."

A hearty slap on his shoulder staggered Asa. The

gambler across from him flipped the cards when the pressure on his wrist was released.

"Two pair? You didn't have a full house! I had you beat!"

"Faint hearts never won the day," Asa said. He turned and caught Desert Pete before the man had a chance to slap him on the shoulder again. "And what do you want, bothering me while I'm working?"

The prospector was covered in dust, as Wash had described earlier. His clothes looked like a perpetual dust storm and his face was streaked with soot.

"Sit back down. We got to play another hand!"

Asa turned deliberately and faced the gambler. He glanced at the man's partners and included them in his cold declaration. "You were in cahoots. I don't mind that. I do mind you trying to tell me what I have to do. We'll likely meet up again. We're all good players. Next time you might smoke me. But that'll be next time."

He put enough steel in his words to make them back off. They huddled together, whispering, and then left without another word. Turning to Desert Pete, he said, "You might have gotten me killed if my sweet talk hadn't soothed them. They lost a pile of money."

"Yeah, sorry, Asa, my man. Sorry. I had to tell you what I've found."

"We've been kicked out of our tent. I wasn't able to pay Breckinridge."

"I know. I got something better all lined up. Come on. Let me show you." Pete herded Asa from the saloon, but not before Asa repaid Wash.

"What's so important?"

"There. The store with the boarded-up door. We go in there, and I'll show you."

Desert Pete was eager, but Asa worried. He touched the six-shooter at his hip. He thought the prospector was harmless, but too many men in Golden Junction turned dangerous at the lure of so much money.

"Is it somewhere that we can pitch our camp?"

"Yes, well, maybe . . . maybe it's not a good idea." Pete hurried ahead, mumbling to himself. Asa thought the man had developed into a fine conversationalist with himself over long, lonely miles in the desert. His actions warned he had gone around the bend.

Pete pushed aside a board and went into the abandoned store with surprising agility. Asa followed, careful not to get his fancy duds too dirty. He coughed at the dust in the air. Cobwebs hung everywhere in the dim interior. Bare counters showed this had been a yard goods store where cloth had been displayed. Asa picked his way carefully behind Desert Pete, then stopped suddenly.

The prospector had vanished.

Asa drew his six-shooter and tried to make out what lay in the shadows ahead. He edged forward and found nothing. Lighting a lucifer would ignite the cobwebs and send the entire building up in flames. Besides, Asa didn't have a match.

"Pete?" He whispered the name and listened hard. The ruckus from out in the street threatened to drown out any reply. The rotting wood creaked around him. He took another step. The boards sagged and nails squealed as they pulled free. A quick jump back saved him from a fall into a dark hole.

Asa shielded his eyes with his left arm as intense light flared in the hole. Pete held up a torch. The expression on his face turned demonic in the flickering light.

"Come on down. There's a ladder. I got to show you this, Asa. It's gonna make the difference."

"Is there a tunnel?" Asa knelt and peered around. "Can we leave town this way?"

"You can't get a horse down here. It'd go plumb wild. No, there's more than that. Come on down."

Asa holstered his gun and carefully took one rung at a time as Pete steadied his descent by leaning against the ladder. The rungs were as rotten as the rest of the wood but held his weight long enough for him to drop to the tunnel floor. He stepped away from Pete to keep from being set on fire by the guttering torch he waved around.

"Lookee here. Isn't this the most beautiful thing you ever laid eyes on?"

The prospector held the torch near the wall. The glitter caught Asa's eye. He bent over, then pried loose the rock and examined it closer.

"Pete, this is iron pyrite. Fool's gold. I know something about chemistry and assaying. You brought me down here to show me worthless rock?" Asa looked down the tunnel. It branched into three other stopes. "This is an abandoned mine. If they ever found gold, it must have played out years ago." He looked back up into the empty store. "They built Golden Junction on top of the excavations."

"There must be gold still here. There has to be!"

"Be careful prowling around. The tunnels might collapse on you. It's been years since anyone shored up the ceiling."

"We lost our tent. We can stay down here. I found a room where the miners had cots and a mess."

Asa patted his coat pocket. He was back in the

game. With so many chips, he could stay in the hotel. The thought of Miss Lorraine tucking him in at night made him blush. It'd be better if he stayed in the livery with his mule. It'd be cheaper, and there wouldn't be as much temptation to explain to his wife when he got back to Meridian.

"I don't cotton much to living in a rock tomb," he said. "But if you're going to stay underground, more power to you."

"I know there's metal here. Look. That's blue dirt. It has to mean they missed a vein or two of high-yield gold ore."

Asa left Desert Pete waxing eloquent about how this was the real jackpot where a clever man would make his fortune.

Asa wished him luck. And he wished himself luck with the cards. *That* was where a fortune was to be made.

CHAPTER FOURTEEN

A SA NEWCOMBE BRUSHED straw off his coat, pulled
out a handful of chips from his pocket and sorted
through them to find a ten-dollar chip. He left it on a
railing in front of the livery to pay for both his and the
mule's night. The price was exorbitant but only compared with the rest of the world beyond the town.
Breckinridge demanded more than that for a night's
stay in a tent now, and Asa vowed to prevent the larce-
nous man from ever collecting one thin dime from him
again.

Besides, the company overnight would be better.
Old Abigail hardly snored compared to Desert Pete.

Asa headed for the Silver Bucket but considered trying other gambling venues. The Oriental Tiger Lair
reputedly had high-stakes games running constantly,
and not just poker. The roulette wheel there spun until

it needed oiling. The squealing made him cringe, even as he wondered how the wheel was gimmicked. The Spanish monte game appealed to him more than potentially rigged roulette. It was quick, bets soared and the players tended to be unsophisticated in the ways of odds. That appealed to him right now when he had to amass a considerable fortune just to get even with many of the other professionals who hadn't been robbed blind by a sneak thief.

A commotion in the street outside the Oriental Tiger Lair drew his attention. Two men stood face-to-face, shouting at each other, fists clenched. The small crowd egged them on, taunting and jeering. Asa knew what followed such a confrontation, and he should have kept walking, but the energy and the utter viciousness of the gathering held him fixed to the spot, watching and dreading what had to happen next.

"Knives!" The smaller of the men thrust out his chest, jutted his chin belligerently and yelled even louder.

"You picked a good way to die. Winner takes all!" The second man stood a head taller and weighed fifty pounds more. From his clothing, he was a mule skinner. His opponent dressed fashionably enough, but Asa suspected he wasn't anything more than a shopkeeper who had come to Golden Junction to make his fortune. More than one sitting at the poker tables had sold their business in another town to get the buy-in. For them it was an all-or-nothing gamble.

Most ended up with nothing.

"I'll cut you up good!"

The mule skinner thumbed his nose and did what he could to gin up support in the crowd. Neither looked capable of lasting more than a few minutes in a serious poker game.

That meant they had to find other ways to corner all the chips. If Asa understood the challenge, one of them was fixing to die. He weighed the strengths and weaknesses mentally. The crowd bet. From what Asa overheard, the smaller of the pair was a two-to-one favorite. He had to have been a known quantity while the shopkeeper was an interloper.

Asa caught his breath when both men dumped their chips on the boardwalk in front of the saloon. The small mountain drew him. A quick estimate made the combined trove worth at least twenty thousand dollars. Asa forced himself to look back at the men willing to kill each other for that much money. It was a princely sum, but to wager your life? Asa shook his head sadly at the fact that anyone had come to such an end.

A long bandanna with knots tied in the opposite ends started the fight. Each took his knot and chomped down on it. The knives they flourished flashed in the sun. The crowd moved the pair into the middle of the street. Men circulated through the crowd, taking bets, giving odds. Asa jerked erect when he saw a familiar face in the crowd—one that wasn't betting. Two men with him shouted and jeered, but their eyes flitted to the bank down the street.

The one Asa recognized was the short, grizzled outlaw from the Mosquito Pass—the man he had tried to gut with his own knife and who turned up time and again like a bad penny. The man didn't see him as he whispered with the other two, who kept up a steady war cry to blend in with the crowd and hide their own scouting of the bank. The distraction worked. No one noticed how the trio paid more attention to the militia patrols than to the slashing knives turning the combatants into bloody ribbons.

Asa touched the butt of his Peacemaker and cut through the crowd to get closer to the trio. He never heard the signal to start. The crowd turned to concrete around him as all attention focused on the fight. The men both lunged simultaneously. A crimson spray showered the nearest in the crowd, and then the fighters spun away, jabbing and trying to grapple. The first to release the knotted bandanna lost. In spite of himself, Asa let out a cheer when the smaller man twisted and deftly brought his knife around in an arc that opened the other's man belly.

The sudden pain made the shopkeeper double over. That was all it took. The mule skinner brought his knife down doublehanded and drove it into the other man's back. The impact of steel against spine popped the bandanna from a now gaping mouth. The shopkeeper dropped facedown and twitched a few times before dying.

"That's it? Is that it? I've won? Snapper Gates! That's my name and I won! You scallywags get away from my winnings!" The mule skinner took the bandanna from his mouth and tossed it high into the air. Several men drew their six-shooters and fired, filling the cloth with holes before it fluttered to the dusty street.

The mule skinner was hoisted onto two men's shoulders, but he forced his way off to land beside the pile of chips he'd won. If the crowd had carried him around in victory, those chips would have vanished. Gates drove his knife point first into the wood walkway and greedily began raking in his chips. When his cloth bag was filled, he took off his sweat-stained denim shirt, tied the arms together and used it as a sling to carry the rest.

Only then did Snapper Gates let the most aggressive in the crowd hoist him to their shoulders once more and parade up and down Main Street.

He leaned back and threw his hands skyward, bellowing, "I'm renewed. Renewed, I say! There's nothing better'n winnin' to make a man whole!" He let out a loud cry of pure victory and began tossing out handfuls of chips to the crowd around him. Their roars of approval drowned out Gates' joyful laughter. He climbed down from his shoulder perch and marched off, the leader of an approving parade.

Once the throng followed to celebrate with the mule skinner, Asa hunted for the three outlaws casing the bank, but they had disappeared the minute the fight ended. The mule skinner heaved the shirt holding his chips over his shoulder like a rucksack as he bounced along. The man grabbed his knife and pointed it, tip up, as Asa stopped a pace away.

"What do you want?" Snapper Gates glared down at Asa as he brandished the knife to show the blood on the blade and hilt.

"Are you putting your chips into the bank for safe-keeping?"

"What's it to you?" Gates kicked hard and dropped off the men's shoulders. He stopped a few inches from Asa and truculently shoved his face toward him, as if daring the gambler to take a swing at him. With the bloody knife clutched in his hand, Gates needed only to shift his weight a few inches to gut Asa or anyone else challenging him.

"I'm heading that way, too. We can watch each other's back."

The mule skinner eyed Asa from head to toe and decided he liked what he saw. A curt nod was all the answer he gave before he set off at a quick pace. Asa trailed Gates, hand on his six-gun. More than one spectator wanted to clap the mule skinner on the back, hoping some of his luck would wipe off or perhaps for a chip to bounce loose.

It took only a few seconds for the crowd to disperse, many on their way to seek other ways of winning, diversions and probably even more deadly games. Asa picked up the pace and walked alongside Gates, keeping an eye out for his old nemesis.

"Who're you looking for?" The mule skinner shifted the knife to his left hand so he could carry the chip-laden bundle in his right.

"I saw three men sizing up the bank. The only reason for them to pay so much attention would be to rob it."

"You asked if I was putting my chips in the vault." The man slowed in realization and stared at Asa. "That's plumb crazy. Why'd they want chips?"

"You're right. What do they have if they took the chips? They'll go for the cash we used to buy in. That's already in the vault."

Snapper Gates pursed his lips and thought this over. "That'd mean it wouldn't do us no good to win if all the gold's gone."

Asa shrugged. That was exactly what it meant. He had to believe Big Ed Edwards and his militia were wary enough to keep it from happening. But somehow, his faith wasn't up to fully believing that.

"You see them varmints anywhere?" Gates swiveled around, as if he hunted whomever Asa had spotted earlier.

"I did before, but I lost 'em." Asa went into the bank ahead of the mule skinner and looked around. He almost expected to see the outlaws waiting here, but the lobby was deserted except for the guards and two tellers in their cages.

"Make way. I got more to put in than you, mister." The mule skinner shoved Asa aside and went to the closest teller. A loud click of chips on the counter set them both to counting.

Asa went to the other teller with his more modest stash. He kept two thousand and got a receipt for the rest, minus the rake-off to the bank. The receipt went into his vest pocket usually reserved for his father's watch. The emptiness caused an ache in Asa that had to be resolved sooner or later. Laramie Frank Gillette would pay for extorting the watch the way he had.

"A hundred dollars," Asa said through clenched teeth.

"What's that, mister?" Gates tucked his receipt away. "What do you say if I buy you a drink? You brung me good luck. There was five hundred more in the winnings than I thought. I never knew killing a man was that profitable. After the big game, I should be a bounty hunter. The pay's better than being a freighter driving mule teams."

"Why not? A drink sounds like it'd hit the spot. I've worked up a powerful thirst."

They left, Asa looking around warily. It almost pained him to leave his winnings in the bank, but after being robbed, this was safer. How much safer remained to be seen. At least the chips were secure for the time being from petty thieves who lacked the imagination to see where the real treasure lay. Anyone robbing the bank would take cash and gold, not chips.

As they walked down the street, Asa had to ask, "From the way the crowd cheered you on, you must live here in town."

"I worked in Big Ed's Glory Bee Mine, haulin' ore to the crusher for nigh on a year. Before it played out, the Glory Bee was 'bout the final one to close. It was about then that he whupped up the idea of this big gambling match."

"You didn't buy in?"

"A hundred or so of us stayed to make a few bucks off the gamblers. It ain't workin' out like I thought. Like any of us thought."

"You're trying to win the final hand?"

"Big Ed let us in without the five-thousand-dollar ante. He knew none of us was good enough to do anything but lose." Gates spit. "I've got money for a stake now. That'll show him what for."

They walked in silence for another couple minutes. Finally, Asa had to ask, "The mines up on the hillside, are those the only ones?"

"The only ones I know of. What are you gettin' at?"

Asa started to ask about the maze of played-out mines beneath the town. Those must have been drilled and dug before those up above the town were proved. Why he wanted to keep Desert Pete's discovery secret was something of a puzzle, but Asa wasn't about to give it much thought at the moment. His mouth had turned into the innards of a cotton bale, and his lips were chapped from the lack of moisture. All he wanted was a beer. Then he'd consider what to do next. He followed the mule skinner into the Silver Bucket and looked around.

The hubbub never died down. The place was as crowded as ever, and the barkeep worked furiously to keep the mugs and the shot glasses filled. Big Ed might have lost his mines, but this saloon was a different kind of gold mine. Not a table lacked a full complement of men feverishly trying to walk away with the pot from the final hand. Three tables had been moved close to the door for dice. Asa nodded in passing to Wash Reynolds, who must have had his feet nailed to the floor behind the faro table. He worked the casebox and took and paid out bets with authority and what seemed to be the rhythm of a Regulator clock. Asa knew that steady, uninterrupted play netted the bank the highest money. The more hands in an hour, the higher the take for the house.

He twisted from side to side to get through the crowd but lost the mule skinner in the crush. It had been a hard day, and his anger began to rise. Telling himself to stay cool failed when a man turned suddenly in front of him. They collided, rebounded and each was knocked back a step.

"You're a clumsy oaf," the man growled. "Why don't you apologize so I won't have to beat some manners into you?"

The crowd began fading away until Asa and the obnoxious gent were standing off in a bubble at the center of the floor. He heard the spectators begin betting

on the outcome. Would he apologize, or would there
be a fight? Odds went up when he shook himself and
squared off.

"You ran into me."

"Are you calling me a liar? You're not only clumsy
but you're a loudmouthed pig rooting around the slop
trough." The man pushed his coat back to free up his
six-gun.

The betting went wild now.

Asa felt rather than saw a man come up behind. A
hand lifted and pointed at his adversary. He recognized the lace cuff and jacket.

"Careful, now. That's Handsome Jack Cochrane.
He's a gunfighter. I've seen him cut down two men at
once. Fast and mean and he never misses. Ever." Wash
tugged on Asa's left sleeve. "It doesn't cost you anything to apologize. It'll cost your life if you don't."

"What're the odds?" Asa was aware of how the furor died down now, as if the bets had been placed. He
sized up the gunfighter. The man was so good-looking,
he was almost pretty. With high cheekbones, a fine nose
and wide-set eyes of the purest blue, the gunman had
come by his appellation honestly. From the way he carried himself, he entertained every compliment as the
gospel truth.

"A hundred to one. Against." Wash pressed closer
and whispered, "Make an excuse to back down, or I
put a bet down against you. I might as well make a few
pennies on a sure thing."

"It was his fault." Asa's temper rose again. The
crowd betting against him capped an otherwise terrible day. They didn't think he could defend himself,
even against a man who looked to be a dandy.

"I'll put up five thousand!" The bet came out clarion clear and cut through the crowd's low buzz.

Asa shifted to one side and saw Frank Gillette behind the gunman. He thought he could see the gambler speaking to the gunfighter because the man rolled his shoulders as if getting ready to draw.

Gillette knew he'd never win against Asa in a fair game. Putting Handsome Jack up to the fight was his way of taking out the competition. That angered Asa even more.

"What's Laramie back there paying you to fight me? It must be a decent sum since he's too cowardly to fight his own battles." Asa stood on tiptoes and tried to lock eyes with Gillette. The shifting crowd prevented it, so he raised his voice even more. "What's the going rate to avoid facing me across a poker table, Gillette? Is it that five thousand you bet? No, you're too cheap for that. He's not paying you but—what?—a hundred dollars? Less than that? You're not worth more than a few cents."

The gunman got riled now. "Laramie's reward for your scalp was a hundred dollars, but you got such a big mouth, I'll do it for nuthin'!"

"Be careful. Don't let Gillette hear that. He'll try to rob you of every dime. He's a cheapskate as well as a coward!"

"Your fight's with me. You ran into me, and I'm not acceptin' any apology from you now." The man slid the leather keeper off his six-shooter's hammer. His fingers tapped against the side of his holster. "You throw down anytime you want."

"He's lightning fast, Asa. You want me to shoot him after he kills you?" Wash sounded sincere.

"What'll you do? Shoot him in the back, Wash?"

"I'm surely not quick enough on the trigger to face him. Shooting him from ambush is about the only way to get rid of Jack and keep on breathing myself."

To the crowd Asa called, "What's the wager against me?"

Snapper Gates pushed his way through the crowd, waving a handful of foolscap. He was taking the bets.

"Got close to ten thousand against you."

"At a hundred-to-one odds?" Asa saw the mule skinner nod, looking a little guilty. "I'll bet three thousand at those odds. Can you pay off when I win?"

"You ain't gonna win," Gates said positively.

"You lay off the bets the best you can. When I win, I'm going to collect my three hundred thousand."

"You're letting the money go to your head just like his lead's going to go to your heart. Sneak out of town while you're still alive," Wash advised.

"Better put a bet down on me," Asa said. He pulled free of Wash's grip and took three steps to go nose to nose with the gunman. They stared at each other until Asa bellowed, "I was the one challenged. That means I get to choose the weapons. Is that right?"

The crowd roared approval.

The gunman sneered. "I don't care how we do this. You're a dead man."

"In the town square in one hour." Asa glanced at the mule skinner. "That'll give you time to get the money together to pay me off. Three hundred thousand dollars to cover my bet."

"That's a passel of chips," someone muttered.

"Get a wheelbarrow for it."

Asa smiled at his opponent, then winked. Before the man reacted, he spun about and strutted from the Silver Bucket. Wash Reynolds trailed behind him. He was the only one who saw how Asa's hands shook like aspens in a high wind.

CHAPTER FIFTEEN

W ASH REYNOLDS LOOKED around uneasily. He kept
the wood box holding the weapons tucked under
his arm until it became uncomfortable. Then he shifted
to hold it under his other arm.

"They're all making side bets," Wash said. "You'll
be the biggest bet so far, and I saw ten thousand change
hands over two men slicing each other up with knives."

Asa felt curiously calm. He had made his decision,
and now that the moment of truth had arrived, he was
good with it. If Gillette hadn't butted in, he might have
apologized to the well-favored gunfighter. From what
Handsome Jack Cochrane said, he'd been paid a hundred dollars to eliminate the opposition. Asa knew
only too well how Gillette played cards. He took it as
a compliment that the gambler wanted to get rid of
him rather than face him across a poker table.

A loud cry rose. A large knot of men moved slowly toward the plaza. Asa jumped up into the ring built for a prizefight to get a better look. His heart beat faster. In the center of the crowd strode Handsome Jack like some conquering hero. A quick look around the plaza showed how many others had already gathered.

Miss Lorraine and a half dozen women huddled together. The madam's sour expression told of her disapproval. She locked eyes with Asa and shook her head. He took off his Stetson and bowed in the courtliest way possible. She hesitated, then pushed away from two girls clinging to her. When she reached the edge of the elevated ring, she looked up. Her expression turned dark now.

"You're a damned fool. I thought you had better sense. That man's a killer."

"Someone that pretty looking can't be as tough as everyone makes him out to be."

"He killed three men in one day, one after another not a hundred feet from here. He's fast, Mr. Newcombe, real quick."

"So I've heard." He looked over at the crowd and its hero. "You might want to step away. This isn't going to go as Gillette thinks."

"Gillette? What's Laramie Frank Gillette got to do with this? You're going to get yourself killed dead by a murderer who doesn't care if he's facing you or not when he pulls the trigger."

"You're wrong, Miss Lorraine," he said. "I've sized him up. Handsome Jack is vain. He wants his victims to appreciate his good looks as he shoots them down."

"Oh, you!" Miss Lorraine spun and stalked off to

rejoin her girls. They chattered among themselves until the crowd parted and the gunfighter came forward. He held out his arms. Two in the crowd slid his coat off to give him a clear grab for his smoke wagon.

"You showed up," Handsome Jack called, sure that the crowd heard his every word. "A yellowbelly like you? I thought you'd be running. Are those your knees knocking together in fright that I hear? Or is the noise from you sweating blood?"

"Is that a bit of rouge on your cheeks? You're wearing women's makeup?"

Asa heard Wash hiss a warning as he taunted the gunfighter.

"Sorry. It's a trick of the light. I was wrong."

Handsome Jack turned left and right, laughing. "He admits he's bumped into me!"

"No," Asa said, pitching his voice to carry. "I was wrong about you wearing a dance hall floozie's makeup to look even prettier than a picture. That's all."

Handsome Jack snarled and climbed into the ring. It didn't surprise Asa when Frank Gillette accompanied him as a second.

"It's too damned late now," Wash muttered. "I can shoot him for you."

"Why would you go and do that?"

"Revenge," Wash said. "I'll see that Gillette pays for your funeral."

"He's not going to do that." Asa shucked off his coat, then unbuckled his gun belt and handed it to Wash. "There won't be a need."

He stepped forward and fought down the urge to punch Handsome Jack and smear his nose all over his face.

"Why'd you get rid of your six-gun? It's not saving your worthless hide. I don't mind putting a slug into an unarmed man." The way Handsome Jack sneered left no doubt about his morals.

"I'm sure that practice makes perfect," Asa said, "but since you challenged me, I get to choose the weapons." He motioned to Wash, who came up with the large wood box.

Handsome Jack's lips drew back in a feral sneer. He unbuckled his belt and tossed it to Gillette. "I don't care what type of gun you've got there. I'm expert with anything that's got a barrel. Been a while since I fired a dueling pistol. This is going to be fun."

"Then let's get it over with," Asa said. "Only my choice isn't a firearm."

Wash opened the box and held it out.

Handsome Jack Cochrane paled as he stared at the contents. He called over his shoulder to Gillette, "What is this? You said all I had to do was gun him down."

"Your choice of weapon," Asa said. "It's going to be a damned shame having your face all cut up. You ever see what a meat cleaver does to a man's face? I grew up using a cleaver. My pa was a butcher, and he had me working in the slaughterhouse from the time I was six."

Handsome Jack edged back. Gillette put a hand in the middle of the gunman's back to keep him from bolting. The gambler whispered furiously, but Handsome Jack wasn't having any of it. Gillette was probably trying to convince Handsome Jack that Asa was lying and that his pa was a gambler. Jack was beyond believing it. He stared at the two meat cleavers as if he were hypnotized.

"If I were you, I'd pick this one." Asa lifted a wickedly sharp cleaver and held it up so the sunlight glinted off the silvered blade. "It's better balanced and swings fast. Just don't overshoot and get off balance. That'll let me cut off your gun hand and then mess up your face." He swung it a few times so that it whistled. "I can take the heavier one. It's harder to use, but I'm used to the weight. I got so I could cut off a pig's head with one whack."

The crowd grew restive when Handsome Jack pressed back into his second. The pair exchanged heated words.

Asa couldn't hear what either said, but he didn't have to. He glanced at the mule skinner. Snapper Gates had stopped taking bets and looked like a trapped rat. When Handsome Jack continued his argument with his second, the mule skinner began yelling for the fight to start. The crowd took up the cry and turned it into a chant.

"Fight! Fight! Fight!"

In spite of the volume, Asa heard Handsome Jack's parting words to Frank Gillette.

"Not my face. I'd be scarred the rest of my life." He jerked his gun belt from Gillette's hands, slipped between the ropes and hit the ground at a run.

For a moment, the crowd noise died down. Then murmurs of discontent built. Asa saw the time was ripe for him. He went to the edge of the ring and bellowed, "He quit. He wouldn't fight, so I'm the winner. And all you who bet on me, be sure to collect."

He gestured. Wash Reynolds came up beside him, pistol drawn, cocked and aimed at the mule skinner.

"You got the chips to pay off? You owe me three hundred thousand."

"That's more than—" Gates turned as pale as Handsome Jack when Wash discharged his gun. The slug ripped past the bettor's head.

"Yeah, you owe me, too," called a solitary man in the crowd. Desert Pete pushed his way forward.

Asa didn't know whether to feel good or sick to his stomach. Other than himself, and he had nothing to lose, only one man in the entire town had bet on him. He jumped down and shook the prospector's hand.

"Glad somebody had confidence in me."

Desert Pete snorted and looked around sheepishly. "Those odds were too good to pass up. If it had been a bet against the sun comin' up tomorrow mornin', I'd've taken the bet, too."

"Are you still exploring?" Asa tried to ask the question in such a vague way that Wash wouldn't get too curious. The abandoned mines underneath Golden Junction seemed important to him, even if he didn't share Desert Pete's enthusiasm for them. "Any sign you can get out of town through them?"

"Naw, but I only just started mappin' them out." Desert Pete gave Wash Reynolds the once-over and sniffed. "You surely are hangin' with a better class of road agent now."

Asa introduced them. They circled each other warily like dogs ready to fight over the same bone.

"Got to get back to work," Pete said, not taking a liking to Wash. He left without another word.

"That was the man you shared a tent with? You can buy the hotel with your winnings." Wash's tone betrayed how much of the prospector's opinion he shared. Neither was likely to enjoy the other's company very long.

"I've found other accommodations," Asa said. He still preferred the mule to anybody Breckinridge recruited for his tent city. "Let's get a drink."

"I've heard tell there's a new show onstage at the Silver Bucket this afternoon. Buy me that drink, and we can see what entertainment Big Ed Edwards has set up for us."

"You ought to buy me the drink. I gave you a front row seat for Handsome Jack's humiliation."

"I lost a hundred dollars betting against you. And you should have warned me about what you were going to try. You took quite a risk facing down a killer like Handsome Jack. What if he hadn't chickened out?"

"There'd have been blood all over the boxing ring, and Big Ed would have figured some way to make me pay for cleaning it up. But I pegged him right. When Cochrane realized that even if he killed me his face'd be all cut up for the rest of his life, he had to back down. If I got lucky, I'd've taken off his gun hand and ended his gunfighting career, to boot." Asa laughed without humor. "I pity anyone crossing his path in the next day or two."

Wash agreed. Jack Cochrane had to win back his confidence and prove he wasn't a coward. That meant others had to die, maybe several of them. If there was any justice, the town militia would take him out before too much blood was spilled.

They pushed through the swinging doors of the Silver Bucket and were almost crowded back out onto the street. The crowd had grown so large, Asa worried the saloon walls would be pushed out, causing the entire building to collapse.

"The show must be about ready to start," Wash

said, "but getting close enough to see anything's not likely."

As he spoke, a few men in front of them glanced back. A buzz radiated through the crowd, and then one spectator shoved out his hand and shook Asa's, forcing it up and down like a pump handle.

"You're 'bout the bravest man I ever did see. Come on in, Mr. Newcombe."

"We want to see the show but—"

"Make way! Make way for Mr. Newcombe!"

If he hadn't seen it, he wouldn't have believed it. The crowd parted like the Red Sea, giving him and Wash a clear path all the way to the row of chairs pressed up against the stage.

Wash made a grand bow and gestured for Asa to precede him. Asa had never been treated like royalty before. He felt self-conscious as men on either side reached out to touch him. One even said, "For luck!" When he got to the chairs and didn't see any empty ones, two men shoved past him, grabbed a pair of spectators already seated and lifted them bodily. They were hustled off before they could protest.

Again Asa caught part of the whispered explanation to the displaced men. ". . . chopped up Handsome Jack with a meat cleaver!"

That wasn't what had happened, but Asa found himself shoved down into the chair by men fighting one another to shake his hand. When he thought his arm would fall off, respite came. Big Ed Edwards strutted out onstage, cleared his throat, saw this had no effect, then fired a pistol into the ceiling. The report and falling plaster got the audience's attention.

"Shut up so the show can start," Edwards bellowed.

When the crowd started hooting and hollering, he fired his pistol twice more. When it got enough quiet, he went on. "You want to see the purtiest filly what ever trod the boards? Here she is, gents. Here's the toast of San Francisco, the lovely lady who performed for the crowned heads of Europe, the one, the only chanteuse . . . Molly Francis!"

Big Ed Edwards left the stage, emptying his six-gun as he went. Amid a shower of plaster, the singer pushed through the curtains and struck a pose. Asa caught his breath.

Introductions usually overstated both beauty and ability. Edwards hadn't come close to describing how lovely Molly Francis was. She was tall, maybe five ten and had hair so blond, it sparkled like silver. The coiffure built her up even taller. Pearls and tiny ruby specks sparkled in the well-formed hair. She blinked so, her long black lashes emphasized sea green eyes. But what startled Asa most was her dress. Red silk clung to every curve of her body. Most women wore corsets and bustles. Molly Francis obviously did not. As she moved, the dress caressed her body and promised more than any other woman ever had, without the benefit of marriage.

If she'd just walked around the stage, her performance would have been memorable. She opened her bow-shaped rouged lips and sang. Asa heard heavenly choirs in her perfectly pitched voice.

"I've never seen any performer like her," Wash said in a choked voice. "Can she be real?"

"Look at her dress. There's nothing fake anywhere. You can see that it's all there."

Asa fell silent as he let the woman's spell wrap him up and move him in ways he had never expected a saloon singer to do.

He wasn't the only one beguiled by her siren's song. The entire saloon had fallen almost silent. The only other sounds in the room were the click of dice and the barkeep pouring beer, but all that was in the background, unheard by the men utterly entranced by the singer. Asa wasn't sure how long Molly Francis sang, but her performance eventually came to an end. When it did he sagged, exhausted at being so focused for so long.

Then applause erupted. The audience jumped to its feet, whistling and catcalling. The songstress acknowledged the accolades, blew a kiss and came to the front of the stage. She held up her hands.

"Please! Let me have a final word." She waited for the furor to die down. "I'm not being paid for my performance. If you could spare a little something, I will be forever grateful." She singled out Asa. "Sir, your hat. Could you please lend it to me for a moment?"

Asa took off his tall-brimmed Stetson and handed it up to her. Their hands brushed, and he blushed at this slight touch. Molly Francis bent and held out the hat to the men crowding close to throw in chips.

The horde of men moved Asa away from the stage. He walked over to Wash, who was talking with Big Ed Edwards, and overheard a business deal being hatched. Edwards offered Wash an exclusive faro table in return for a cut. Before Asa could offer up his opinion that Wash was better off teaming with him, he felt a hand on his shoulder. A long-fingered pale hand with crimson-painted nails stroked his shoulder back and forth. He turned to look up at Molly Francis.

"Come on backstage so I can return your hat." She smiled, winked and then lithely slinked away. Several men tried to scramble onto the stage to follow but were pulled back by men with red armbands. Edwards' militia had moved in to protect the entertainer.

Asa doubted they would let him backstage. He almost turned back to find a poker game, but something moved him around to the side and up the steps onto the stage. Two militiamen gave him the once-over, then stepped aside to let him pass. Curious now, he pushed through the heavy curtains and looked around the deserted backstage area. Large flats painted with desert and city scenes leaned against the back wall. He walked slowly to the far side, where three doors marked with stars told him these were dressing rooms.

Two doors stood ajar before empty rooms. The third was closed. He knocked. No answer. He almost left, but on impulse, he opened the door and called out, "Miss Francis?"

His words echoed into the empty dressing room. He started to leave, then saw an envelope thrust into the frame of a large mirror above a dressing table. His name was written on the envelope in a precise hand.

Asa looked around guiltily, as if he shouldn't have been there. A quick flip of his thumb opened the unsealed envelope. He took out a folded note scented with lilac. He couldn't keep from sniffing the note; then he opened it and read:

> Mr. Newcombe, I am waiting in the King's
> Palace. Join me if you want your hat back.

The elaborate initials confirmed the note had been left by Molly Francis. *MF*. He took a deep breath, nostrils flaring at the delicate scent.

Then he went to find the King's Palace and the awaiting chanteuse.

CHAPTER SIXTEEN

ASA MADE A quick search of the area behind the curtains. The stage was deserted. He looked again at
the note, inhaled it, then tucked it into his pocket. Wan-
dering about, he sniffed like a bloodhound to follow the
delicate scent down a ramp into a storeroom. A door at
the far end stood ajar, letting in a sliver of wan yellow
light. He cautiously opened the door to carpeted stairs
leading to the second story. At the top of the flight of
steps, he saw another door, this one ornately carved and
decorated with an Oriental pattern of writhing dragons
and other strange creatures he didn't recognize.

Curiosity devoured him now. He went up the steps,
every footfall cushioned by the thick red carpet. At the
top he studied the door. Not Oriental as much as it was
Egyptian, he decided. Or a crazy artist's mixture. He
pushed it open. An antechamber filled with Egyptian
artifacts extended to either side. An arched, carved

doorway ahead was flanked by statues of animal heads that appeared to stand guard. In the room beyond were more familiar furnishings.

A green-baize-covered poker table dominated the room. Only two chairs were pushed in. As he wondered what was going on, a vision of beauty languidly stepped from behind an ornately painted screen. Molly Francis held two glasses in her hands. She raised one in silent salute to him, then daintily sipped.

"Come in, Mr. Newcombe," she said. "Share a drink to celebrate my good fortune."

The blond vision set both drinks on the table, bent and lifted his Stetson. She dumped the contents on the table. Chips rolled everywhere. Without seeming to hurry but moving with expert ease, she trapped the errant chips and scooped them up. Using a few quick motions usually reserved for professional gamblers, she built six equal stacks of chips in front of one chair.

"A game, Mr. Newcombe?" She gestured to an empty chair. "You will find it quite exciting, I assure you."

He walked slowly, trying not to show his true eagerness. Although her beauty was hypnotic, he took in as much of the surroundings as possible. The room had been outfitted for gambling. No windows, impeccable furnishings, a bar stocked with several bottles of whiskey. He didn't have to see the labels to know this wasn't the tarantula juice served downstairs. This was top-drawer liquor reserved for the elite who managed to find their way between the two statues outside the door.

"Anubis," she said, as if reading his mind. "The Egyptian god with the head of a jackal." She moved to her chair and waited. He took the cue and held it for her. She gracefully sank into it. As he walked to the chair across from her, she explained, "Anubis was the god of the tombs—and the weigher of hearts."

"Not diamonds or spades?" Asa sat and tasted the whiskey in his glass. It slipped smoothly down his throat and pooled warmly in his stomach. At least he thought it was the liquor. Every move Molly Francis made could as easily have been responsible for the warmth he felt.

"What is your pleasure?" She looked up, feigning shock. "I mean, what game do you wish to play?" From somewhere she produced a deck of cards. Her painted fingernails flashed as she shuffled, fanned the cards, picked them up and shuffled a few more seconds before placing the deck on the table between them.

He cut. "You have a game in mind, I'm sure. You're the hostess. You choose."

"Oh, what a gentleman you are, sir."

She squared the deck and dealt five-card stud. The last card dropped. She looked up, a faint smile on her painted lips. "Stud suits you."

Asa fished about in his pockets and found a considerable fortune in chips. Snapper Gates had been unable to pay the winnings after the duel with Handsome Jack Cochrane but promised to deliver when he could. Three hundred thousand was a spectacular amount for Asa. He had almost a third of that on him and put it on the table, his piles of chips matching those Molly Francis had collected from the appreciative audience.

"My, how big," she said. "Your pile of chips."

Asa lost the first hand and hardly cared. The betting was timid for two players with so much in reserve.

Her shining eyes never left his as she dealt cards, bet and won the second hand, too.

Asa realized what was happening. He could appreciate her beauty and watch how her nimble fingers worked to deal and move chips—or he could play serious poker. He settled down and began thinking about the game rather than how Molly Francis filled out her clinging dress or how she smiled just for him. She was quite expert at both distraction and gambling.

"How did you let Big Ed sign you up as a headliner?"

"My troupe fell on hard times in Denver. My manager engaged in an unfortunate altercation that left him . . ."

"Dead?"

"Unable to continue on our tour. Then the driver decided to steal both the wagon and all our props. The three other performers booked engagements around the city, leaving me on my own." She pushed forward her chips. Asa counted quickly. Two thousand dollars was a princely sum to bet on what might have been a bluff. He worked out the odds on her actually completing a straight and immediately pushed forward enough to call.

"Let's make this a little more exciting," she said. She reached down and added her golden slippers to the pot. "You can call with your boots. I noticed them. They are very nice. You have good taste."

"I won them in a card game," he said. Asa shucked off his boots and balanced them on the edge of the table. "They need polishing. If you win them, I'll see that they shine like mirrors again."

"Oh, to see up my skirt? Naughty boy."

"You have to win them for that to happen."

Another round of betting convinced Asa she was bluffing. With their footwear and close to eight thousand in chips riding on the last turn of the cards, he found himself as interested in the woman as in the winnings.

Her expression when she failed to make her straight told him more than if she had won. Molly Francis wasn't the least vexed at taking such a huge hit to her stake.

No gambler worth his—or her—salt was cheerful after losing a hand like that. Something more than a game with such sexual overtones was going on.

"Another drink?" He poured from the bottle at his hand. She sipped at the whiskey, her eyes peering at him over the rim of the crystal glass.

"We both know why you came here."

"Into the King's Palace?" Asa made a sweeping gesture encompassing the room with all its treasures. He had gestured at the hoarded archaeological wealth but knew Molly Francis was the real prize. More to the point, she wanted to be the prize.

"Gambling takes many forms. With a woman it is different than for a man." She smoothed her silk dress, accentuating her curves. "But the final play doesn't mean we both can't win."

"What are you suggesting?"

"Everything I have against . . . your wedding ring."

Time froze. Asa heard his heart slow. Air flowing into his lungs turned to syrup, moving slowly, ever so slowly. A brief bout of dizziness passed. "Why?"

Molly Francis looked surprised—a real reaction, if Asa was a judge. "Men die for what I am offering you. Don't you find me desirable?"

"You know that I do. I'm not dead. But I am married." He tapped his ring against the table.

"Are you confident enough in your cards? Everything." She moved sinuously as she pushed all her chips forward. "And I mean everything against your chips—and ring."

Asa sat stock-still, his mind racing. She was undoubtedly right that men had killed to be with her. And quite a few thousand dollars in chips lay on the table. Whether he ever collected the full bet from winning his duel with Handsome Jack was questionable. This was real, not fairy gold.

Fairy gold. He turned his ring around a few times. Rebecca meant more than winning the money to save Meridian. But long-buried instincts had been resurrected in him since coming to Golden Junction. The thrill of a bet won reminded him of his former life, and it had been a good one until . . .

"You have a pair showing," he said.

"Why, yes, I do." Molly Francis pushed herself up and leaned forward so he got a good look at what he stood to win—if he beat her pair of queens showing.

There had to be more in her down cards. Another queen? A queen and a pair for a full house? Molly Francis was no novice at this game—at any game she played with him. He couldn't beat a full house but knew she didn't have trip queens. Two of his down cards were queens, accounting for them all. He had another pair, but low. Treys. One card left to deal.

"All I have except the ring."

"Oh, Mr. Newcombe, don't be such a prude. The ring. Or fold and lose everything else on the table. That's, oh, two hundred thousand dollars? And my promise for a delightful evening afterward will also be lost."

"Priceless," he said. "I must count that as priceless."

Molly Francis' lovely face hardened just a tad. "Bet or fold. Your choice."

"Call."

Asa watched as she peeled off the top card and dropped it facedown on the table in front of him. She then dealt herself a card. With exaggerated care she placed the remainder of the deck to one side. The blond gambler flipped over her cards.

"Two pair. Queens and tens. Show me what you have, Mr. Newcombe."

He turned over the pair of treys and then tapped the card she had just dealt. A quick move turned over the third trey.

A full house.

Rather than exultation at winning, he felt a letdown that almost robbed him of all strength.

"You win . . . everything." Molly Francis stood and ran her hands down her hips and across her firm thighs, reached down, filled her hands with a wad of silk dress and began lifting it to expose creamy legs. When she got to her thigh, Asa held up his hand.

"I accept this as all that you owe me."

"But—!" She almost sputtered.

He held up his left hand with the ring.

"I *am* married."

"She is a lucky woman." Molly Francis lowered her skirts and smoothed the wrinkles the best she could. "But you positively destroyed my reputation by not claiming your winnings. Are you sure I can't entice you, just a little?" She puckered up and closed her eyes.

Asa leaned across the table and gave her a quick peck on the cheek. This surprised her as much as him not claiming his full winnings.

"Tell your admirers anything you like," he said.

"And what will you tell yours?"

He laughed. It was amusing to think that he had admirers. If anything, he had enemies willing to cut his throat. "A gentleman does not speak of his personal affairs."

She sighed. "I wish there had been an affair. Allow me to help you."

Together they scooped up the chips on the table. Asa didn't mind the way she rubbed up against him like an affectionate cat. She was only playing now. They both understood the limits he had set.

His pockets bulged, and his Stetson almost overflowed with chips. He looked at them and said, "Is it true that Edwards made you perform without a guarantee? Your singing is superb."

"I'll make more. I have several more acts scheduled before the final game."

He pulled out five black chips and held them on the palm of his hand. She looked at them, then at him and smiled. With great deliberation she took the chips and dropped them down her décolletage.

"You are a true gentleman in every way. I said I envied your wife. It is much too easy to hate her for having won your affection."

Molly Francis offered him her arm. Together they left the King's Palace. At the top of the stairs, she took her arm away.

"My room is at the rear on this floor. May your luck be as great as your honor, sir."

He bowed slightly, then went down the stairs into the main saloon. The crush of men smoking and swearing and drinking contrasted so greatly from his time

upstairs with Molly Francis that he had to look back up
the stairs to assure himself it had not all been an opium
dream. Asa caught his breath when he saw her arguing
with a man. He almost went back up to her defense,
then stopped.

Whatever her business with Laramie Frank Gillette
was her concern, but Asa thought he knew now who
had arranged the private game in the King's Palace.
Gillette had dangled more bait in front of his rival and
had again come away a loser.

That made Asa a winner even more than the mother
lode of chips he had won.

CHAPTER SEVENTEEN

ASA NEWCOMBE HAD been at the table for more than seventeen hours. He had found an open seat at this table immediately after his private game with Molly Francis and discovered his luck still ran high. When he had a streak going, it took a team of horses to pull him away. Unlike many gamblers, Asa knew how to recognize the signs of Lady Luck turning fickle, and he always cashed in then, but he had no idea when that would be. He had added close to six thousand more to his hoard, cleaning out nine players since sitting down.

The four he faced now were grim-faced, determined men. Two were professionals. He knew by their dress, the way they watched every card coming off the deck and the way they bet. One, who wore a huge walrus mustache, mumbled to himself. Asa caught snippets of what the man said. He ran down the cards on the table and calculated odds. Asa listened hard and used the man's talent against him when he added in his own cards for his personal reckoning.

The other three were nowhere near as astute as the man with the bushy mustache, but Asa watched one powerfully built man with hands the size of Mason jars because he had tried to deal seconds more than once. He was practiced at cheating this way, but his immense hands were better at hiding what he did than at actually dealing. Asa said nothing and used this as another way to have an advantage over his opponents. He wasn't cheating, but he allowed others to do it.

The ethics of that had once bothered him. Not now. The sooner he collected all the chips and cashed them in, the sooner he saved his hometown and got back to his wife and family.

"Is it true you were with the lady singer? The one who performed last night?" The walrus-mustached gambler thought to distract the others in the game although the question was directed at Asa.

"She is something special," Asa said. The cards wheeled out to land on the table in front of each player. The ham-handed dealer had dealt himself a pair of aces—Asa wasn't above ace sequencing to figure out what hands the others held.

"What's she like?" The question drew the attention of all the others in the game. Asa watched Walrus Mustache slip two of his cards off the table and replace them with cards that had been stuck under the table edge. This hand was rife with cheating.

"I do not gossip, sir," Asa said, but he lowered his voice and leaned in to include the other players in his bit of private, salacious knowledge. "But if you are lucky enough to play with her, be warned. She is a formidable opponent and one of the most expert card players I have ever faced. It is possible that none other than Charles Cora taught her the game."

"They hung Cora," protested one player.

"And with him went all the secrets of a masterful gambler—expect for what he taught Miss Francis."

This tidbit caused them to mutter and exchange whispered comments. Not once did they question the honesty of the revelation. Asa had no idea if Molly Francis had ever met the famous San Francisco gambler, much less been his willing student. Anything he said was part of the game. Amuse the others so they lost concentration, anger them or simply cause an unusual emotion to gain an edge. Those were tricks of his.

Before the betting began, a loud commotion at the front of the saloon drew their attention. Asa put his hands over his cards, to be certain no one tried to switch them. His arms circled his chips for the same reason.

"I am the bringer of sad tidings," the man dressed in a long black frock coat and tall silk hat bellowed. "You are all going to purgatory for your sins!"

He barreled in, pushing men to the side. He stood tall, topping six feet without the silk hat, and stepped up on the brass rail at the bar to give himself even more height. He swept a half dozen empty glasses from the bar.

"This demon rum is leading you astray. It will rot your guts and tarnish your soul. Do not taste its vile poison. You will regret it when your immortal soul is consigned to the lowest levels of hell!"

The barkeep lunged to stop the errant preacher from upending a bottle of whiskey and letting it drain into his mouth. He coughed and then spit a fountain of the liquor back into the air.

"I reject the devil's brew! Do not partake of Satan's ejaculate!"

"Get out of here, or I'll throw you out!" The bartender grabbed at him again and missed. He regained his balance and fumbled around under the bar for a bung starter. By the time he hefted it with the intention of bringing it down smack-dab on top of the man's hat, the preacher had swung away and raced to the stage. He vaulted onto the area where Molly Francis had sung her heart out the night before. This message was wildly different.

"Save your souls from perdition. Repent! Give up your evil ways. Do not imbibe of the whiskey and brandy and beer. Alcohol clouds the mind and blackens the soul!"

"Will somebody shut him up?" The question came from Walrus Mustache across the table from Asa. "He's ruining my concentration. I got a hot game going here."

"A hot game, that sinner says! It will be hotter where your immortal soul will be sent for an eternity of harsh punishment! Do not tempt fate with your games of chance. Give them up immediately! Let me take temptation away from you and help preserve your souls."

Someone threw a chip at the preacher. Then another and another. The man dropped to his knees, beseeching some higher power to cause a deluge of chips. He almost got them. The white chips turned to red and then blue as the gamblers found the range. They pelted him until he bowed down to protect himself.

"That's shut him up. Now, let's get back to the game,"

Walrus Mustache said. He pushed chips into the pot to open.

Asa peered at the corners of his cards, then pushed them in. Too much card handling beyond his control went on. He watched the betting until he was distracted by the preacher gathering the chips thrown at him. Something felt off.

"I've been in the game long enough." He swept his chips up and stuffed them into his pockets. As he stood, the preacher raced past and shot through the double doors to the street.

Asa followed at a more leisurely pace. He reached the saloon door in time to see the black-clad man running toward the town square. A glance over his shoulder at the Regulator clock on the wall behind the bar told him it was past noon.

Walking briskly, he went to the plaza and saw the preacher counting out his chips to Snapper Gates and getting a betting slip in return. Asa had to laugh. The man had a skill at replenishing his coffers for a big bet. He doubted there was any real objection to the rotgut whiskey served in the Silver Bucket or even condemnation of the games being played. It was only a different confidence game being acted out.

A crowd began forming. A man climbed into the ring and shouted, "The fight commences in fifteen minutes. Place your bets on the fight of the century. The fight of the century, and it's right here in Golden Junction. Get your bets laid now while the odds are still good!"

A large chalkboard, probably taken from the town's school, was propped against the ring. Asa was too far away to read the fighters' names, but the odds were writ large. One carried a five-to-one advantage, but even as he watched, the mule skinner wiped the odds out with his sleeve and changed it to three to one.

This produced a new round of betting.

Asa yawned. He had been up for too long and needed to sleep, but the fight was almost ready to begin. A shady spot in front of a shuttered bookstore afforded him a clear view of the ring, now with several men walking around in it. He suspected these were the trainers for the fighters. A smallish man ordering them around had to be the referee. The trainers were already arguing with him. When the fight started, there would be even more words exchanged.

Asa looked around for the preacher to see how he occupied himself until the fight he had already placed all his chips on. The man had moved away from the ring and climbed up to precariously balance on the sides of a watering trough. Nobody paid him any attention except Asa until he used his stentorian voice to begin a different pitch.

"I've got the finest soap in all of Colorado territory! Only one white chip for a bar."

"Who's got time to take a bath?" The man shouting the question looked around and repeated it when he got no action from the crowd the first time.

"This isn't just any soap. It's Lucky Miracle Soap that can make you rich as well as clean."

"Tell me, good sir, how is that possible?"

Asa paid more attention now. The preacher and the man asking the questions were in cahoots.

"Buy a bar of Lucky Miracle Soap and see for yourself. Here, take it!"

The shill took the bar and unwrapped it. He held it up and shouted, "There's a fifty-dollar bill wrapped around this bar. Give me another, sir. Give me five more!" He tossed up a red chip to the preacher, now soap vendor.

A second man shouted that he had a five-dollar bill wrapped around the soap he had purchased for a dollar chip. That brought the crowd rushing over, thrusting chips at the preacher. He and the first two men who had struck it rich with their soap wrappers fell into a pattern, taking the chips and handing out soap from boxes stacked behind the preacher.

Asa was the only one to notice that none of the sales after the first two had paper money wrapped around the soap. A general store sold such a bar for a nickel. In a boomtown such as Golden Junction had been, the price might have been two bits. The preacher improved the hygiene with his sales, but he did nothing to pad the pockets of the men with the Lucky Miracle Soap bounty in the form of paper money.

Before anyone complained at the lack of money along with their soap, the ring announcer rang a bell to get the crowd back for the fight. Asa saw the preacher divvy up the money his scheme had netted with his two assistants. Then all three hurried to the ring to place bets on the fight.

Asa started toward the ring when he heard a familiar voice. He spun and saw the soap-selling preacher talking with the outlaw who had tried to kill him on the trail to Golden Junction. The would-be killer balanced a box on his shoulder. From the ease with which he carried it, all the soap that had been in the box was already sold. A quick check reassured Asa his Peacemaker was ready. He dodged men on their way to watch the fisticuffs.

"Hey!" he called out to stop the outlaw from vanishing as he had so many times before. In spite of their sharing the trail from the Mosquito Pass depot and fighting almost to the death between Meridian and Golden Junction, Asa had no idea who the outlaw was. He had marked the man good with more than a single knife thrust. From the way he swung the empty box around, the wounds didn't slow him down anymore. Asa vowed to change that with a bullet between the man's eyes.

He dodged the preacher and then saw he had lost his quarry once more. Asa grabbed the preacher's arm. A jerk pulled him free.

"Don't touch me, mister, unless you want to lose that hand." The preacher pulled back his long coat and showed a sheathed knife at his belt.

"Who was that?" Asa pointed after the outlaw. He saw more was required to spring the information. "He owes me money from a bet he welshed on."

"Tough. I don't know him."

"You were talking to him." Asa stepped around to block the man's retreat. Standing on tiptoes, the man looked anxiously over Asa's shoulder toward the ring. "Tell me and I'll let you go."

The preacher shoved Asa out of the way and reached for his knife. Asa moved faster than he had in years. He cleared leather, drew, cocked and shoved his six-gun's muzzle into the man's midriff.

"Answer me."

"I paid him to move some boxes. That's all I know about him."

Asa sensed that he was drawing attention. Ever since he had faced down Handsome Jack Cochrane, he had become something of a celebrity. The crowd wanted nothing more than something new to bet on. He wasn't going to give it to them. All he wanted was to keep a low profile and keep accumulating chips until he had a chance at the big prize.

He put his thumb on the hammer and slowly lowered it. The preacher sneered, pulled his coat around him and stalked off. Asa considered how easy it would have been to shoot the confidence man in the back. Instead of taking the shot, he returned his six-shooter to the holster. Stride measured, he followed the preacher. The man placed a new bet with Snapper Gates, who somehow had become the official bookie for the sporting events; then he stepped away to get a better view of the ring.

"Wearing the red sash, Killer O'Malley, known as KO for his record of two hundred wins and no losses." The announcer made a grand gesture toward the far corner, where a hairy bruiser let his trainer tie the red scarf around his bulging waist. Two assistants worked to mop sweat off the fighter's naked torso. He pushed them away, raised his fists high over his head and let out a bull-throated roar of challenge.

Asa looked at the other fighter. He was smoothly muscled, not as hairy, and he looked out of place in the ring. His trainer couldn't get the yellow sash knotted. The fighter yanked it from the man's trembling fingers and secured it around his waist himself.

"And in the other corner, wearing the color of cowardice but showing bravery facing KO O'Malley is none other than Golden Junction's pride and joy, gold miner and newcomer to the ring, Hard Rock Rodriguez."

"What're the odds?" shouted someone at the rear of the crowd. The men closest to the blackboard surged closer.

Gates worked to erase numbers and add new ones. He answered, "KO is a six-to-one favorite."

This brought a new wave of betting.

Asa ignored that activity to study the fighters. He didn't doubt O'Malley had fought more than two hundred times, but his scarred face and cauliflower ears betrayed hard fights and likely losses. Rodriguez carried a few scars, more likely earned through his work as a miner. The crowd expected to see O'Malley's victory, after a drawn-out, crashing exchange of clenched fists. Winning was important to the onlookers, but seeing blood flow kept life from getting too boring. Asa knew very few of the crowd thought they'd win the big prize. All they wanted was a diversion on the way to the final game—the final game where they'd merely be spectators.

The real question came to Asa. Was the fight rigged? The obvious fix had O'Malley taking a dive so the underdog cleaned up with high odds. That was how fortunes were made. But if the fight wasn't long enough and bloody enough, the crowd would string up anyone they thought responsible for cheating.

Asa hoped the fight promoters were clever enough to avoid that. The mule skinner still owed him a mountain of chips.

The ringing bell startled him out of his ruminations. The fighters advanced, fists raised. Rodriguez made a few tentative jabs and was rewarded with a runaway locomotive of a punch to his forehead. The miner's head snapped back, and he toppled flat on his back, staring at the sky.

The bell rang, ending round one.

Asa started to leave to find a more civilized poker game to make his money when he saw something that stopped him dead in his tracks. The fight abruptly took on more interest for him.

CHAPTER EIGHTEEN

MOLLY FRANCIS SAUNTERED toward the ring, spinning a parasol that kept the bright noonday sun off her fair skin. She wore a dress so white, it appeared to glow. Though she hadn't worn a bustle or hoop skirts for her performance the night before, she did this afternoon, and every twitch and turn captivated the crowd.

It certainly kept Asa's attention. She was helped up into the ring, where she abandoned her parasol and took up a sign with the numeral 2 on it. Aware she had become the center of attention, she strutted around the ring, holding the sign high to show the upcoming round. She hesitated, smiled broadly and blew a kiss in Asa's direction.

"You made quite an impression if she's doing that in public."

Someone took his arm and pulled him closer. Miss Lorraine grinned wickedly.

"Has she stolen you away from me? At least I've lost you to powerful competition. How was she?"

Asa blushed. He laid his hand on Miss Lorraine's to give it a polite pat before pulling his arm away, but she clung to him so he couldn't move. His only recourse without causing a commotion was to stay and watch the rest of the fight. If the quick knockdown in the first round was any indication, O'Malley would have no trouble finishing off the plucky miner.

"She's only acknowledging that I complimented her singing."

"That's not what the gossip says. The two of you spent considerable time together in Big Ed's upstairs harem."

"Harem?"

"I don't know what else to call a place he has outfitted for orgies. You and Miss Francis were there, weren't you? For a couple hours."

"She's an accomplished gambler."

"I'm sure games were played. Oh, Asa, stop looking so uncomfortable." She leaned in to lay her head on his shoulder. Such a public display would have been talked about in Meridian for weeks. Here no one noticed.

"She's getting out of the ring. The fight's about to continue."

"You want to help her down? I'm sure she helped you up last night."

"Please." Asa cleared his throat. He stared straight ahead and ignored Miss Lorraine's chuckle. He was glad his wife wasn't here to see two women such as Molly Francis and Miss Lorraine vying for his attention. "The next round is beginning."

A bell rang. The miner lumbered forward, his fists

not raised quite as high as before. The first round knock-down had taken the starch out of him. KO O'Malley showed no hint of tiring. And why should he? The few punches Rodriguez landed weren't anywhere near enough to make him react, much less bruise him.

"Do you have a bet on the fight?" Miss Lorraine used Asa to pull herself up to get a better view over the heads of men closer to the ring.

"I couldn't figure out if the fight was fixed."

"It's not. I've got a small bet on Mr. Rodriguez. He's as close to being a gentleman as there was in Golden Junction—before you came to town, of course."

"O'Malley has fought a lot of men. He looks like he can take whatever punishment the miner can deliver."

"You're wrong, Mr. Newcombe. I have it on good authority that O'Malley was on a bender last night. If Mr. Rodriguez is clever, he can bring down the giant with only a few punches."

"O'Malley was at the Everest last night?"

"All night long, drinking heavily." Miss Lorraine stifled a cry when Rodriguez staggered from a heavy punch to his chest. "There is another, more vulnerable area, if a low blow is delivered."

"He has the clap?" Asa had to laugh.

"My girls were careful with him, but I do worry."

"I might have something to help." He had finally gotten the upper hand. She looked at him curiously. "I have drugs that might help. I'm an apothecary."

"You are a man of many talents, I am sure, Mr. Newcombe. Whatever you can part with would be appreciated."

Asa had the feeling Miss Lorraine's appreciation would extend as far as Molly Francis', but the chanteuse had been put up to it by Frank Gillette. Miss Lorraine's motives were still something of a mystery to him.

"Oh, oh!" she gasped as Rodriguez took several sledgehammer blows to the gut. Then she pointed to Rodriguez's trainer. "He knows the way to win."

The trainer jumped up and down and shouted to his fighter. In spite of being groggy from hammer blows to the belly, Rodriguez reacted swiftly. He ducked a heavy punch, worked underneath and pelted O'Malley with a flurry of blows to his belly. For the first time, the big fighter reacted. He grunted and clutched his stomach, giving Rodriguez the chance to land an uppercut. The exposed chin jolted upward just slightly under a blow that should have downed a bull. Rodriguez's move confirmed Miss Lorraine's secret about O'Malley. Asa saw the low blow and how O'Malley reacted.

With the air knocked out of him, he let out a whoosh, stumbled back and fell. This ended the second round.

"Rodriguez can be disqualified for that," Asa said. "But if he doesn't fight dirty, he'll die in the ring."

"There's a bonus being offered if there is a death," Lorraine said. "I don't cotton much to such things, but watching those brutes actually fight is rather exciting."

Asa's attention drifted back to the ring. Molly Francis carried a new sign proclaiming a third round was on the way. The way she speared him with her gaze told him she had seen how Miss Lorraine was hanging on to his arm. Whether she was jealous or saw this as losing control over him, which Gillette had paid her to get, was a question he wasn't too keen to answer.

He glanced at Miss Lorraine and then back at Molly Francis as she climbed down from the ring. If he hadn't been married, being fought over by two such lovely women would have pleased him. Now it was far beyond uncomfortable. Gillette had used the singer to gain an advantage over him. He didn't think Molly Francis would harm him but keeping him mentally off-balance would give the other gambler an edge when they met over the poker table.

Asa found himself anticipating that meeting to end the fuss caused by the two women. Once the big pot was won, the militia would let everyone go free. He intended to be the first one riding out of town, whether on Old Abigail the mule or on his own horse. Gillette shouldn't be allowed to keep the gelding, even if punishing him for the theft wasn't in the cards.

The next few rounds were longer and caused more blood to flow. The low punch slowed O'Malley but did nothing to bring him down. That resilience bothered Asa. Edging around the ring, with Miss Lorraine still hanging on to his arm, he found a place to watch what KO's trainer did between rounds. The way he furtively dipped a rag into a bucket and then wiped O'Malley's face looked suspicious.

"Are you well, Mr. Newcombe? You're wheezing like a lunger." Miss Lorraine sounded genuinely concerned for him.

"There's an odor in the air that shouldn't be . . ." Asa took another deep whiff and wobbled about. A sudden breeze from O'Malley's corner carried the sweet smell.

"You don't look good. Should we go back to the hotel so you can lie down?" She gripped his arm harder when he recoiled. "Just to lie down and rest. Nothing more." She smiled wickedly. "Unless you want more, of course."

"You don't smell it?"

Miss Lorraine daintily sniffed, then frowned. She turned slowly and homed in on the same bucket and rag Asa had noticed by O'Malley. "I've no idea what that is."

"Ether. His trainer is using ether to kill the pain. That's why the low blow didn't drop him like a stone."

"Ether like doctors use? I've heard of its use during the war. Some dentists even use it before pulling teeth." She touched her jaw and smiled ruefully. "I wish the dentist who yanked out a couple of my back teeth had done something to kill the pain."

"I've got some laudanum," Asa said, distracted. He shook off the cloud descending over him. The trainer finally covered the bucket, giving Asa a chance to suck in pure air.

"That would be useful for my girls," she said. "Some have pain that cannot be reached any other way."

"There. Look! See how O'Malley is weaving about? This is where the fight ends."

The words barely escaped his lips when Rodriguez stepped up, deflected a roundhouse blow and began pelting rapid-fire punches to the larger man's belly. Rodriguez swung with such fury, the veins stood out on his forearms and he turned red in the face from exertion. One of the blows ended O'Malley's bid to win another fight. He doubled over. Rodriguez lifted his knee hard and caught an exposed chin. It wasn't a legal blow, but it ended the fight and the referee concentrated on counting O'Malley out rather than on disqualifying the miner.

"The winner by knockout!" The ring announcer grabbed Rodriguez's wrist and hoisted his hand high in victory. A cheer went up and drowned out the groans of those who had lost their bets.

"Come back to the hotel. We can have some lemonade and talk. You look half past dead." Miss Lorraine's concern was evident.

"I've been up all night," Asa said.

"Are you sure *she* didn't keep you up all night?" Miss Lorraine's concern changed to disapproval as she looked down her nose at Molly Francis.

Asa stared at the singer, too, but found himself more interested in how she and Big Ed Edwards started arguing. The people in Golden Junction he distrusted most all hovered around Molly Francis. At least Frank Gillette hadn't joined the conversation. She stamped her foot and poked Big Ed with her parasol. Whatever she objected to was swept away by Edwards' grabbing her by the upper arm and shaking hard. Her head rocked back and forth as surely as if one of the fighters had clipped her on the chin.

Asa started to go to her aid but the mule skinner cut him off.

"Mr. Newcombe, here's more of your winnings from the other day. By my count, you still got a hundred thousand coming. I'll get it to you in a day or two."

Asa stared at the bag of chips. Trusting Snapper Gates to give an accurate count was foolish, but he was distracted. He took the chips and sagged under the weight.

"Thanks. Be sure to get me the balance in twenty-four hours."

"If you'd have another duel, I—"

"No. You figure how to pay me. I have my own business to tend to." Asa took a step around the mule skin-

ner to go to Molly Francis' rescue, but she had vanished
as quickly as a mirage in the desert.

"Come along, Mr. Newcombe, just for a while. You
need to rest." Miss Lorraine tugged on his arm.

"Will you do me a favor?" He looked at her. Her
lovely face brightened as if the sun had come out after
a rain shower.

"Why, of course. What do you want me to do?"

He handed her the heavy bag of chips. "Keep these
for me until I can deposit them in the bank."

"There's so much here. You trust me with them?"
She looked honestly startled at this.

"You have an honest face. Excuse me, Miss Lorraine. I'll come around later to collect the chips."

"Should I wait up?" she asked uncertainly. Then,
with more determination, "I *will* be up whenever you
come by."

He mumbled thanks and worked his way through
the remnants of the crowd, hunting for Molly Francis.
Wearing that pure white dress and carrying the parasol should have made her stick out. Nowhere did he see
her. He slowed and watched Big Ed Edwards as he
talked to the preacher and one of his henchmen. He
waited to see if the outlaw who had dogged his tracks
from Mosquito Pass showed up. The trio palavered another few minutes, then went in different directions.

Asa trailed Edwards until he realized the other
man was heading back to the Silver Bucket. By that
time it was too late to go after the preacher and find
what he was up to. More than gamblers had come to
Golden Junction for the big game. Those who lived by
their wits and duping others out of money had rushed
there, too. The game ended when all the players' chips,

not spent on hotel rooms, booze, whores and the other fees, went into the final pot. It was like a parimutuel betting pool, only with a single winner.

Breckinridge alone raked in hundreds of dollars a day. Edwards owned the Silver Bucket and probably the Oriental Tiger Lair, as well. Those funneled a river of money in the man's direction. Did the winner have to clean out Big Ed Edwards, too? Asa doubted the chips not on the final table had to be collected—that was Big Ed's way of walking away a rich man off the game.

Asa's steps took him up one street and down another, away from the crowds in the saloons. He stopped outside the abandoned store where Desert Pete had found the way underground. What the old prospector hunted in the played-out mine shafts puzzled him. Before he went to the storefront, he caught movement from the corner of his eye. Asa put his hand on his Peacemaker, then relaxed.

Molly Francis had entered a store down the street. She leaned out the window and gestured to him. The first thing he noticed was how filthy her white dress was. In the few minutes since she had announced the rounds in the prizefight, it looked like she had rolled around in filth. The first thought that he had was about the argument she'd had with Edwards.

He waved to her and stepped up onto the boardwalk. The wood yielded under his feet. This section of town had been abandoned quite a few months ago and hadn't been maintained like the area around the saloons.

"Miss Francis! Are you all right?"

She gestured more urgently and ducked further into

the store. He wondered how she had entered the building. The door was jammed. He applied his shoulder
and knocked it off its hinges. Stumbling in, he regained
his balance and faced her. She stood at the back of the
room, eyes clamped shut and trembling.

"What's wrong?"

Asa took a step forward; then the lights went out.
Someone dropped a bag over his head and yanked a
drawstring tight around his neck. He fought to tear it
free. Then a hand clamped over his mouth and nose. A
whiff of ether was all it took to make him pass out.

CHAPTER NINETEEN

A HEAVY BOOT TO his side caused Asa to roll over and groan. Fireworks exploded in his head when something blunt crashed into his temple. He sagged. Strength ran from his body like beer from a cracked mug. A little here, a lot there, he let consciousness slip away because it proved too hard to hang on to.

". . . shoot him."

The voice came from a thousand miles away. He recognized it. Then another voice said, "No," and he recognized that one, too. Asa knew when he was teetering on the edge of exhaustion. Everyone he saw looked the same. Their features blurred, and he began forgetting names. The year before when Meridian had suffered a typhus outbreak, he had worked around the clock after the doctor died. Being the closest thing to a medic, he had mixed and prescribed and passed out what medicine he could from his shop. The apothecary ran empty after forty-eight hours, and Asa wandered around town, saying things to suffering people he didn't remember and being worse off than many of the sick.

Rebecca had corralled him and put him to bed. By the time he recovered, the epidemic was fading. The weather turned cooler, and the fleas carrying the typhus were few and far between.

It had taken him two days to recover his strength. He felt worse than that now. Trying to lift his arm became more than a chore. It was impossible. A quick sniff made him cough. It also carried the scent of ether.

"Gassed," he muttered through chapped lips and a dry mouth. "Somebody gassed me and clubbed me."

He grunted when another kick to his belly doubled him up. This time hands pulled him erect. He tried to stand straight, but pain bent him at the waist. Again he tried to lift his hands. Enough sense returned for him to realize his hands were fastened behind him. The bag tied over his head kept him from seeing the men surrounding him, but he knew their voices.

"Gallant," he coughed out, "stop hitting me."

"What do you want me to do, sir?" The militiaman jerked Asa around and held him upright. Strength of will stiffened his legs and allowed him to remain standing under his own power.

"What do you want from me, Edwards?" Asa had recognized the other voice first thing.

"I want to string you up for what you did, you—"

Asa winced as the bag was yanked from his head. The cord tied around his neck choked him and then broke under the force of wresting it free. He blinked dirt and grime from his eyes. The blurry images focused. The pain in his belly came from shock this time.

"Molly!" He stared at her body. Her throat had been cut with such savage force that her head dangled to one side. In spite of the brutal death and the blood that drenched her once white dress, she remained beautiful.

"Why'd you have to go and kill her, Newcombe?"

He swiveled around in Lou Gallant's grip to face Big Ed Edwards. The man's normally florid face was pasty white. His hands shook, and his eyes stared at the body. Whoever had killed Molly Francis, it wasn't Edwards. In that instant, Asa realized the owner of Golden Junction had loved the singer. Her murder stunned him as much as it did Asa.

"I didn't kill her. She called to me, I came in and she was still alive. Then someone put that bag over my head and used ether to knock me out. From the way my head feels, they must have clobbered me, too."

"His hands were tied behind his back when I found him," Gallant said. "But that don't exonerate him. He might have seen us coming and done all that to give himself an alibi."

Asa looked hard at the militiaman. The only way anyone came up with such a cock-and-bull story was if they'd done the crime and wanted to place blame elsewhere.

"None of that makes a lick of sense, Edwards. Look at how my hands are tied." Asa almost threw his shoulder out of place trying to turn and show the tight bonds around his wrists.

"He's a crafty one. Sneaky like a hungry fox getting into the henhouse," Gallant said. "I heard others talkin' about him and how he outsmarts them at the tables."

"That's my style. I don't kill them. I outsmart them. Look what I did to Handsome Jack. Fighting him would have been suicide. I made *him* run so no blood was spilled."

"You did that very thing," Edwards said. "But we found you in a room with a dead body." His voice cracked as he spoke. "Nobody else was spotted."

"Who told you to come here?" Asa thought he knew the answer but wanted Big Ed Edwards to come to the same conclusion.

"Laramie warned Lou here. He found Molly Francis and called me."

"Frank Gillette," Asa said bitterly. "He's more likely to have done the deed than anyone else I know in town."

"I've known Laramie for a year or two. He's a sharp gambler, but he's always played fair with me." Edwards motioned to the militiamen. "Get him out of here and throw him in a cell." He swallowed hard. "And get Purcell. He can take care of her body."

Asa heard Gallant whispering the orders. Purcell had to be the town undertaker. Gallant finished with "Toss him in jail. Don't be gentle."

Two of the militiamen grabbed Asa by the elbows and dragged him from the empty store. To his surprise, the sun balanced on a distant peak and moved slowly higher in the bright blue Colorado sky. He had no idea how long he had been in the building with the murdered woman.

Gallant made no effort to quietly take Asa to the town's jailhouse. By the time they got to the building just off the main plaza, a crowd had gathered. He heard Snapper Gates taking bets and running odds on when he would be hanged. Nothing in Golden Junction went unwagered.

Asa wished he could put all his money on the outcome. Unfortunately, betting that he would swing was close to a sure thing, and winning wouldn't do him one whit of good. Gallant kicked open the door to the calaboose, dropped Asa flat on the rough-hewn planks in the floor and unlocked an iron gate. He went in and pulled open a cell door. His men dragged Asa in. Not one but two sets of bars held him securely.

"Are you going to untie me? My hands are numb." Asa wiggled his fingers and barely felt them. They had swollen to twice their usual size, which made the bonds even tighter around his wrists.

"Gnaw through the ropes like a good rat." Gallant stormed from the jailhouse. His henchmen trailed him. From the parting looks they gave Asa, his execution wasn't likely to be delayed too long.

It was sunrise now. He wondered if he'd last until sundown. It hardly seemed likely.

They had taken his Peacemaker and the knives sheathed in his boots, but the knife in the spring-loaded sheath on his left arm hadn't been touched. The only problem he had was the tight rope around his wrist prevented him from tensing his forearm and sending the knife sailing into his grip. He got his knees under him and flopped on the cot. If he intended to escape, this was the perfect time.

He groaned as he strained to get the knife free. Asa looked up when he heard the outer jailhouse door creaking open. Propped against the wall, he heaved a sigh of relief when Miss Lorraine came in.

She was held outside the second set of bars. She stared at him, then shook her head sadly. "You can't stay out of trouble, can you?"

"It makes for an interesting life." He kicked himself

upright and came to his feet. Judging distances convinced him he had no way of sticking his hands through the bars of his cell to have Miss Lorraine reach through the outer bars to help him. "You didn't bring a cake with a file in it?"

She snorted in disgust at his attempted humor. With a dismissive wave of her hand, she said, "You should have come by the Everest for that lemonade."

He had to agree. But the situation was dire, and he needed help escaping.

She held up her hand to keep him quiet. "You didn't kill that floozie. Even Big Ed saw that, but he was too heartbroken to let you go. He wants someone to hang for the killing."

"Can you convince him that hanging the wrong man is worse than anything else he can do? Hang me and the real killer is free to do it again."

"Big Ed's not concerned with other deaths, just Molly Francis'. Do you have any idea who did the dirty deed?"

"Gillette is my guess." He explained how he had been knocked out with ether and how he thought Gillette had supplied the ether to O'Malley's trainer.

"There's no proof. You didn't even catch sight of him before the sack was tied around your head." She sighed.

"Something?" Asa tried to hold down the rising fury. He knew what that was. "How big a bribe to let me go?"

"He'd call it a fine, if he calls it anything at all. And it's all the chips you have on you as well as the ones in the bank. He thinks that'd wipe you out."

Asa stared hard at the woman. She knew the mule

skinner owed him a considerable amount, and she had taken a large bag of chips to hold for him.

"Whatever must you think of me, Mr. Newcombe? The . . . material . . . you gave me for safekeeping is just that—safe."

"Make the deal with Edwards. Give him all I had on me, and he's probably already seized my account at the bank. Is there anything else he wants from me? I won't confess. I've already told him what I know."

"He's not a stupid man. He won't ask for a confession, but he will expect you to track down that woman's killer."

Asa wondered if Miss Lorraine had had the gumption to kill Molly Francis in such a brutal fashion. She had shown nothing but contempt for the singer. The way she spoke of her made that clear. Was it anything more than petty rivalry? But for him? Or for Big Ed? Asa was a latecomer to the intrigues of Golden Junction, and he had no idea about the personal histories of those who had remained for the big poker showdown.

"He's got me pegged right."

She made a disgusted sound and left. Asa waited impatiently for more than a half hour until Lou Gallant came in. He glared at his prisoner, opened the two barred doors and shoved Asa out.

"Untie me." Asa held his hands up behind his back the best he could.

Gallant made a rude gesture and left the jailhouse, Asa's ropes untouched. At least he had left the door open. Getting outside would have been taxing if he hadn't. The sun beat straight down on Asa. Noon. He saw Miss Lorraine in the shade of a nearby overhang protecting the boardwalk in front of the general store. He hobbled more than he had anticipated. They hadn't been gentle dragging him to the jail.

He silently moved his bound hands around for her. She drew a small knife with a wicked two-inch blade and sawed at the ropes. He cried out when they dropped free. The circulation returning to his hands proved more painful than he had expected. Rubbing his wrists got some feeling back into his fingers.

"It'll take a while before you're dealing off the bottom of the deck again," she said. She reached into her purse and pulled out the large sack holding the chips he had given her for safekeeping.

"I won't forget this," he said. He looked around. "I need my six-gun and knives back."

"I'm ransoming them." She held open her large bag. Two knives gleamed in the sunlight. The cold blue steel of his Peacemaker rested under them.

"Ransom?"

She grabbed either side of his head and pulled his face down to hers and planted a big, wet, juicy kiss on his lips. He tried to pull back. She broke off, then went back for a second longer, deeper kiss. Asa gave up fighting her. Miss Lorraine stepped away.

"You act like I'm cutting off your—"

"It was good," he said. "Thank you."

"There should be more to get these back, but it's my bad luck to find a man who is actually married." She handed him the knife and finally the heavy Colt.

He opened the gate, spun the cylinder and made sure the gun carried six rounds. He snapped shut the gate and dropped the gun into his holster. Looking at the reflection in the plate-glass window caused him to straighten. He forgot all his aches and pains. Behind him across the street was a familiar face.

"I see the little twerp," Miss Lorraine said, pressing close to him and whispering. "The one that always interests you when you spot him."

"I've stabbed him and shot him, and I can't seem to kill him." Asa watched the outlaw's reflection move away. He glanced over his shoulder and saw the man duck down a side street.

"He was waiting to see if you got out of jail. You're heading into a trap, Asa." She clung to his arm. Seeing his resolve, she released him. "Come by the Everest when you are done sticking your head into a bear trap, Mr. Newcombe. We can share some lemonade."

He surprised her with a quick kiss on her lips, then pushed away to arm's length. The impulsive behavior caused him to blush, thinking what Rebecca would have said if she had seen him. But Miss Lorraine offered good advice, and he trusted her judgment. He smiled weakly at his indiscretion, hastily turned away and strode off after the outlaw who had filled so much of his life since the trip from the Mosquito Pass depot. He might have been walking into an ambush, but he had reached the point where action was demanded. The image of Molly Francis would haunt him for a long, long time. He owed it to her to bring her killer to justice—in the sights of his Peacemaker.

CHAPTER TWENTY

A SA NEWCOMBE HAD second thoughts about going
after the outlaw when he saw that the other man
headed for the eastern part of town. Mostly deserted,
the buildings there afforded numerous places for an ambush. All the outlaw had to do was go into one store,
draw a bead on a place in the street and wait for Asa to
come by. The gunshot wouldn't even disturb the boister-
ous gambling going on at the Silver Bucket and the Oriental Tiger Lair and other places on the southern end of
town, where a few people congregated.

He pressed against the rough storefront and tried to
see the glint of sunlight off a metal barrel. Nothing. Asa
edged along, aware that the outlaw could have been
halfway to Missouri by now.

"Patience," he told himself. "Don't rush things. It's
like a good hand. You can't hurry, or you'll spook the
other player."

He was about to give up the hunt as futile when he saw three men come out of an old stable down the street. The preacher, O'Malley's trainer and the outlaw chattered like magpies. Asa was too far away to overhear them, but whatever they discussed caused the trainer some consternation. He shook his head often. The other two exchanged looks that excluded the trainer. They might have been a gang, but Asa watched one of them being dealt out of whatever mischief they were cooking up.

They went back into the stable. He moved closer. The muffled gunshot sent him scurrying for cover. He dived and rolled behind a rain barrel, Peacemaker ready for action. In a few seconds, the preacher man and the outlaw emerged. Without a word, they went in separate directions.

After they disappeared, Asa cautiously advanced on the stable and poked his head inside. A pair of boots, toes down in the straw, were visible in the back stall. Gripping his six-gun, he moved quickly, darting from one empty stall to the next until he reached the trainer, who lay dead as a doornail. He had been shot in the back of the head.

"What was it you backed out on?" He mumbled the question to the dead man and jumped when he got a reply.

"Now, that's a mighty astute question, gambler man."

Asa went into a crouch, spun and fired. He couldn't see the outlaw in the doorway. Gun smoke filled the closed space and choked him. Eyes burning, he went to the back of the stall and kicked like a mule to knock down the outside wall. Bullets tore past his head. The outlaw realized Asa was in the stall but not where. Bullet holes appeared all over the divider to the next stall. Asa counted six holes and knew the outlaw had to reload. A final kick knocked a hole in the wall big enough to crawl through.

He wiggled in the dirt outside the stable, got to his feet and raced to the front in time to see the outlaw's back vanish inside. It was a foolhardy move, but he swung around, six-gun leveled.

He faced the outlaw, who had his weapon trained on the spot where Asa appeared. They both fired at the same instant. Asa's aim was a tad better. He hit his target and caused the outlaw to jerk, missing a clean shot. Still, the slug tore past Asa's arm. It felt like a bee sting but had done little more than tear the fabric of his coat and shirt. A thin red line soaked through, showing the minor extent of his injury.

Firing steadily, he drove the outlaw to the rear of the stable, where he had already left a body. Asa intended to add a second to the pile.

"Why won't you mind your own business?" The outlaw peered around a divider and fired a couple more times. Asa had taken refuge behind a hay bale.

"You're the one trying to kill me. Does the knife wound in your gut hurt?"

"Not near as much as the bullet you just put into my leg. The blood's running down into my boot. I'm bleeding to death. Come put me out of my misery."

The man's voice was too strong to believe he had been seriously injured. Asa cursed himself for not turning the knife more once he'd driven it in. The man had the constitution of an ox.

"You're planning something with the fake preacher." That didn't provoke any reply. "Why'd you go and kill Molly Francis?"

"I was told to, but I couldn't do it." The outlaw cursed when that confession slipped from his lips.

The exclamation was all Asa needed. He jumped over the bale and ran forward, six-shooter blazing. He reduced the stall divider to splinters. His Peacemaker came up empty, but now his left hand was free and the spring worked perfectly. Again he had a chance to use that knife on the outlaw. It came into his grip with a click and *whish*!

He burst around the stall. Other than the dead trainer, it was empty. The outlaw had ducked out through the hole Asa had made for himself. He sheathed his knife, reloaded and retraced his steps out of the stable. Peeking around the corner, he saw the hole. The outlaw was long gone.

Asa poked around for a few minutes, hoping to get an idea where the owlhoot had gone. He had missed another chance to end the man's miserable life. He wondered if the outlaw had murdered Molly Francis, or if he had blurted out the truth about not committing the crime. Not knowing the truth rankled him even more.

"Who told him to kill her? And why didn't he do it?" That question burned in his mind. Gillette was the obvious one. Asa had no idea about the connection between Gillette and Molly Francis, but he had seen them that night of the King's Palace card game. They had known each other, and the woman had been ordered around by the gambler as if he owned her.

Asa decided it hardly mattered anymore. Bringing justice to the likes of Frank Gillette would come in its own sweet time. Acting as judge, jury and executioner hadn't been anything Asa had expected when he agreed to the cockamamie scheme Mayor Dutton and the others had forced on him. But the way he felt deep in his gut told him he and Gillette would do more than face each other over a card table.

Still furious over losing the outlaw, he wandered through the deserted section of Golden Junction. At one time there must have been more than ten thousand people here to support so many stores. Now that the gold mines were played out, Big Ed Edwards had to come up with ploys like the winner-take-all gaming to keep Golden Junction in existence a few more weeks— or a few more days. When the last card turned, the town was dead.

"Hey, psst. Asa! Hey!"

Asa whirled, his six-shooter in his grip. For a second he wasn't able to find who had called his name. Then he made out a shadowy figure in a doorway of a store whose roof had partially collapsed.

"Don't sneak up on me like that, Pete." He shoved his six-gun back into his holster. "I might have shot you."

"All keyed up, are you? Come on over here." Desert Pete motioned for Asa to join him.

As he stepped through the tilted doorframe, he saw that Pete had worked like a beaver. The far wall was braced, and a dark hole in the floor showed where the underground empire Desert Pete had discovered opened to the world.

"Look down there. Go on, Asa, take a gander."

He leaned forward. Pete had a couple lanterns glowing, their pale yellow light showing how he had been hammering away at the tunnel walls like some berserk woodpecker. Specks of brightness glittered, but Asa remembered the other hunk of rock Desert Pete had shown him. Iron pyrite. Fool's gold. The only thing that could be said about the prospector's work was that it kept him out of the sun.

But was sunstroke preferable to being plumb loco?

"You've been busy," Asa said cautiously. "You didn't happen to see where the man who shot at me went?"

"That little wart? The one what hangs out with Joshua?"

"Is that the bogus preacher?"

Desert Pete nodded like his head was mounted on spring.

"Where are they hiding? They have most of a town to pitch camp." Asa stared into the emptiness below. "You haven't run into them anywhere underground, have you?"

"Nope. These tunnels are a secret."

Asa doubted that. Anyone who had been in Golden Junction very long had to know the first mines stretched for miles beneath the town. These shafts had been drilled and come up empty. Then the mines gnawed out of the mountainside had given vast wealth before being exhausted.

"Don't tangle with them if you see them. Let me know. The one you called a little wart was paid to kill Molly Francis. He said he didn't but never told me who committed the crime."

"Killed? She's dead? Now, that's a waste. Don't recall ever seeing a purtier lady. She had quite a set of pipes on her, too. Lovely songbird."

Asa refrained from telling Pete to get out more to keep up with the goings-on in town. The more the prospector explored the subterranean maze, the more likely he was to find a way out of town. Despair took

Asa when he realized how many fortunes he had already accumulated, only to lose them to sneak thieves and Big Ed Edwards, as if the town's champion wasn't a step above being a petty thief himself.

"I'll buy you a drink," Asa offered. "Join me at the Silver Bucket."

"You go on. Let me root about awhile longer. I'm close, Asa, real close to a big strike. I feel it in my bones."

"Don't starve down there." He slapped the miner on the back. A small cloud of dust rose. As he left the dilapidated store, he wiped the dirt off his hand. His once spotless gambler's garb was torn and as filthy as Desert Pete's.

He prowled about a half hour more, hunting for Joshua and "that little wart," and gave up as the sun sank behind the distant mountains on the far side of North Park. He paused just inside the Silver Bucket as he sized up the action. The poker games looked to be penny-ante. After so many prize seekers had been cleaned out, this surprised him. Those listlessly moving cards about weren't the ones Asa needed now. Go big. He wanted to accumulate enough to become a contender in the final game.

"Join me," Wash Reynolds greeted. "I can use someone on the casebox, at least for a few hours."

He went to the faro table. This was where the gamblers who still had a pile left gathered. The bets they made were big enough to become campfire legends. Asa saw that one bad run would wipe out Wash. He wanted to lay off the bets to avoid going bust.

"My pleasure." Asa dropped his bag of chips onto the table where Wash kept his bank.

The man's brown eyes went wide at the sight. "You

keep surprising me, Asa. I heard tell Big Ed had cleaned you out with a fine."

"It takes more than a failed mine owner to stop me." He looked around the crowded saloon. "You see the fake preacher this evening?"

"Been too busy taking these poor fools' money." Wash lifted his chin to indicate that Asa ought to do the same. Thousands of dollars rode on every turn of the card now.

"How long are we staying partners?" Asa swept the losing bets in, paid off the winners and saw the gamblers wanted to let the bets that neither won nor lost ride. That suited him fine. The bettors weren't figuring the odds with every hand dealt.

"From what I hear, it'll be this time tomorrow night that the big game starts. I've seen bets of a hundred thousand become commonplace."

Asa nodded. The big blowout would bring desperation and euphoria. Those were the most dangerous times. And the most thrilling.

He realized he had fallen back into old habits from before he had met his wife and started a family. The bets he placed weren't for his own benefit but to save Meridian from the fate befalling Golden Junction. Meridian had never been a mining town, but the railroad bypassing it doomed it as surely as if it was and its mines failed to produce the metal they once had.

Trying to tamp down his excitement as the bets at the faro table grew, Asa came to a crossroads.

"Last three cards. Odds are four to one," announced Wash.

"Then I'm in for every chip I got," said a man dressed

in a pin-striped suit. "I take risks building railroads. Compared to the money I have riding the rails every day, this is . . . exhilarating."

"That's a hundred thousand," Wash said in a small voice. "I can't cover the bet. We'll have to close the table rather than accept it."

"I'll take the bet, then," Asa said. His heart hammered so hard, it might have exploded in his chest at any instant.

"You can't cover four hundred thousand if you lose!"

"You fellows finished jawing? I want to make the bet. You covering it or not?" The railroad man began stacking chips on the table. A single turn of the cards determined whether he cleaned Asa out . . .

. . . Or if Asa had the stake for the really big-ante games.

"Covered." Asa felt a curious calm. His hands didn't shake, and his voice came out strong and clear. This was his destiny. He and his father had gambled up and down the Mississippi and would have become legendary, if it hadn't been for . . .

He touched an empty vest pocket. Gillette had taken his pa's watch. It had never been a lucky talisman for Asa, but he needed luck now.

Wash dealt the three final cards facedown. Asa studied the railroad magnate and paid no heed to the cards. He would know the result by the man's reaction. And he was almost right. The man's eyes widened slightly, then closed.

Asa kept from letting out a whoop of relief. There wasn't any need to see the cards to know he had won.

"Another round, sir?" Asa pulled in the losing bet

and stuffed it directly into his bag. Wash had backed out when it mattered, and he wasn't entitled to even a white chip.

"That cleans me out. Thanks for the honest dealing." The railroad magnate thrust out his hand. Asa shook. Then he was alone, no matter how much the crowd around him hooted and hollered and tried to slap him on the back for winning such a large hand. In his victory he stood atop Mount Olympus, a god among gods, soon to be the grand winner in Big Ed Edwards' game to end all games.

CHAPTER TWENTY-ONE

IT WAS A foolish thing to do. Asa knew better than to bet in any game controlled by a mechanical device. Chuck-a-luck cages hid magnets. Roulette wheels had brakes and shaved wooden balls with some slots in the wheel slightly larger than others. But the Monkey Magician Gambling Device appealed to his sense of whimsy.

"That contraption's been brung all the way up from the Iron Front Saloon down in Austin just for your plea sure. Step right up. Place your bets," the operator called, "and make a fortune. Take chips from the house—if you can make the monkey your partner."

"Partner?" A half-drunk gambler stared at the device. "I had a wife who looked like that."

This drew an appreciative chuckle from the crowd gathered around the table at the rear of the Silver Bucket. Asa circled around to get a better look at the machine. A fake bower with intricately wrought metal flowers arched above a mechanical monkey garbed as a Persian magician. In its paws was a small cage, where the dice rattled about once the spring mechanism in the broad base was released. A key wound it up like some kind of clock. It shook all over until the dice came flying out of the cage on their own. It might have been in the snap of the fingers or as long as thirty seconds before the gyrating Monkey Magician rid itself of the dice.

Bets ran the gamut from under and over to exact rolls. The current operator demanded that the rules of craps be followed.

"Seven's your lucky number. Pass? Don't pass? Put down your bets, and let the monkey make you a fortune."

The dice were loaded into the cage clutched between the monkey's hands. The operator wound the device up and supervised the betting.

"Cast your spell, Magic Monkey!" He yanked the switch at the base. The monkey gyrated. Its floppy magician's hat bobbed about and the cage rolled back and forth until, unexpectedly, the dice came tumbling out.

"Seven's the winner!"

Asa watched the man load the device again. He bet a thousand dollars on *pass*.

"That's the way to do it, sir! Why, you're Asa Newcombe, ain't you? The man who faced down Handsome Jack the other day. Are any of you other gents willing to take on our hero?" The operator continued his spiel. For some reason most of the gamblers bet against Asa, as if all his luck had run out after the duel.

Thinking on it, he wasn't inclined to argue. The gruesome image of Molly Francis flashed in front of him. Thoughts of all the chips he had lost to theft and fines haunted him. And then there was the outlaw Desert Pete called the "little wart." He, Joshua, and Laramie Frank Gillette had been doing better than he had since the duel.

The bet with the French-built clockwork dice-rolling machine was going to reverse that. He had seen the gimmick. How the operator flipped the activating switch determined the outcome. With so many betting against Asa, the operator had to be inclined to let him win just to rake in the majority of chips.

"Make those ivory cubes dance! There it goes. The monkey has spoken!" The operator did a little dance of his own as the dice tumbled about and came to rest.

A groan went up from those who had bet against Asa. He collected his money, gave the Monkey Magician a parting pat and went to find a more honest game. As he turned from the table, he saw Big Ed Edwards watching him. The man glared. It didn't take a genius to know who collected the winnings off the gambling device. Big Ed was anything but a neutral observer. He collected fees at every turn, sat on the real money in his own personal bank vault and was likely to be the ultimate winner, no matter who laid down the winning card.

Once Asa cashed in the chips and claimed the prize— a million dollars? More?—walking away from this ghost town and its barren mines would be a sight easier.

Every step he took, he rattled from the bag stuffed with chips. Asa considered putting some in the bank, but he had a poor record of keeping them there. Better to hie on over to the Everest Hotel and let Miss Lorraine keep them for him. She had taken a fancy to him,

and she was as honest as anyone in town. He had made
it clear that there would never be more than casual
friendship between them, so she wasn't likely to get
angry at having a broken heart. He would never reject
her because there was never going to be more.

Asa shivered in the cold wind blowing off the Front
Range to the east. The calendar might have said it was
summer, but winter touched the breeze early this year.
All the more reason for him to finish the great poker
showdown as quickly as possible.

He walked faster down the street, then slowed and
halted in the middle of the street. Dark figures sneaked
about, heading toward the bank. For some reason he
thought of scurrying rats hunting for piles of garbage.
With no intention of going to the bank, even if it had
been open at this late hour, he still found himself following the trio of skulking shapes. He pressed into a
doorway and watched.

He caught his breath as one of the trio stepped out.
The rising sliver of moon cast a pearly light that high-
lighted the preacher's face. Joshua motioned to the
other two. Little Wart appeared, the very man who had
tried to end Asa's life before he even got to Golden
Junction. Asa drew his six-shooter and took aim. He
owed that outlaw more than a simple noose would have
ever repaid. He had overheard him confess to knowing
who had killed Molly Francis or at least having been
told to kill her. If all he had done to Asa over the past
week wasn't enough, being a party to that vile murder
alone forfeited his life.

Asa rested his gun hand against a post. He drew
back slowly on the trigger, then paused when the third

figure showed himself. A powerful lot of shooting was in store this night. Frank Gillette joined the preacher and Little Wart. He lowered his six-shooter when Lou Gallant and two of Edwards' militiamen hurried to join the others.

They pointed and gestured at the bank. Gallant drew something in the dirt with the toe of his boot. A long discussion followed, Little Wart kneeling to use his finger to add to the dusty picture. Then they split into two groups, each going in a different direction around the bank building. Asa took a deep breath, then dashed from his hiding place to look at what they had sketched in the dust.

At first he couldn't make heads or tails of it. He circled it slowly until it finally made sense. The crude drawing of the bank showed the position of the guards inside. Tiny Xs had been marked through three of them. The vault had been circled so that it appeared a halo floated around it. The intent was obvious. Gillette and the others intended to rob the bank.

In a way Asa wished they would do it. He had no love for Big Ed Edwards. But if Gillette and the gang made off with the cash in the bank, his entire reason for coming to Golden Junction disappeared. More than that, the outlaw he had shot and stabbed and almost caught had taken revenge on him by being party to killing an innocent woman.

The sound of the bank robbers returning sent him scampering for a hiding place. He crouched by a chair on the boardwalk. If it had been daylight, they would have spotted him right away. In the dark, as long as he didn't stir, they would pass him by. A half dozen men trooped past. He waited a full minute and then trailed them. The more he learned about the robbery, the better he could thwart it.

He let them keep a full hundred yards in front of him. His mind raced as he darted from one hiding spot to another in case one of them checked his back trail. There'd be no point telling Edwards that his own militia commander intended to rob him. What if Edwards was behind the robbery? Throwing in with Gillette didn't seem too far-fetched. There'd be gunplay after the robbery, but Asa had no idea how the sides would be chosen.

Someone else might be the winner of the big pot, but if the money was stolen before that, Asa had no chance at all. Better to go down with a busted flush than let the likes of Gillette, the outlaw and the others take the money.

They made a beeline for the eastern part of town with its deserted buildings. Passing the livery stable where he had shot it out with the outlaw, Asa began closing the distance. A light flickered in one tumbledown house. He waited for the gang to enter and sneaked to the rear. Asa crawled close against the house and sat under a busted-out window so he could eavesdrop on everything said inside.

"First thing. Let them open up. The head teller opens the vault to check it, then locks it up. Then's the time we hit. We take out the guards like we planned, grab the money and ride like the wind."

"For Montana," Gallant said. "I'll have the patrols all posted to the south of town. That'll let us get out to the north before anyone knows where we've gone."

"Won't they get suspicious, all the guards to the south and none to the north?"

Asa recognized Gillette immediately. He touched the butt of his Peacemaker, then relaxed. As satisfying as it was thinking of gunning down the men, he knew he wasn't that fast. Or that good a shot. If he singled out one of them, the rest would ventilate him. Even with a Gatling gun he had no chance of taking them all out. Better to catch them as they left the bank. They'd be overconfident and think their plan had worked to perfection. Walking into a barrage would fix them good—but Asa needed a small army backing him up. This wasn't a fight for a solitary man.

They started arguing over the best route north. Asa took his leave, moving quietly. He tried to come up with a decent plan to catch the robbers. He finally decided catching them red-handed wouldn't be as good as being sure the money stayed in the bank. Whether Big Ed Edwards backed the men or not made no difference. The more he thought, the more Asa became sure that Gallant and the renegade militiamen were double-crossing their employer. If Edwards wanted the money, all he had to do was take it.

Still, that would have been too obvious. Everyone would have gone after him. This way Edwards needed only to feign innocence. The gang would be blamed.

That made sense, but Asa knew men like Edwards too well to think he'd split the money so many ways. Even if Gallant and the others patrolling for Edwards shot their partners, the money was going to be spread thin. Even a million dollars.

Asa's head hurt from trying to figure it all out. By the

time he stood on the steps in front of the Silver Bucket, he had come to a decision. He went inside. Wash was working the faro table.

"Where's Edwards?"

"Upstairs in the King's Palace. He's got a big game going."

As Asa started for the stairs to the second floor, Wash called after him, "It's invitation only. I don't think you're in his good graces."

"I'll tell you what's going on later. Keep after them." Asa pointed to the bettors lined up three deep around Wash's table. All were eager to lose their money. The race to win all the chips was speeding up. By now most of the men at the faro table knew they had no chance. That meant the final game was going to be their entertainment.

Asa wondered at anyone paying five thousand dollars just to watch the game.

He took the stairs two at a time to the top. Two armed guards, in addition to the towering Anubis statues, blocked his way. Asa felt his temper rising. The last time he had been here was after the five-card stud poker game with Molly Francis. He wasn't in any mood for the militiamen to slow him.

"You can't go in. Private game," the nearer guard said.

Asa cleared leather and smashed the Peacemaker's barrel alongside the man's head. Before that guard crumpled to the floor, Asa moved on the second guard. He crammed the muzzle into the man's belly, doubling him over. He lifted his knee with as much force as possible. The other man's chin connected squarely, snapping his head back. He joined his partner on the floor.

Hardly breaking stride, Asa threw open the door to the King's Palace. His sudden entry caused six heads to swivel about. At the far side of the round table, Big Ed Edwards reached for his vest pocket. From the outline pressed into the cloth, he carried a derringer.

"I need to talk to you, Edwards."

"You have the floor, sir," Edwards said in a cold voice. "These are friends. Anything you have to say to me can be said in front of them."

Asa opened the floodgates, spilling all he knew about Lou Gallant and the others casing the bank to rob it. He held back from accusing Gillette and wasn't sure why. Somehow it felt wrong to let Edwards know everything he did. When he ran out of details, he clamped his lips shut and waited. His reading of Edwards proved dead-on.

"Get yourself a drink, sir. Downstairs. On the house. You've been up too long without sleep or, possibly, a decent meal." Edwards turned icy. "Your earlier escapades undoubtedly sparked this wild accusation. Now leave."

"They'll rob the bank and steal every penny in it. That's all our money, our actual cash money." He tried to read the other five players. Two were confused. Two showed some outrage at having their game interrupted. Those two had the most chips piled in front of them. The final one shifted in his chair to reach a six-shooter in a cross-draw holster. This player was firmly on Big Ed Edwards' side, no questions asked. If Asa had to guess, this gambler and Edwards had teamed up, unknown to the others, to fleece them.

Behind him the two guards moaned and rubbed their heads. A quick glance warned Asa he'd be trapped between the players at Edwards' game and the militiamen.

"I warned you!" He stepped over one guard and went down the staircase, fuming mad. His buy-in money was in that bank, and he couldn't get it out.

If Edwards refused to protect the bank, for whatever reason, Asa had to take matters into his own hands. Wash Reynolds looked up as he approached. The expression on the man's face was one of resignation. Asa knew he had one ally in his mad scheme.

CHAPTER TWENTY-TWO

"THIS IS CRAZY. We can be killed. And for what?"
Wash Reynolds fidgeted. He leaned his rifle
against the wall of a bakery and brushed dirt off his
fancy French cuffs. Desert Pete told him that smooth-
ing wrinkles from his coat made him look fussy. This
bickering grew steadily in volume.

"Quiet, you two. This is serious—deadly serious,"
Asa said. He stared so hard at the bank that his vision
began to blur. The sun was sneaking over the far mountains, and the bank opened in only a few minutes.

"Are you sure they won't wait until after everyone's
gone? It's dangerous to take out a bank when there're
so many guards in the lobby." Wash looked around
nervously. His calm demeanor while running a faro
game had evaporated completely. That was gambling,
this was lead flying with lives at stake.

"I overheard their plan. They're going to shoot

three guards, meaning a couple of them in the bank lobby are in on the robbery. They intend to hit when the head teller checks the vault. He opens it and does a quick inventory on everything in it."

"Now, why would he do that? There's no money comin' in, and by that, I mean spendable money." Desert Pete scratched his crotch, then yawned mightily. Two of his back teeth glittered bright gold. That was the first hint Asa had that Pete was what he claimed— a successful prospector. He'd had the buy-in money to get into Golden Junction, but he had never shown a hint of having a dime more to his name.

"He's got a point," Wash said. "They can stack the chips in a box outside the vault. All they need to do is keep good records of who's banking their chips and how many."

"There might be more to the robbery than it appears," Asa said. "The chips are as good as money until there're no greenbacks or specie to back it." Ways that Big Ed Edwards parlayed that to his own advantage tumbled about in his head, but it was too deep for him. Keeping it as simple as possible meant the robbers took real money from the vault and ignored the boxes of chips Edward had given out.

"No matter what, all we stand to get is an ounce or two of lead in our bellies," Wash said. "There's no reward for this, is there?"

"The reward is keeping a chance at winning the big money." Asa's irritation with the two men grew. He'd give them this, though. They had come along, and they hadn't seen what had happened to Molly Francis. They had accepted his brief, bloodless description and were ready to take on bank robbers only because they were his comrades—friends, even. He started to step out into the street, but Desert Pete grabbed his collar and yanked him back.

Three riders rode slowly toward the bank. They pulled up bandannas to cover their faces. One checked his watch, looked up and signaled to his partners. Both suddenly whipped out their guns and started shooting into the air.

"What's going on? They—" Wash shut up when gunfire from inside the bank echoed out. The guards inside joining the robbery had taken care of those who weren't. By now the head teller was being herded back from the open vault door for the robbers to steal all the money.

"This isn't going down right," Asa said. "Why aren't they helping the ones in the bank?"

The trio was still mounted and made no effort to help their partners inside the building. Stranger, they didn't have spare horses for the other robbers.

Asa trained his rifle on the one who had given the signal. This must have been the leader.

"That's the one I call Little Wart," Desert Pete said. "The far one fixin' to ride away."

Asa shifted his aim from the leader to the man who had taken part in killing Molly Francis. It made no sense to start the robbery, then ride off without the loot. Whatever the plan, he wasn't going to let the killer escape this time. He had stabbed him and shot him. Now it was time to end his life. Asa's finger drew back. The rifle bucked back into his shoulder, and the robber slumped forward in the saddle.

"You got him!" Desert Pete did a victory jig.

The two remaining outlaws turned their guns toward the bank entrance. Asa saw that they thought their partner had been shot by someone inside. He raised his rifle to take out another, but Wash stopped him.

"Stay back. Listen!" Wash pulled both men back and pointed to the bank. Shots continued to echo from inside. Shouting told of the pandemonium reigning, and a bullet broke a windowpane. Shattered glass rained down on the street.

The sudden silence was as startling as the first shot.

Asa tried to figure what was going on. Three men marched from inside the bank, hands in the air. The mounted leader pulled down his bandanna. The other man with him did the same.

"That's Gallant," Asa said, frowning. "He's got the drop on the men coming from the bank."

"That's Edwards bringing up the rear. He's got a six-shooter leveled at them. He and Gallant look to have captured the robbers." Wash sounded relieved that the danger had passed so quickly.

"He knew. Lou Gallant went along with the robbers to catch them red-handed." Asa gripped his rifle tighter. At least he had put another slug into Little Wart. The way he had taken off before the robbers inside had been herded out spoke to his intuition about trouble brewing around him. Asa tried to figure out what was going on. It amounted to Edwards double-crossing the men who had been on his side. He had used them and now was eliminating them. Gallant walked at Edwards' side right now, but if he didn't watch his back, Edwards would take him out.

Asa stared at the dust cloud showing where Little Wart had hightailed it. Could he depend on Edwards tracking him down to tie up that loose end, too?

"The militia's taking the robbers off to the calaboose," Desert Pete said. "But there's something else going on. I swear, I can smell gold, and there's a big stench risin' from that there bank now."

"Edwards is leaving. Looks like he's going to the Silver Bucket," Wash said. "No reason why we shouldn't head that way, too, since that's where we can rake in enough chips to take the money out of that bank legally and Gallant captured the robbers."

Asa, deep in thought, trailed after his friends. He stopped dead in his tracks when he heard four shots from the direction of the jailhouse. While he wondered if Gallant had shot the robbers in his custody, he didn't want to know. Word would spread fast enough without bloody proof.

"What if Gallant thought his boss knew about the robbery and turned on his partners?" He spoke aloud. Neither Desert Pete nor Wash paid him any attention. But it made sense. Gillette was nowhere to be seen. If he had learned that Edwards had discovered the plot, he'd have held back, too. He might even have put Gallant up to double-crossing his fellow robbers.

In a way, Asa cared nothing about all the dealing and double-dealing. He had put a bullet in Little Wart. Let him die of lead poisoning.

"Gentlemen!" Edwards' voice boomed from inside the saloon. Asa tried to get in, but the crush inside kept him in the doorway. Wash had found his wonted spot behind the faro table. Desert Pete had disappeared into the throng. "Drinks on the house!"

The roar of approval deafened Asa. He had worked up a thirst waiting for the bank robbers but wasn't thirsty enough, even for free liquor, to push into the Silver Bucket. When the furor of getting liquor for free died down, Edwards rambled on, enjoying the sound of his own voice.

"Bank robbery is a terrible crime," he called out "But my militiamen caught the outlaws responsible They have been dispatched, even as we stand here talking about it."

Asa nodded unconsciously. He was right that Gallant had shot his coconspirators. Now that he was firmly in Edwards' good graces, why shouldn't the king of clubs try again? The failed robbery worked in his—and Gillette's—favor. From the performance Edwards gave, he was in the catbird seat and invincible. What better time to rob the bank?

Then Asa's scheming took a different route. What if he beat Gallant and the others to the treasure trove in the bank? He wouldn't need any help if he planned right. There wasn't any reason to get Desert Pete or Wash involved, even if they'd go along with such a ridiculous idea. There wouldn't be enough of a head start before Edwards and every man in Golden Junction came screaming after him. The mental picture of Miss Lorraine coming after him with a sharpened knife chilled his enthusiasm for such a venture. Disappointing her was more of a crime than stealing the contents of the bank vault.

"Many of you have gone bust," Edwards rambled on. "That means the final game's not far off. Get out there, boys. Win, gamble, get ready for the big showdown. It's going to be spectacular!" Edwards lifted his glass in a salute. The cheer that went up told more of the thrill of seeing many hundreds of thousands of dollars change hands than any possibility many in the crowd would be at the final table.

Asa patted the pockets holding his chips. It was time to bet big or go bust. He still failed to push into the saloon. He stepped away and considered going to the Oriental Tiger Lair or some other gaming house when he saw Edwards hurrying away. He had left the Silver Bucket by a back door. The way he furtively looked around to see if anyone noticed him held Asa's attention.

Rather than fight his way in or find another game, Asa shadowed Edwards back to the bank. While that wasn't an unexpected destination for Edwards after the abortive robbery, that he had tried to be sneaky about returning was. Asa surreptitiously settled in a chair across from the bank entrance to see what happened. It didn't take long.

A man pushed a wheelbarrow around back. When he came back a few seconds later, he wasn't using the barrow. Asa let him go about his business and then peeked around the corner of the bank. He caught his breath when he saw Edwards struggling with a large mailbag. He dumped it in the wheelbarrow, looked around to be sure no one saw him and ducked back into the bank, only to return with another equally large canvas bag. He dropped this one with a loud clang. Asa had a good ear. He knew the dulcet ringing of gold coins. He wasn't a judge but thought those two bags plus a heavy third one might hold as much as a million dollars.

Big Ed Edwards was robbing his own bank.

Asa drew his six-gun, then thought better of confronting the man as he pushed the wheelbarrow away. The stable was in the opposite direction. While he might have had a wagon waiting to take the heavy cash and greenbacks, Edwards hadn't had time to arrange

it after the robbery attempt. But he had known about
it and might have prepared for it. Declaring the dead
robbers to be the actual culprits wouldn't hold water.
Something else was afoot.

The man maneuvered the wheelbarrow as if he was
an old hand. Asa suspected Edwards had worked the
mines himself, carting out loads of ore all day long. He
had been successful enough hauling ore to buy himself
the entire town.

Edwards deftly kicked in the door of an abandoned
store and pushed the barrow out of sight. Asa cautiously approached and peered inside through a knothole in a wall. He pressed closer and moved around
until he saw Edwards shove a brick under the wheel
and upend the barrow. The three sacks tumbled down.

But they didn't land on the floor. They vanished.
And then the man followed them.

"Well, well, well," Asa muttered. "Of course Edwards knows about the tunnels underneath Golden
Junction, too."

He waited ten minutes for a dirty Big Ed Edwards
to leave. The wheelbarrow stayed inside the dilapidated store, ready to wheel the money out later. When
Edwards headed back in the direction of the bank,
whistling tunelessly, proud of a good morning's work,
Asa slipped into the abandoned store.

The hole leading underground was plugged with
several long boards and a heap of debris. He moved
the boards aside and felt around in the dark. A rope
ladder let him down into the old mine shaft. Groping
around, he followed a wall until it suddenly disappeared.

Moving to take advantage of what little light fell

through the opening, he saw how the tunnel branched out. Not ten feet away he found three large canvas bags filled with money.

Asa sat on the money, wondering what to do. He had considered risking his life to rob the bank. Edwards had done it for him. Wrestle the money to the surface, load it on his mule and another packhorse, then shoot his way out. He growled in frustration. Getting away with the money presented the hardest part. The militia still patrolled the town's perimeter.

Once the money was discovered gone, there'd be a hue and cry. Unlike the other robbers, he couldn't hightail it for parts unknown. Gillette, if no one else, knew him. Tracking back to Meridian would occupy a decent bounty hunter for only a day or two. Putting his family in danger was out of the question.

He had to leave the money.

Or he could move it and ransom it back to Edwards.

But first he dug around in a sack and removed five thousand dollars. If he failed to win, he'd at least be able to give back the seed money provided by the good people of Meridian.

CHAPTER TWENTY-THREE

"THAT'S ABOUT THE dumbest thing I ever did see," Desert Pete said. "I been out in the desert without water, plumb out of my head, and I never thought to do such a thing."

Pete and Asa walked into the middle of the street and stared at the men lined up on the Silver Bucket's roof. They dodged an empty whiskey bottle that hurtled down from above. Whoever had emptied it no longer needed it for being reckless.

"All the way!" Snapper Gates harangued the crowd, and egged on the participants atop the saloon. "You got to jump the whole danged way! Take a running start if you like. Do it from a standing start. It don't matter. You make the distance, you win the pot!"

"Like betting on the horses," Wash said, "only the horses are smarter. That's got to be close to thirty feet across. No man can jump that far."

"No man who's been drinking as hard as they have."
Asa saw the majority of bets were placed on not making the distance. To him, that was a lead-pipe cinch.

"They're puttin' on quite the show. When are they fixin' to actually jump?" Desert Pete rubbed his hands on his shirtfront. Asa knew the reaction. The prospector wanted to bet but had been cleaned out. He considered loaning the man a few dollars and then heard how the crowd responded. No matter how Desert Pete bet, Asa would hate the outcome.

"Put a bet in for me," Wash said, handing Pete a blue chip. "Get good odds."

"That he makes it? That there's Jumpin' Johnny Jensen. He's got legs like steel springs. If any man can step across this divide, it's him." Pete ran his finger around the chip rim.

"Bet on him making it," Wash said. "You're likely the only one who thinks he can jump that far."

"That there man's danged near a mountain goat. I've seen him—"

"Make the bet," Asa said irritably. By staying, he contributed to this suicide. He wouldn't bet, but his morbid curiosity kept him frozen in place. As much as he loathed the idea of seeing a man fall to his death, studying the crowd helped him understand what made them bet and how to get absurd table stakes.

Desert Pete hurried off and got his betting slip from the mule skinner. He clutched it in his hand as he rejoined Asa and Wash. He joined in the crowd chanting, "Go, go, go!"

Jensen waved to the crowd, then disappeared. The sound of his boots hammering against the saloon roof echoed until he suddenly exploded into view. As if he kept running, his legs pumped against thin air. His arms flailed, and a scream ripped from his lips. Asa closed his eyes a split second before Jensen slammed into the side of the mercantile store. The impact sounded like a rifle shot. Silence fell over the crowd, which had been urging him on. Asa opened his eyes. He let out breath he hadn't known he was holding.

Jensen clung to the edge of the store roof. A few kicks battered the wood front. He let out a grunt and heaved himself onto the roof. Hands clenched, he held them high above his head. The crowd's shock at him making it across faded. A cheer for the conquering hero went up.

"Lemme collect." Desert Pete rushed to the mule skinner and collected his five-to-one odds. He handed twenty-five to Wash. "Thanks. You staked me again. You intendin' on banking the faro game again?"

"Come ahead. I'll be happy to take what you didn't pay me." Wash tucked the chips into his vest pocket.

"Here comes another human rocket! Better than fireworks, he's aiming to duplicate the greatest jump of all time." The mule skinner whipped up enthusiasm in the crowd to bet even more heavily on the spectacle.

"Gonna do it one better!" The potential jumper began a spiel on how great he was and how he had beaten every jumping frog in a fair match. The crowd started their chant and drowned him out.

"Are you betting again?" Asa asked Desert Pete. He wondered at what the next man intended. He fumbled and turned around and around for no good reason.

"That's Crazy Harry. I might chip in a few dollars for his funeral, but then again, I might not. He hasn't been too kind to me."

"Here he comes, folks! He's taking it to heart to be a human rocket." The mule skinner took in bets and wrote receipts for another few seconds until the crowd gasped.

All eyes turned upward. Crazy Harry looked as if he were on fire. Men on either side of him used lucifers to light fuses wrapped around his body. Then he launched himself just as the fireworks began going off. Firecrackers and Roman candles lit him up. Halfway across his jump, his clothing caught fire. He screamed from the exploding firecrackers, and then he screamed even louder when he missed reaching the goal by fully ten feet. Crazy Harry plunged to the street, the fireworks still erupting sparks. His cotton shirt turned to ash, revealing blistered skin.

Asa cursed under his breath when no one else ran to aid the injured man. He caught a thrashing arm and flipped Harry onto his face, then kept him rolling in the dirt. The firecrackers sizzled and sparked for a few more seconds. Snuffing out their fuses wasn't possible; they'd have burned underwater. The only thing that saved the man was the last of them detonating. Asa kept rolling him in the dirt until he shoved the man into a mud puddle. That caused a huge plume of steam to rise. Asa pulled him upright to keep from drowning in the shallow pool.

He had seen his share of dead men before. He eased Crazy Harry to the ground.

"A loser!" Snapper Gates bellowed the verdict. "He failed. He didn't make it. Collect on your bets."

Asa reached for his Peacemaker. A hand on his shoulder prevented him from shooting the mule skinner. He looked up. Wash shook his head. He kept his hand on Asa's shoulder until it became obvious Asa was not going to open fire on either the handicapper or his crowd all demanding to be paid off.

"I'll pay for his funeral," Asa said. When Gates paid him no attention, he lunged, grabbed the man and shook hard enough to rattle his teeth.

This brought angry retorts from the crowd waiting to collect. Then they saw the towering fury waiting to be unleashed.

Through clenched teeth, Asa grated out, "I said I'd pay for his funeral." He crammed a black chip into the man's hand. "See that he gets a good send-off."

"It was his doing," Gates started. He shut up when Asa drew his fist back. Again Wash kept him from making matters worse.

Asa jerked free and pulled back. His breathing calmed, and he no longer snorted angrily. When Gates went back to his work, Asa turned away.

"Go gamble. Get your mind off it." Wash hesitated. "Did you know him?"

"Never saw him before in my life. He shouldn't have been so stupid, but he doesn't deserve to be treated like a circus act."

Wash muttered something, but Asa had begun walking away. His pulse hammered in his ears and shut out the ruckus all around him. The heat of his fury made others get out of his way as he entered the Silver Bucket. The faro table stood empty since Wash was somewhere behind him. But he needed a game to vent his ire. The click of dice drew his attention. His hand brushed over the butt of his Peacemaker when he saw Laramie Frank Gillette working the chuck-a-luck cage.

He stacked a couple thousand dollars in chips on

the table in front of him. Gillette looked up, tensed and reached for a vest pocket. Asa saw the outline of a hideout pistol.

"The rules are anybody can gamble, if there's space at the table." He pointedly looked left, then right. Gamblers faded away to give him elbow room.

Gillette smiled. It wasn't pretty. He gestured at the dice layout on the table.

"You got any objection to me running the game?"

Asa shook his head. He watched Gillette load dice into the cage, then spin it around a few times before yanking the bottom clear to send the dice tumbling. They rolled out. Seven. Gillette reloaded and called for bets. Asa pushed his chips onto the DON'T PASS line.

He won.

Asa got into the flow of the game, estimating his chances and winning steadily. An hour later the other players had drifted away. Asa faced Gillette on every roll.

"Let's make this interesting. Everything. There'd be fifty thousand each on the line." Gillette egged him on.

Asa looked up and studied every line in the other gambler's face. Gillette thought he wasn't gambling. That told Asa what he needed to know.

"I'm out."

"Yeah, I thought so." Gillette made no effort to keep the contempt from his voice. "You're like your old man. He quit, too, when the stakes got too high."

Asa paused. He knew the trick. Gillette wanted to make him mad so he let his emotions take over. Men who lost their temper were easy marks. That told him even more about the next roll of the dice. He had been right to back away.

It was the smart thing to do. Asa turned back and shoved his chips forward.

"Let's roll the dice."

Gillette laughed harshly. He loaded the cage, spun it this way and that, then released the cubes. They tumbled over and over and came up snake eyes.

"Your point is two." Gillette bet against Asa and started to drop the dice back into the cage.

Asa moved like a striking rattler. He grabbed Gillette's wrist and twisted hard. Then he leaned forward so the other man's hand crushed down on top of the dice.

"What're you doing? Let me go!"

"I remember my pa saying you were careless."

"What's that mean?" Gillette tried to pull free. Asa held him too securely.

"He noticed how you lost the dice you played with. Drop them on the floor. Brush them away with your cuff. Sometimes you got to coughing so hard, you had to cover your mouth with a handkerchief—the same hand holding the dice."

Gillette struggled. Asa leaned forward, putting even more weight on the trapped hand.

"If those dice come up with snake eyes again, I win. Anything else, you win."

"That's how the game's played."

"The game's played with the dice in your hand." Asa jerked Gillette's hand around and forced open the palm. The pair of dice rested in his palm. Asa forced the gambler to drop those dice into the cage.

Then he watched him like a hawk. Gillette hesitated. He would have protested, but the tiff had drawn the attention of gamblers from all over the saloon. He massaged his wrist. Asa's fingers had left fiery red marks on his pale skin.

"Turn the cage. As many times as you want. You want to give the crowd a show, don't you, Gillette?"

The gambler cursed under his breath as he turned the handle. The cage vibrated as the dice ricocheted around inside. Then the bottom opened. The crowd sucked in a collective breath. Asa didn't watch the dice. He locked eyes with Gillette. He had seen hatred before in his life but nothing like this.

"Glory be! Newcombe won! Snake eyes! Twice in a row!"

"Fancy that," he said, raking in all the chips.

"Never seen luck like that," one of the crowd marveled.

"It wasn't luck, was it, Laramie?" Asa grabbed the dice and flung them over his shoulder. Men in the crowd scrambled to grab a bit of the fabulous luck.

"You made your point. We'll meet again. Next time you won't be so lucky."

"Luck had nothing to do with it," Asa said. "But you know that since they were your dice. When we meet again, make sure your six-gun's loaded, not just your dice."

Gillette snarled and left the table. Asa let him go. Then he called out that he was buying drinks for the house. It wasn't his money. It was Gillette's. And soon the rest of the man's chips would be Asa's.

Soon.

CHAPTER TWENTY-FOUR

Y OU NEED A wheelbarrow to carry all those chips."
Asa Newcombe bit his tongue to keep from saying more. He still pictured Big Ed Edwards moving all the cash from the bank and stashing it in the tunnels under Golden Junction.

"I've got a strong back and a weak mind." Wash Reynolds grinned. "Leastways, that's what my papa always told me." He counted quickly by making thousand-dollar stacks of chips. Some tottered and threatened to fall, but he expertly shored them up. A second count caused an even bigger smile. "Forty-five thousand here. I'm well-heeled for a big game now. With what I stashed in the bank, there's over a hundred thousand for my stake."

Asa looked around the saloon. The pace wore down the men who weren't suited for such pursuits. That made winning off them all the easier. Many were miners and thought eighteen-hour days of swinging a pick and moving tons of ore qualified them for an equal amount of time at a poker table. The skills were different. Asa was nowhere near the physical specimen of those men, but he had learned how to remain alert. Their minds slipped into a comatose state. His became sharper and more focused, and he thought his skills improved the longer he played.

His take for the night matched Wash's. The victory over Frank Gillette had given him the energy to play on for another day or two. The longest he had ever sat at a table was close to thirty hours. Memory of that game—his last before coming to Golden Junction—gnawed at him. There were good reasons he had quit gambling.

"So . . . so?"

He jerked back to what Wash said.

"You're so tired, you're asleep on your feet," Wash accused. "I'm putting my chips into the bank for the day, taking out the whole lot before closing this evening, and then I am going to clean out every last fool who'll set opposite me at a poker table."

"Stud?" Asa hadn't seen Wash play anything but faro. He wondered what the man's game was, the one that a gambler always went to when winning became necessary. "Three-card monte?"

"Draw poker," Wash said. "It's simple and gives decent odds to the man who knows how to play. Is that you?"

It was Asa's turn to smile.

"You'll find out in about eight hours, I suspect."

Wash wrapped his chips up in a sheet and slung it over his shoulder, lugging it away. He laughed as he left. With such a hoard he was going to be in the final game.

Asa started toward a table with a few players who looked like easy marks; then he saw one man at the bar elbow his partner. The two knocked back their whiskeys and hurried after Wash. If their attitude had been more relaxed, Asa wouldn't have noticed. These two looked like men with a mission.

Asa veered from the table and followed them into the street. As he feared, they were focused on Wash and his bag of poker chips. He drew his six-gun and checked the cylinder for a full load as he walked. If he'd had a lick of sense, he would have just shot the pair in the back. His sense of fair play kept him from taking this easy way out.

The two broke into a run and grabbed the gambler, one on each arm. They lifted and shoved him to the ground. His chips went into the dust, but Wash had figured out that his life hung in the balance. He went for his S&W carried in a shoulder rig.

"Stop!" Asa shouted, and fired into the air. It didn't deter the attack on his friend.

One robber swung his six-shooter and caught Wash on the wrist. Even at twenty yards back, Asa heard the snap of a breaking bone. Wash let out a shout of pain and fell away. He stared up into the muzzle of the robber's pistol.

Asa fired, this time targeting the robber. In his haste he missed, but the bullet flying past his head caused the robber to jerk about. When he fired, he missed putting a bullet in Wash's chest. Before Asa fired again, he had to deal with the other robber. Lead flew all over. One bullet caused Asa to wince. It hadn't blown through him but came close enough to make him dodge. He fell forward onto his belly and rested his elbows on the ground to steady his aim. This time Asa took out the second robber.

The first robber jerked around as his partner fell. This caused him to make a fatal mistake. He couldn't decide between finishing off Wash and firing at Asa. As the robber swung back and forth hunting for a good target, Wash pulled a Remington derringer and put a .41 caliber slug into the indecisive shooter. The robber fumbled to get a better grip on the Model 95 and failed. The gun fell into the dust. He stood like a statue, paralyzed from the shock of Wash's bullet.

Asa lifted his six-shooter. He fired, but there was no call for it. The man fell like a tree sawed by a lumberjack. Standing at attention, he toppled onto Wash, pinning the gambler to the ground. Asa scrambled forward, ready to shoot. Wash struggled to get out from under the dead body. His broken wrist hindered him until Asa tossed the corpse to one side.

"You dropped your chips," Asa said.

For a moment Wash stared at him, both men breathing hard from exertion; then he laughed. Asa heard a touch of hysteria in the other man. While Wash calmed down, Asa gathered the chips and tossed them into the makeshift bag.

"I need a doctor more than the bank," Wash said, finally getting to his feet. He held his right wrist in his left hand. "This hurts like hellfire."

"There's not a doctor in town. Not that I heard of, but I know someone who might take care of you."

"Not Desert Pete. I heard him going on about how he cut off a partner's leg before it got infected."

"Not him." Asa steered Wash toward the Everest Hotel. As they got closer, he waved to Miss Lorraine, who was sitting on the second-story balcony.

She called to someone inside. By the time they reached the front door, a pretty young woman was there to open it for them. Asa saw Miss Lorraine coming down the stairs, a doctor's bag clutched in her hand.

"Gunshots?" She peered at them and how Wash held his right wrist. "A break. I'll need a splint."

It wasn't clear whom she spoke to, but Asa heard footfalls hurrying away. He didn't doubt suitable splints would be found and brought into the sitting room.

"You two ought to be paying for other services here, but, no, you have to do everything the hard way."

"I'd be welcome?" Wash looked at her.

"You're well-dressed." She wrinkled her nose as she glanced at Asa. "Better than him now. You've got manners. Why not?"

"And you've got money," Asa added.

"There's that. This is a business like any other. We have to make a profit. Turning away paying customers isn't the way to do it." She cinched a bandage around the wood splints on Wash's wrist until he winced. "Don't be like that." She tied off the bandage and sat back to study her handiwork. "It will take a few weeks to heal. The bone was broken but didn't get to moving around. A greenstick fracture, they call it."

"I can't use my fingers." Wash tried to wiggle his fingers. They twitched. "I can't deal or hold cards."

"If you want, I can cut off your hand to give you a real excuse."

"You sound like Desert Pete," Asa said.

"Him? Never!" Wash leaned back, closed his eyes

and muttered to himself about getting back in the game. Miss Lorraine laid a soothing hand on his forehead, then stroked his hair gently. Wash's mumbling quieted as he drifted off to sleep.

Miss Lorraine kept Asa from waking him. She gestured for him to follow her upstairs. They went out onto the balcony, where she sat in a chair, looking down the main street. From here nothing that went on in what remained of Golden Junction bypassed her. Asa settled down in a chair on the other side of a table set with glasses and a pitcher.

"Lemonade?" She held up the pitcher. She saw his expression. "The lemonade's free. If you want sugar in it, that'll be one dollar."

He fished about and dropped a red chip on the table. "Give me five spoonfuls."

"My, aren't you the sweet one?" She added two heaping teaspoons from a sugar bowl, then leaned back and sipped at her own glass.

Asa tentatively sipped. It was much better than drinking what was otherwise pure lemon juice. He glanced sideways at the woman. She was a handsome one, he thought. He started to ask a question—one that she probably had heard far too many times—but she cut him off with a deep sigh.

"I should have left before Big Ed's crazy scheme. I don't like being cooped up in Golden Junction. The town felt like a box before. Now it's a prison."

"Where would you go? Denver?"

"Somewhere that I could earn money without having to be a madam. That's better than working the cribs, but depression gets to me just as it does the girls."

Asa fished around in his pocket. He had come prepared with stock from his apothecary. He placed a bottle of laudanum on the table.

"Thank you," she said. "That helps some of the ladies, but it causes problems in the long run. But for now, well, thank you."

They sipped their lemonade in silence for a few more minutes. Asa finally blurted the question that had gnawed away at him. "What hold does Edwards have on you for you to have stayed?"

She turned and studied him, then smiled ruefully. "You are so much more than a gambler, Mr. Newcombe. You cut right to the heart of my problem. Last year a flu epidemic hit Golden Junction. I had twenty girls working for me. Six died and another ten were deathly ill. Without Big Ed's help, they all would have died. I sold him the Everest, and he still has a thousand-dollar note I signed."

"To save your employees?"

"Whores," she said. "There's no need to pussyfoot around, Mr. Newcombe. I could renege on the loan, but I'm not that kind. I honor my debts."

"We all have our crosses to bear." He drained his lemonade and considered another glass. She decided for him, pouring and then adding more sugar. When she handed it to him, their hands touched for a moment. He pulled back almost guiltily.

"You are a man of mystery, Asa. What is it that eats at you?"

He stared at the men in the street. Most of them had gone bust but were trapped in the town until the final hand. From the rumblings, too many of those men depended on charity from the ones still in the game. Flat broke and dependent on handouts.

"I try to be better, but I can't."

She said nothing. He felt sucked into the silence. Duty had always been paramount for him, and he felt it more now than ever before. If he failed, the best that happened with Meridian was getting their money back. He patted the pocket where he had put the buy-in money stolen from Big Ed Edwards' hidden stash. After the attempted robbery, hiding it in the subterranean maze had been a smart move, whether he just wanted to keep it safe or intended to steal it and blame it on the would-be bank robbers.

But Asa had considered stealing it all. That was one moral failing he had triumphed over. But so many others piled up on top of him.

"I gave up gambling when my pa died."

"It has something to do with Gillette, doesn't it? I hear it in your voice when you mention him. And Gillette has been a visitor here a few times over the past week. All he wants to talk about is you."

"We were in a game aboard the *Dixie Queen*, one of the biggest riverboats on the river. They carried plenty of cargo, but from the Texas deck down to the waterline they ran more games of chance than anywhere outside New Orleans." Asa's mouth turned dry as a cotton bale shipped on that stern-wheeler. He tried to stop the flood of words but couldn't. They had been dammed up too long.

"We were in a game with Gillette. Him, my pa and me. Gillette cheated, and my pa caught him. Gillette went for a gun. So did my pa. Only Gillette wasn't drawing. He only took out a tin of lucifers to light a cigar. I grabbed my pa to keep him from shooting down . . . that man." Asa sucked in a deep breath and let it out fast.

"We wrestled, and his gun went off. The bullet went through his pocket watch."

"What happened?" Miss Lorraine spoke in a voice so low, he almost failed to hear her.

"The bullet went through the watch and into his heart. I killed him. If I had let him cut down Gillette, he'd still be alive today."

"You saved Laramie and think you were responsible for shooting your own father?"

"Time for me to win the last hand." Asa finished his lemonade in a gulp and stood.

Miss Lorraine pushed the red chip across the table to him.

"Use this to win. Clean out Gillette."

"I'd do more than that, given the chance." He slipped the five-dollar chip into his vest pocket, where his pa's watch ought to have been. "For luck."

They locked arms, then silently went downstairs. Wash Reynolds snored softly, his head still draped back over the back of the settee. His broken wrist was propped up on a padded arm. He looked peaceful enough to stay there in the brothel's parlor for a long, long time.

"You want to let your friend sleep some more?"

"Let him rest so he'll be wide-awake when I clean him out."

Miss Lorraine shook her head. "You are an arrogant one, aren't you, Mr. Newcombe?"

"It's not bragging if you can do it. I've watched him at the faro table, and I know how he thinks. He can beat most of the gamblers left."

"But not you?"

"Not me." Asa took the woman's hand and kissed it, bowing slightly before heading toward the Silver Bucket.

Along the way he saw two dead bodies and a third in the making. Two men had bet all their chips on the quick draw and first shot. He tried not to cringe as he walked past and heard the gunfire followed by the thud of a body hitting the ground.

Asa wasn't looking forward to facing the victor of that contest, but he would if it meant winning. The people of Meridian depended on him. As he stepped into the Silver Bucket, he realized he needed the win to justify his own existence.

CHAPTER TWENTY-FIVE

ASA DECIDED TO let the two gamblers face off against each other. A quick glance showed almost a hundred thousand on the table. The way they bet, there'd be a mistake made that wiped out one of them entirely. He watched intently to get hints about their play when a gunshot rattled the saloon. With a move like a striking rattler, he had his Peacemaker out and ready for action.

Looking around, he saw a half dozen other men also hunting for the source of the gunfire. Like a weather vane, he turned and stared into wind coming from the rear of the saloon. A second shot rang out. Several men with drawn guns who stood closer to the rear slipped their six-shooters back into their holsters. Whatever went on, they didn't see a threat.

Asa slid his six-gun back into place and walked away from the poker game to find out what new commotion was going on at the rear, where a half dozen pool tables stood. A man jumped up onto one table, gun drawn. He shouted something Asa failed to understand, then fired. The bullet ricocheted off a pool ball to bury itself in the side wall.

A cheer went up.

"You done it, Herk. You sunk the eight ball!"

Several onlookers went and slapped the man on the back as he dropped to sit on the edge of a second pool table.

Asa took in the scene with a single glance. The loser forked over a small mountain of chips and slunk off. The victor opened the gate of his Colt and reloaded.

"Who else wants to challenge me? I'm the best bullet-pool player in the whole of Colorado. Ain't nobody better. And none of you milksops can come close to beating me."

"What's the stake?" Asa asked.

For a moment the challenger failed to answer. Asa repeated his question.

"You? You're challenging me, Herkimer Cody, to a game? What's a big enough bet to make you wet your fancy pants, mister?"

Asa had no idea who spoke.

"Fifty thousand."

A hush fell over the saloon. Asa looked around and realized he was the one who had named such a ridiculous bet.

"You got more sand in your gizzard than I'd credit." Cody looked Asa up and down and shook his head. "You ought to save your money and buy new duds. Your finery's all torn up and dirty."

"A hundred thousand."

Again Asa wondered who had spoken. And again it hit him he was upping the ante. If he lost, there wouldn't be enough left to get into a game that mattered. But if he won, he'd be among the handful with the most chips. The more he had stacked in front of him when he sat at the final table, the better his odds of winning. Other than cheating, a big stake along with acute talents gave a gambler the best chance of triumphing. Everyone had a losing streak. That was luck. Enduring the down hands required a deep pocket in order to come back.

"You ain't kiddin', are you?"

"Odds not high enough?"

Cody held up his hand. He looked around and saw that the men who had cheered him on now egged him on. They wanted to see this showdown, and they didn't care if Cody or Asa won. Seeing so much money change hands was the next best thing to bloodshed for them.

"All right. Nine ball? You get to keep shooting if you sink a ball."

"Is that a hundred thousand for the game or for each ball?"

Again silence fell. Everyone stared at Asa. Then whispers started until word passed throughout the Silver Bucket. Other games meant nothing compared to this one. If the first shooter ran the table, he'd win almost a million dollars.

"You got that much?" Cody peered at Asa suspiciously.

"Do you?"

"Let's shoot for break." Cody looked around and then pointed to a deer head mounted on the back wall. "Whoever gets closest to the eye."

Asa moved in a swift, easy movement. He drew and

fired by an instinct hidden away for a decade. Once he had been as good as any gunfighter, and that skill had kept him alive. It returned in a flash.

His bullet hit the deer's right eye. The glass shattered and showered down on the pool table. He brushed it off, then inclined his six-shooter in the direction of the deer head.

"There's the other eye. All yours."

"I intended to take out the one you shot."

Asa fired again. The second eye exploded. "Pick another target."

"I'll break," growled Cody. "I'm running out of ammo."

"That's all right, Herk. All you'll need is nine rounds to run the table." A man standing beside Cody slapped him on the shoulder to encourage him. Asa saw that he had spooked Cody. But he wasn't ready for the break.

Cody aimed at the rack and fired. Three balls went spinning off and into pockets.

"You want to pay up now and avoid a bigger loss?" Cody strutted around the table, chest puffed up as he blew the smoke from the muzzle of his gun.

"You want to double the bet?" Exhilaration filled Asa. Everything was on the line. Only he could pull on past any fear and win.

"I'm not giving you a chance to fire, not even once. I'm running the table." Cody circled like a wolf sniffing out its prey, aimed and fired.

Pieces of the ivory ball flew all over the table. Rather than being nudged along by the bullet, the pool ball exploded.

"My turn," Asa said. He saw Cody start to object. "You didn't pocket a ball. Or any part of it." Asa brushed away the dust and broken pieces as he lined up his shot.

He fired. The ball rolled straight and true into the pocket.

The next two rounds also pocketed balls. He could tie up the game with one last shot. Four-four and the ball that had disintegrated when Cody struck it off center. Asa cocked his Peacemaker, sighted and fired. For an instant it looked as if the ball rolled true, but at the last instant, it veered away and bounced back and forth in the pocket mouth.

Before anyone said a word, Cody fired. The ball finished its journey into the pocket.

"Five-three. You owe me two hundred thousand."

Asa stared at the table. He should have gotten a push. A tie. A draw. That would have satisfied him.

"Pay up. Now." Herk Cody swung his six-gun around and pointed it over Asa's head in obvious threat.

"You cleaned me out," Asa said in a choked voice. He came up short by two hundred chips.

"Owe me." Cody bellowed, "Drinks are on me!" He fired his pistol into the ceiling, causing a shower of plaster. When he came up empty, he reloaded and stared at Asa with a mixture of pity and contempt. He pushed past and went to the bar to enjoy his newfound notoriety.

"You got the strangest ideas about winning I ever did see." Wash Reynolds perched on the edge of the pool table. He appeared more refreshed than when Asa had left him. "I'm not loaning you a single chip this time. It's too close to the final table."

"I'm not completely cleaned out," Asa said. He drew out the red chip he'd tried to pay Miss Lorraine with.

"Quite a ways from that to buying into a real game. Come on. Let's take Cody up on that free drink."

"Go on," Asa said. "I've got some gambling to do." He looked around. The only game taking such a low bet was a faro table.

"I'd wish you good luck, but you're better off if I wish that you get a lick of sense." Wash went to the bar and tapped on it with his splinted wrist to get attention and demand his free drink. Cody came over and the two of them were joking like old friends as Asa went in search of a game.

A few players with small stakes played Spanish monte. Asa dropped his single chip on the table and said, "Deal me in."

Three hours later he had turned the red chip into that much over a thousand. All the while he was aware of the five thousand dollars he had stuffed into his coat pockets, his buy-in stolen back from Big Ed Edwards' hidden stash in the mine shaft under the town. No matter how he fared, he vowed that the money rightfully belonged to the citizens of Meridian. His last bet at monte won him another three hundred.

He scooped it up, looked around the saloon and found Herk Cody at a high-stakes poker game. With chips in hand, he stood beside the man until Cody noticed. Then he counted out two black chips and said, "We're even."

Cody sputtered and started to come after him as he walked away, but the others at the table called the gambler back. Asa smiled as he went to the bar, got himself a shot of whiskey and then saw that Wash had taken his place behind the faro table once more. He

dealt awkwardly with his splinted wrist, pulling cards
from the casebox, and he had a player shuffle for him.
Asa stood directly in front of him.

"I told you. No more loans," Wash said as soon as he
saw Asa approach. His friend's dark eyes widened when
he dropped his thousand dollars' worth of chips on the
table. "I see you got somebody to stake you. You're going to owe them a passel before you're done here."

"Deal," Asa said. He watched the cards and did the
odds. An hour of play saw him ahead by five hundred.
In two hours, he had a quarter of Wash's entire stake
of chips.

At five hours, they were even.

"One of us is going to walk away with a bag full of
chips," Wash said. "We can keep nibbling away at each
other or make a single bet. What's your pleasure? It
makes no never mind to me, but it's almost dawn."

"High card?"

Wash counted through the chips. He was almost as
dexterous using his left hand as he was with his right. He
pushed the stacks out where they both saw the amount.
"Forty thousand each. All in?"

"All in," Asa said. He had lost everything but the
single chip before. This time even the chip from Miss
Lorraine would be at risk. "You first. You're the one
with the gimpy hand."

"My wrist is broken, but my luck's intact."

Wash used his left hand to cut the deck. He turned
it over. A slow smile crossed his dusky face.

"Luck is riding at my shoulder. The suicide king.
Your death, friend Asa, your demise at my hand."

Asa took a deep breath and cut. He hesitated, then
turned over the deck.

"It's suicide, all right. Yours. The ace of hearts."

Without a word, Wash lowered his splinted forearm to the table and shoved the hill of chips toward Asa. Then he reached under the table for a carpetbag large enough to hold all the chips.

Eighty thousand. Asa had his ante for the big deal.

CHAPTER TWENTY-SIX

"I NEED TO GET some food and take a long nap," Asa said. He yawned, as if this proved how tired he was. Again, he tried to remember how long he had been awake and couldn't. Caught up in the gambling, he had gone from shooting pool balls to monte to faro, all in what seemed now to be marathon sessions. He remembered the old aches and pains in his back and legs, and he had been ten years younger when he had plied his trade on the riverboat casinos.

A stentorian call for attention caused him to turn. Big Ed Edwards stood on the stage. The man hooked his thumbs in the armholes of his vest and reared back. His words came out loud and clear.

"Gents, it's time for the final table. The showdown. The big deal. It'll be a simple enough game. Draw poker. And the stakes? For everything, my friends, for every last loving chip. Winner take all!"

"How much's that?" Herk Cody shouted from the bar. "You keep sayin' there's a big pot. I got more'n a quarter million in chips. How much do I stand to win?"

Edwards paused for effect, then lowered his voice to make sure everyone hung on every word.

"How much, you ask? How much? The winner will ride out of Golden Junction with a million and a half dollars in cash and gold. One million five hundred thousand dollars to the winner!"

Wash let out a low whistle. "That's more than I guessed from counting chips on all the tables. Good luck." He awkwardly reached out, his left hand turned so he could shake Asa's hand. "Remember me in your will. I was the one who made it possible for you to get into the final table."

Asa barely paid attention. He had eighty thousand. Cody had three times that amount. The others moving toward a table in the center of the saloon all dragged bags of chips. One man sashayed to the table, as if this was just another game. Asa saw the tension around the man's squinty eyes. He looked nonchalant, but Asa knew that inside, he was a volcano ready to erupt. Big Ed Edwards hopped down from the stage and made sweeping motions. Lou Gallant and another militiaman lugged large boxes of chips over and put them beside an upholstered chair that Edwards immediately claimed as his own.

Asa considered asking for a similar chair. They were likely to be at the table for a long spell, but he decided an uncomfortable straight-backed wooden chair suited him better. The more uncomfortable he was, the easier it was to stay awake. Even drifting a little, letting exhaustion dull his senses for one hand, might prove calamitous. Cody was to his right, Edwards in the chair next going counterclockwise, and a gambler he didn't know to his left. The chair directly across from him was empty.

"Who's the final . . . ?" His voice trailed off when he saw Laramie Frank Gillette enter the saloon. The double doors swung behind him, causing a small breeze to gust in from outside where dawn cracked the sky.

"Mr. Gillette, just in time. The final chair is yours." Edwards made a grandiloquent gesture. "We will play draw poker until one player has all the chips."

"What if we wanted to play another game?" Cody thrust out his chin belligerently. Asa resisted taking a swing at him. He could double his money with a bet that his punch floored the man.

"You've had your chance to do that. If you don't wish to play, your chips are forfeit, and I wish you a fond goodbye, Mr. Cody."

"You can't do that!" Cody half rose, then saw Gallant and the other guard put hands on their six-shooters.

"It looks as if he can," Asa said dryly. "Shuffle up and deal."

He stared across the table at Gillette, who eyed him like a vulture spotting something dead. Cody won the cut to deal first. Asa tapped the deck after Cody shuffled rather than cut it again. If he had somehow stacked the deck, this might throw him off. But Asa hadn't seen anything but a straight shuffle. Cody dealt quickly—honestly, from all Asa could see from his vantage point.

He peeked at the corners of his cards. Two pair. Low. He anted one hundred dollars and the betting began. Rather than pursue the pair when he got nothing to help, he folded. Only a few hundred lost, but Gillette took the pot. Asa was aware that of the players, he had started with the fewest chips.

As the play circled the table, the tides of chance pulled more and more away from the man to his left. Asa faced him down over a pot worth almost a hundred thousand. In his hand he held three tens. Not great but good.

The final card was dealt. His opponent took one card. Asa got nothing with his two-card draw to help. The other gambler smiled slowly, then turned poker-faced.

"I'm going to bet the ranch on this one," he said. "Everything I got." He pushed a mountain of chips into the center of the table.

If Asa called and lost, he'd be out. But the tiny crinkles around the man's eyes told a story different from the fleeting elusive smile. That tell had been planned. He meant for Asa to see it and think he had drawn a big hand. From the play, the gambler wanted Asa to call what might be a straight or a flush. There might be a full house hidden away behind the man's big hands. Or there might be nothing.

Asa thought he bluffed. Forcing himself to calm down, his hands almost shaking, he shoved all his chips into the center of the table.

"Let's see what you got." The instant he spoke, Asa knew he had won. The man silently dropped a single pair of kings. "My trip tens take the pot." For a moment, he stared at the chips he had won. This put him even with Gillette and slightly ahead of Edwards. Cody was far back in the chip count now.

Asa took Cody out in the next hand with a full house. That left him matched against Big Ed Edwards and Frank Gillette.

And even this proved unequal. Both he and Gillette chipped away at Edwards' stake. By the eighth hour, he and Gillette were almost equal, with Edwards having fewer chips than Asa had begun the contest holding.

However low on chips he got, Edwards proved tenacious. Another hour. Another two. Asa began to feel the lack of sleep. He finally accepted a shot of whiskey although it would do more to put him to sleep than invigorate him. As the others looked at their cards, he drew out a small bottle from his coat pocket. A quick thumb flick took out the cork. He poured the contents into his whiskey. Running an apothecary shop had its advantages. He knew the drugs that helped for sleep, and he knew others that kept a man awake. Those had been sold mostly to stagecoach drivers and engineers on trains.

More than one railroad man at the Mosquito Pass depot had bought the drugs from him. He knocked back the bitter shot and made a face. It was potent stuff.

"What'd you drink?" Gillette cast a gimlet eye on him. "You're not supposed to take anything the rest of us can't."

"I don't remember hearing that in the rules. Is that so, Mr. Edwards?"

Big Ed Edwards frowned as he stared at his hand. He looked up, glowering at Asa. "I don't care what you imbibe. Drinks are on the house."

"He took some kind of drug!" Gillette protested.

"I can beat him, no matter what he takes. Are you going to bet or fold?" Edwards glared at Gillette.

Asa felt the effect of the Hoffman's Anodyne he had taken almost immediately. His heart beat faster, and his blurred vision cleared. His hands trembled now, but

ne felt like a racehorse at the starting gate. Any fatigue
ne'd felt before evaporated like mist in the sun. Asa
wanted to fight his weight in wildcats.

In spite of feeling as if he was fresh as a daisy, Asa
ost the hand. He sat back in this uncomfortable chair
and looked at his two opponents. The drug made him
feel invincible. He wasn't. He had to use the edge the
drug gave him to beat the pair, not let it lead him astray.

The next hand forced the matter.

He and Edwards faced off. The way the betting went
convinced Asa his opponent was bluffing. His own
hand was weak. A pair of eights against . . . what?

"Let's bump it up ten thousand," Asa said.

"And another twenty thousand." Edwards looked
smug. But the small twitches showed the pressure he
was under. More than ever, Asa believed he was facing
a bluff. But if he called with a weak pair and Edwards
topped him with another pair, not as small, he was out
of the contest. A quick look at Gillette across the table
convinced him. Letting Laramie Frank Gillette win
was a personal insult.

"Everything. All in." Asa shoved his chips into the
middle of the table. As he built the pot, he saw the
panic on the town owner's face.

"I fold." Edwards tossed his cards onto the table.
He had one black chip left. One chip. One. It rested on
the table, a silent testimony to bluffing and failing.

The game was now between Asa and Gillette.

Even with the huge pile, Asa was behind in chip count.

"What'd you have?" Gillette looked hard at him.

Asa smiled and shook his head. This was something
another player had to pay to see. He was itching to find
what Edwards had held, but he had folded. It was

enough to win. Vindication came later, when he fin
ished off Gillette.

"If you gents will excuse me, I need a drink. A stif
one. It's not every day I lose this big." Big Ed Edward
pushed away from the table. Asa ignored the man's de
parture. Gillette's presence was all that counted now.

He was close, very close, even if Gillette had twic
the chips he had. Asa tried to remember when he'd bee
in a game where having a half million in front of hin
made him the underdog. He'd never seen a game wher
there was a million on the table, much less all in on
player's stake.

They played, carefully at first, feeling each other ou
as if this was the opening hand and they had no ide
how the other played. Then betting got wilder and th
pots bigger. Asa lost track of time. He knew they ha
started the showdown at dawn. It turned dark outside
then light again. That meant they hadn't moved for
full day. His legs ached, and his arms had turned t
lead. Without the anodyne, he would have passed ou
long ago.

But he didn't have any more of the potent potior
Everything he had stashed in his pockets was gone
used, given away. He was just as glad he had given Mis
Lorraine the laudanum for her girls. Killing the pai
pulsing through his legs with it tempted him. It als
would have dulled his senses and turned him just
little loco.

It was bad enough he did things like bluffing with
out even a low pair. He won that hand and then lost th
next when he had a full house. Luck could be fickle
Countering that he had to be smart.

And then he was dealt a hand that caused a flush t

rise in his face. He hoped Gillette hadn't seen his reaction. A straight flush, jack of clubs high. This was the stuff of legends, and he held it. He stared at the million and a half in chips on the table. So many chips the table threatened to buckle under the weight. That was his imagination, but that'd be the way he told the story to his grandchildren. That was how he'd tell Mayor Dutton and the rest of Meridian's citizens how the last hand had played out.

"You think you have something that can beat me, don't you?" Gillette sneered at him. "We're pretty much equal on the table. Everything on this hand?"

Asa knew Gillette wasn't bluffing, either. It came down to whose hand held the higher cards.

"Everything?" Asa felt woozy. His head spun, and his stomach knotted. Back in the old days along the river, he had never reacted this way to any hand. But never had there been so much on the line.

"I don't think you're up to it, though, Newcombe. You always back down. You're never there when people need you." Gillette sneered. "Too bad Molly Francis isn't here to put her hand on your shoulder to give you support."

Asa gritted his teeth until his jaw muscles throbbed. The woman's death had been unnecessary. Gillette hadn't slit her throat, but his henchman had.

"But you don't care about women, do you, Newcombe?" Gillette played with a stack of chips, letting them click together until it sounded like a six-gun cylinder being spun. "You don't care about anyone after you murdered your own pa."

Silence fell over the crowd watching the game.

The anger Asa felt as Gillette taunted him exploded

like a volcano. He started for his Peacemaker, but a
hand caught his wrist and held it so he wasn't able to
draw. In his ear Wash whispered words cautioning him
to ease back. He twisted free and went for the gun
anyway. This time another hand rested on his shoulder.

"He wants to make you angry," Miss Lorraine said
quietly. "If your hand's good enough, take him out."

He looked up at her. She was under as much strain as
he was. Asa saw the crowd sided with him, too, but that
wouldn't matter if he tried to gun down Gillette. Seeing
the man dead on the floor, the sawdust soaking up his
blood as he died, would be satisfying. Having Gillette
live with the knowledge of losing was even better.

"Everything," Asa said.

The crowd let out a collective held breath. Miss
Lorraine squeezed his shoulder, and Wash pressed in
on the other side. Even if he lost, he had made friends
in these two. But he wasn't going to lose.

"Got you," Gillette said. "Full boat, aces full of
kings." He dropped the pasteboards on the table and
reached for the pot. Asa tossed his straight flush on top
of the chips.

There wasn't any need to say a word. The expression on Gillette's face was worth as much as the million and a half he had just won. Almost.

"Wait." Gillette shouted over the roar of the cheering
crowd. "One more hand. Everything on the table
against this." He reached into his vest pocket and pulled
out the watch with a bullet hole through it. "Let's see
how much you value the memory of your old man. He
was trash, and you killed him."

"I tried to keep him from killing you," Asa said in a
voice dipped in acid. "I'm sorry I did."

"You shot him. You turned his own gun into his heart and pulled the trigger." Gillette held up the watch so the hole through it was obvious. "His luck ran out. Even his watch couldn't stop that bullet."

"Asa, no, don't. It's not worth it. You won. *You won!*" Wash's advice fell on deaf ears. All Asa saw was the watch, now slowly spinning at the end of the chain.

"I'd say it's an even wager. The chips on the table against this. You sold it to me for a hundred dollars. It's time to see how much it's really worth to you, Newcombe."

Miss Lorraine and Wash argued. She warned Wash to let the bet go ahead. He felt gratitude to her for understanding what was in his heart, what ate at his very soul. She was a rare woman.

"High card wins," Asa said. "There's no need to draw this out."

"I enjoy drawing it out. Seeing you suffer is half the fun."

"Whose chips are those sitting right there?" Asa knew the right goad to hit him.

"High card," Gillette said angrily.

The deck was shuffled and put on the table. Asa reached over, cut the deck and flipped over a card. A sigh passed through the crowd. Someone behind him began softly crying. It might have been Miss Lorraine, but it could just as well have been Wash.

"A four," Asa said in a choked voice, staring at the card in disbelief.

"I got you, Newcombe. I got you good." Gillette cut a card and turned it without looking.

For an instant the crowd was deathly quiet; then a cheer went up. Soon the saloon echoed with cheers and laughter. All Asa was capable of doing was staring at the trey. The odds had been against him, and he had won. Gillette's luck had run out.

The gambler turned deathly pale and collapsed into his chair. Then he heaved himself erect and left the Silver Bucket amid jeers. Asa tried to revel in his victory. Somehow he had turned into a hollow man, with nothing left inside.

"Where's Edwards? This man's won your poker tournament. Give him his money! Give him his money so he can buy everyone a drink!" Wash kept pounding on Asa's back, and dozens of other men joined in. Bruises would show up later. Nobody cared.

Edwards came over and looked at the mound of chips. Then he reached down and picked up the single hundred-dollar chip he'd left on the table. Holding it high, he made sure everyone saw it.

"I'm still in the game. Mr. Newcombe here didn't clean me out. I propose one more hand."

Asa frowned. He had a million and a half dollars. Sheer attrition of so much money against a mere black chip made him the eventual winner. However Edwards valued that single chip, Asa had a thousand more to trump it.

"You might ask what's on the table worth your considerable winnings. I am betting the entire town of Golden Junction against your cash. All the buildings, all the land, everything. You can be ruler of your own town, Mr. Newcombe."

Asa laughed harshly. He had won. Why would he want to own Golden Junction? It was a failing town; half the buildings were falling down because the people had already started to leave. It was a cautionary tale of what Meridian would turn into if he didn't take the money back to build the railroad spur line.

Before he contemptuously denied Big Ed Edwards his one last winner-take-all hand, Desert Pete tugged at his elbow with urgency.

"Do it, Asa. Do it, if he throws in the mineral rights. You won't regret it. You won't!"

He shook his head. With the money he'd won, he could buy out the mortgage on the Everest and let Miss Lorraine move on. Giving a large piece of the action to Wash Reynolds rewarded him for his help getting here. This much money greased a lot of rails.

"Asa, I'm not wrong." Pete's eyes blazed, and his smile went from ear to ear. His hand shaking with excitement, he held out a small rock shot through with black streaks. He pressed it into Asa's hand. "I'm not wrong!"

"Do you want time to think it over, Mr. Newcombe? One hour. We'll return to this table then, and you can give me your answer."

The crowd buzzed at this turn of events.

"To the bar, boys. Drink up. Get ready for the real showdown!" Edwards had one more hour of selling his rotgut.

Wash and Desert Pete had to help Asa stand. The least he could do was find what the old prospector thought he'd found.

CHAPTER TWENTY-SEVEN

"IT'S CRAZY TO make a bet like that." Asa walked carefully, stretching his legs. After so long at the poker game, he felt more dead than alive. The one thing that worked at high speed, though, was his brain.

He had won! And nothing Pete said changed that or made him willing to throw it all away, at least not without further examination. The Silver Bucket seemed like another world to him, much like his memories of being a riverboat gambler. The present elbowed away the past, even when that was only a few minutes ago.

Miss Lorraine, Wash and Desert Pete walked with him in the bright morning sun. He closed his eyes and, like a newly blooming flower, turned his bare face to the light. It warmed him and made life worthwhile again.

"Look at it, Asa. That's all I'm askin'." Desert Pete fell silent for a moment, then said, "It's not all I'm askin'. You got to take Big Ed up on the last hand and win the whole danged town from him. With mineral rights. You have to be sure mineral rights go with the deed." He thrust the hunk of ore at Asa and kept poking it into his gut until Asa took it.

"What is this? It looks like a rock. A sooty rock."

"That's acanthite. Silver sulfide. About the richest hunk I ever did see, and believe me, I've seen some rich strikes."

"Where'd you find it?" Wash looked over Asa's shoulder but made no move to touch the rock. "There must be mountains of that around here for Asa to risk all his money."

"There are. In the tunnels under the town." Pete hopped up and down in his eagerness to share his news. "A million dollars? That's nothing, Asa. Prove the silver, and you can take that much out in a month. And keep doing it for years. There's a fortune under our feet—and it's not what they call a young fortune. You can be the richest man in Colorado."

"I never heard of silver being mined here, only gold," said Miss Lorraine. "The mine shafts were abandoned before I came to Golden Junction. They played out."

"Of gold. They mined out all the gold. There's signs everywhere of them following the drifts along the gold veins, but that's all they wanted. Gold. This is a hint of the silver to be mined. I know it!"

"If Edwards knows the silver's there, why does he care about the money from the poker game?" Asa tried to work through all the possible ways the town's owner could rook them. "And there's no reason to risk everything. What if I offered him a few thousand dollars for Golden Junction? He organized the poker game, so he's made enough money to move on. He's done with the place."

"It don't matter how you get the deed, but you have to if you want to be really rich. *Really* rich." Desert Pete shoved the silver sulfide ore in Asa's hand again. "You said you were a chemist. Assay the ore."

"I'm an apothecary, not a mineral-assay chemist."

"I found the assay office. The chemist just walked off and left all his chemicals and mugs and things."

"Beakers," Asa said. He slumped. The stimulant potion he'd drunk hours earlier had worn off, leaving him bone-tired. "Show me. I might prove that this isn't anything more than a dirty rock."

"You won't regret this, Asa. You won't." Pete looked skeptically at Miss Lorraine and Wash. "You two can come along, I reckon. If you convince him to win this whole town, you'll be doing yourselves a favor."

"You'd cut us in?" Wash laughed. "Why not? I'm dead broke. Every penny I bought into the game." He looked at Miss Lorraine.

She nodded. "If Big Ed loses the deed to the town, whoever owns it will be my new landlord. I can be on lots better terms with someone like you, Mr. Newcombe." She took his arm and swung him around. "The assay office is down this street."

Asa knew when he was being ganged up on. The easiest way to get them to forget Desert Pete's fool idea was to show the rock was worthless. Pete had already pulled away boards from over the door. The four of them bent, twisted and entered the land-and-assay office. The acrid odor caused Asa to wake up. He remembered such smells from working to learn how to formulate drugs.

"There. There's the equipment." Pete blew dust off a retort. He pulled out bottles filled with noxious chemicals and lined them up on a workbench.

Asa ignored those. He worked his way down a shelf filled with books. A chemistry book gave the recipe for the assaying of silver ores. He lost himself in reading the instructions to perform qualitative analysis, then searched the shelves for the proper chemicals. While Desert Pete watched anxiously, Asa poured the nitric acid into a beaker, added some pulverized powder and stirred the mixture with a glass rod. He finally got a white-powder residue at the bottom of the beaker.

Pete let out a sob. "That ain't silver. It's white. And I thought I had the right mineral."

Asa glanced at him and his other friends. They were as disconsolate as the prospector. He ignored their behavior and asked, "Can you find a balance—a machine that weighs things?"

"That looks like the scale the owner of the general store used to weigh out gold dust to pay for everything," Miss Lorraine said, pointing to a rusty device on a back table.

Asa moved it to the worktable, sloshed the liquid and white powder around in the beaker, then added ammonia drop by drop. The sediment hardened to the point he could use tweezers to move it to one of the pans.

The analytical-pan balance was hardly functional, but he did what he could to weigh the silver from the ore. He looked up the numbers in the book, then started over with another sample. A third time gave him the same results.

By now his friends were antsy.

"Well? Is it silver? You can't keep me hangin' like this, Asa. You can't." Pete almost cried.

"You got a white powder, so it can't be silver," Wash said. "Let's get on back to the Silver Bucket so you can tell Edwards to piss up a rope. Take the money you won."

"Wait," Miss Lorraine said. "There's something you're not telling us. Isn't that so, Mr. Newcombe?"

"The first test caused silver chloride to form. That's the white powder at the bottom of the beaker. I added some ammonia to sediment out the metal. This is what I got." He tapped the analytical-balance pan, then slowly added weights from a small wooden case until the pans hung even.

Desert Pete crowded close and looked at the silver chemically extracted. "So it *was* silver! What's it assay to?"

"The book says a decent mine yields eight ounces of silver per ton. That's not what I found in your ore." Asa rubbed his finger over what remained of the rock Pete had given him.

"It's no good?" Wash shook his head. "It's my luck."

"I make it to be more than forty ounces per ton. I'm probably wrong, but not that far off. An experienced chemist needs to run the assay to be sure."

Silence fell as what Asa said sank in. Desert Pete had found a major silver strike under their feet.

Finally, Miss Lorraine spoke. "There's no time to find one to be sure. Big Ed only gave you an hour. More than half that's gone."

A nagging thought haunted Asa. Big Ed Edwards wasn't above salting a mine, but from everything Asa had ever heard, this wasn't how a mine was salted. Pete had dug the ore from a larger vein. It wasn't silver dust loaded into a shotgun shell and fired into the walls.

"I want to see where you found this." Asa dusted off his hands.

"You want to be sure I'm not joshing you about how much of this is down there? I spent close to a week tracing veins and being sure of what I found. Asa, this isn't even the richest hunk of ore down there. It just happened to be handy when I picked it up."

"Time's almost up," Wash said. "My watch works." He held it up for Asa to see the intricate face and the inexorable ticking away of the seconds.

Asa pulled out his pa's watch with the bullet hole through the middle. It would never tell time again, but it reminded him of better days—and worse ones. What advice would his father have given him about the game, the chance to take a million and a half dollars or risk it for what might turn out to be worthless rock in a dying town?

Although his three companions chattered away, Asa kept quiet. His thoughts were a thousand miles away. He left them behind in the land office as he ran out. Before he realized it, he pushed through the Silver Bucket's double swinging doors and went straight to the table where Edwards sat. The man's watch lid lay open on the table in front of him to show the intricate face. He looked at Asa, picked up the watch, pointedly snapped shut the cover and tucked the timepiece into a vest pocket.

"You had one minute to spare."

"One hand. Draw poker." Asa sat opposite Edwards. Big Ed motioned. Lou Gallant brought over a sealed deck of cards and handed them to his boss. Edwards shoved the deck across to Asa.

"You deal."

"The mineral rights," Desert Pete whispered urgently. He was out of breath from running after Asa. Wash and Miss Lorraine pushed closer a few seconds later. "The mineral rights have to be part of the deal."

"My friend's anxious over what's being bet. All my money"—Asa's hand swept in a wide circle to take in all the chips—"against the deed to the town. All its buildings, the land, the mineral rights, outstanding loans, everything."

"I own pretty near everything. The one or two businesses that aren't mine aren't worth a bucket of warm spit. You can buy them or bring in shopkeepers for competition." Edwards got a cagey look. "The mineral rights now— You know the gold mines are played out?"

"The mineral rights have to go with the deed. Pete here says there's a new extraction process that can get a couple ounces a ton out of tailings." Asa hoped the lie sounded credible. If Edwards started asking questions, he wasn't sure how long he could dodge the issue of metal other than gold being mined.

"Do tell? I haven't heard of any such procedure, but then I've been absorbed in arranging for this poker game."

Asa opened the deck and riffled through the cards, looking for obvious marking. He squared them and shuffled a few times, trying to find shaved cards. That would benefit him, not Edwards, if he dealt. A fan on the table, another shuffle, and he pushed the deck to the middle for Edwards to cut.

"It's agreed? All of Golden Junction, including mineral rights. And water rights, too?"

"You drive a hard bargain, Mr. Newcombe. Agreed." Edwards cut the deck twice.

Asa squared it and dealt slowly. Everyone watched his hands to be sure he didn't deal seconds or off the bottom. He put the deck down and quickly looked at the corners of his cards.

It was going to be a hard-fought game. He didn't even have a low pair. Five unmatched cards. Not much chance for a straight.

"Three cards."

Asa dealt them to Edwards and considered how to proceed. Bluffing wasn't going to win the day. Big Ed Edwards wasn't the kind to run for cover. Besides, with all the chips in the pot the usual maneuvering of small bets followed by larger ones and trying to scare the opponent wasn't going to work. Both of them had to rely on having the best hand.

"Four."

Asa peeled off the cards. He didn't bother looking at them. Instead he watched Edwards' hands. The man started to reach under the table but checked himself when Asa drew his Peacemaker and laid it on the table beside him. Silence reigned in the saloon. The only sounds were the building settling and a fitful hot breeze tripping down the street beyond the double doors.

"Full house," Edwards announced, then turned over his hand. "Fives and sixes."

For a brief instant, Asa felt as if he were floating. His body remained at the table, his fingers pressing down on the fresh cards while he looked down from high above. The giddy sensation passed and his soul rejoined a numbed body. He turned his cards over one by one.

He wasn't sure who was more surprised.

He had kept a jack—and had drawn three more.

Big Ed Edwards let out a sound like a stepped-on cat. He rocked back in his chair and put his hands on either side of his head, as if this held in exploding brains. Words jumbled. He stopped, took control of himself and finally said in a voice flat and clear enough for everyone to hear, "Golden Junction is his. Asa Newcombe owns the town."

"And a million and a half dollars." Asa picked up his six-gun and slipped it back into the holster. "Now that the game's over and won, call off your militia. Folks can come and go as they see fit."

Asa hunted for Lou Gallant, but the head of Edwards' posse was nowhere to be seen. After he had handed his boss the sealed deck, he had vamoosed.

That bothered Asa, but he had no chance to pass along his concern. The crowd of failed gamblers who had vied for the big pot all crowded around to touch him, shake his hand and shout out improbable business deals that no man in his right mind would have considered. As that crossed his mind, he broke out laughing. He had bought into the craziest scheme ever.

He waved to Desert Pete, who huddled with Miss Lorraine and Wash. They made their way through the crush to circle him so he could breathe.

"Let's get to the bank. I want this over with."

"You won!" Pete crowed. "You're settin' on a mountain of silver, mark my words. What's in the bank is a measly fraction of what that silver will earn you!"

They got to the door, where Asa called out, "Free drinks until sundown!"

As oppressive as the crowd around him had been, the earsplitting cheer that went up and the sudden abandonment in favor of the promised whiskey became even more oppressive. One instant he had been buffeted about; the next he was almost alone. He and his friends reeled into the street.

"Edwards! Wait!" He waved to Big Ed Edwards as the man hurried toward the bank. Asa ran to place himself between Edwards and the bank. "Let's see the money."

Big Ed's insincere smile told Asa all he needed to know. He signaled to Pete and Wash to be ready. Even Miss Lorraine reached into the folds of her skirts. He hoped she carried something more than a two-shot derringer, though any firepower would be appreciated.

"I never expected you to win, Newcombe. No, sir, I did not."

"You're not penniless. You raked in a ton of money selling to the gamblers you penned up in the town."

"You're right. I made a few dollars, but nothing like winning my own tournament. You have to redeem all the chips taken in by businesses, and that includes my saloons. As much as a half million might be paid out to me and the other merchants for all the services and sales since the game began. That's just a guess, but it still leaves you a million." Edwards looked around wistfully. "I spent the last five years buying up Golden Junction. It's a loss to give up on it."

They went into the bank. Asa's quick eyes darted about. The guards were gone. Only one teller stood on duty.

"This here's your new boss, Fuller. Open up the vault and get him his money."

"You're leaving with it?" The teller's surprise turned to panic. "What's going to happen to the bank? My job?"

"First things first," Asa said. He rested his hand on his gun. "Open the vault."

Both Wash and Miss Lorraine cried out in anger when the heavy steel door swung open to an empty vault. Asa watched Edwards like a hawk.

The former bank owner cried out, "We've been robbed! How'd that happen, Fuller? Did you steal all the money?"

Asa drew his six-gun and pressed the muzzle against Edwards' temple.

"Don't go getting all scared, Mr. Fuller. I know you didn't steal it."

"My job?" The teller had a one-track mind.

Asa put his worry to rest. "I'm promoting you to bank president. Can you do the job?"

"Why, yes. Yes, I can. President?"

"Shut down the bank right now. I'll tell you when you can reopen. By then there'll be money. And I'll expect to see the books. All of them, if Edwards has kept a second set."

"Why, I don't know. I . . . I'll find out, sir!"

Asa shoved Edwards from the bank, his gun never leaving its spot against his temple. The sun was warm, and Edwards sweat like a hog. He trembled as he tried to make his lie sound more plausible.

"Gallant. It had to be Gallant who robbed the bank. We can get a posse together and track him down before he gets too far."

"Shut up. Gallant is many things, but he didn't rob the bank this time."

Asa steered his prisoner around to the back of the bank and along the trail taken earlier. Edwards began blubbering when he saw the wheelbarrow he had used to move the money leaning against the side of a building.

"He took the money?" Miss Lorraine held a small-caliber S&W five-shot pistol. "If he lost, he'd claim the money was stolen and keep it all for himself? I knew he was a skunk, but this is too much." She raised her pistol and cocked it, ready to shoot.

"Hold your horses. We're going down into the mine shaft Desert Pete found. You explore this section of the drifts?" Edwards balked and tried to back away.

"Can't say that I have," answered Pete. "Did this varmint dump the cash money here?"

"Let's see." Asa herded Edwards into the tumbledown building and down the rope ladder into the abandoned mine.

Wash and Miss Lorraine trailed behind, whispering to each other about what they wanted to do to Edwards. Asa, for his part, enjoyed watching Edwards squirm. He kept his prisoner covered as Edwards huffed and puffed and went down the ladder. Pete, Wash and Miss Lorraine proved more agile. They pressed into one another because of the narrow mine shaft.

"Why are we here? I have a fear of tight places. I want to get back to the surface. I can't breathe! Gas damp!" Edwards' excuses fell on deaf ears. Asa prodded him with his six-shooter along the tunnel to the alcove where the cash had been stashed. An instant of fear cut through him. What if the money wasn't there? But it lay as he remembered, waiting for its rightful owner to take it.

"This looks like the money you claimed was stolen from your bank," Asa said. "How do you think it got here?"

"By wheelbarrow, from the looks of it," Miss Lorraine said acidly.

"You are right, Miss Lorraine. I watched him haul it from the bank and stash it here." Asa pointed his six-gun directly at Edwards to keep him from bolting. The man sputtered and tried to deny it.

"Nobody's going to believe you, Big Ed," Miss Lorraine said. "All anyone's going to hear is how you tried cheating everyone out of their money."

"We can make a deal. There's plenty for all of us." Edwards saw Asa's rock-steady hand holding the gun and swallowed hard. "Look, take the money. Let me go. You won it. You take it and—"

"Grab a bag, Edwards, and help get it out of the mine." Asa gestured with his pistol.

"This isn't what it looks," Big Ed said. His protests lacked any hint of truth. "It had to be Gallant who brought it down here. Me and him look alike. You confused us when you say someone wheeling the money here." He sputtered some more, trying to come up with better excuses when he saw this new lie fell on deaf ears.

"And mineral rights to all this," Desert Pete cut in, ignoring Big Ed. "Don't you go forgettin' the mineral rights."

"I won't, Pete. I won't." Asa gestured with his gun. Edwards got the idea. He grunted as he hefted the nearest sack of greenbacks. He staggered under the weight. Wash and Desert Pete began dragging the other two canvas sacks laden with gold.

"I'll go up the ladder and keep him covered," Miss Lorraine said.

"He's not going anywhere. He can barely walk with the bag on his shoulder. Trying to run isn't in the cards, is it, Big Ed?" Asa poked him with his gun. All he got was a muffled curse.

Miss Lorraine climbed the ladder. Edwards followed her, grappling with the heavy bag. He hoisted it the last foot or two. A hand reached out to lift the bag—and the hand didn't belong to Miss Lorraine.

"Look out!" Asa shouted the warning. Too late. A shot rang out, and Big Ed Edwards scrambled off the ladder and disappeared above Asa.

Miss Lorraine screamed.

Then things got worse. The mine shaft began rumbling and collapsed all around Asa, with rocks and dirt falling to the ground in crumbled heaps. His eyes and nose and mouth filled with dirt, and the weight of the world crashed down on him.

CHAPTER TWENTY-EIGHT

A SA GAGGED ON a mouthful of dirt. He tried to warn the others of the cave-in, then realized they had to know. Thinking straight proved harder than ever before. Arching his back opened a small air pocket beneath him. He spit and gasped and tried to wiggle free of his unintentional tomb. The weight pressed him down too heavily. The harder he strained, the weaker he got and the less air he had to breathe.

He collapsed under the strain, sure he'd die. Then a gust of musty air revived him. Hands dragged him out until he flopped over onto his back. He looked up at a match flickering in Wash Reynolds' hand.

"We thought you were a goner. You've got Pete to thank for us not giving up."

"I didn't believe you'd died, not for an instant." Desert Pete crowded close and began brushing dirt off of Asa's face.

He batted the prospector's hand away and sat up. Propped against a wall, he tried to find a glimmer of light above showing how they were going to get out. He reached back. His hand found one of the remaining bank sacks filled with gold and greenbacks.

"Did Edwards cause the collapse? I didn't hear an explosion, so he didn't set off a dynamite charge."

"Miss Lorraine let out a scream. From the sound, she fired that popgun of hers. Then everything fell in on our heads." Wash helped him to his feet. "We're in a pickle. Digging out looks like a fool's errand."

"You fellows are always such Job's comforters. I spent a week prowling around, mapping these tunnels. I know where the best ore deposits are." Desert Pete made a futile attempt to brush off his clothing. Seeing he only kicked up more choking dust, he subsided.

"And the ways to get out of this maze?" Asa had run with a lucky streak at the poker table. Having Pete there continued his winning streak.

Wash cursed when the match burned his finger. A second light flared and showed more of the tunnel. Asa saw that only one of the three money bags was gone. He pieced the situation together. Edwards had carried it up to where Miss Lorraine waited. Then there'd been gunfire, and everything had fallen in on them.

He was still well-heeled enough to save Meridian. First, he had to save himself. From the flickering match light, he saw the tunnel running off at an angle.

"Lead on, Pete. And be quick about it. Miss Lorraine probably needs help."

"By now she's got Big Ed hog-tied and is using him as a footstool," Wash said.

Asa wanted to see that with his own eyes. They hurried along until they came to a juncture where a coal oil lamp sat in the middle of the shaft.

"I left these all over so I wouldn't have to lug them around. Put that match to the wick so we can get better light," Desert Pete mumbled as Wash tried three times to light the wick.

"You should have trimmed it. I was down to my last match. What if we—"

Asa cut off Wash by pointing ahead to a ladder disappearing into the ceiling. Pete hurried over and held the ladder.

"This here's the old barbershop. The ladder goes up to the back room. We'll be a block or two away from where we went down."

Asa scrambled up the ladder. The rungs held him, but he still reached back and helped Wash up since he weighed more. Then Pete joined them. All three were a uniform brown from the dirt. Asa made no attempt to brush it off. He had to find Edwards and settle the score with him.

Through a side street, they edged toward the bank, went around it and found the spot where the ground had caved in. Miss Lorraine lay to one side. Asa held the other two back as he studied the scene. He silently pointed. A shoe stuck out from under a fallen beam.

"Edwards?" Wash started forward again. Once more Asa kept him from rushing out.

"Watch my back. Something went on I can't explain." He drew his Peacemaker and pressed through the broken wall. Gun trained on the unmoving Edwards, he went to Miss Lorraine. She breathed raggedly. He brushed dirt from her face. Her eyelids fluttered. She came awake with a start. A quick grab caught her wrist and kept her from shooting him. Panic crossed her lovely face, then died when she recognized him.

"I shot him. I hit him."

"Edwards is dead. He was mashed by a falling beam. Where's the money bag?"

"No, not him. I didn't shoot him. Gillette! He was here waiting for us when I came up out of the mine. I fired first, but he's quicker than a striking snake. He fired and hit Edwards. The roof collapsed." She stared at the depression in the floor. "The shaft collapsed, too. Everything, all at once. I must have gotten caught up in it somehow."

Asa called in his friends. They dragged Edwards' corpse from under the ceiling beam, then hunted for the money.

"Not a trace of it, Asa," Desert Pete said. "If what Miss Lorraine says is true, that owlhoot Gillette musta taken it."

"It's a heavy bag. Even after slinging it over a packhorse, he won't get far." Asa stared at Edwards and wondered if anyone would contest him owning the town now. No papers had been signed, but there'd been a saloon filled with men who had heard the deal and watched the cards fall in his favor.

Every step he took caused a cascade of dust around him. By the time he reached the Silver Bucket he felt like a dust devil whirling across the plains. Asa drew his six-shooter and fired once into the ceiling.

"Big Ed Edwards has been murdered. Laramie Frank Gillette shot him down and tried to kill Miss Lorraine." He stepped aside so the gathering throng saw her. "She winged Gillette, but he got away. I want a posse to get him and bring him back to stand trial."

The men milled around. The professional gamblers knew better than to volunteer for a posse, but enough others had bought into the game and were now flat broke so that the obvious question came up.

"How much you payin' fer the varmint?"

Asa rattled off the first number that came to mind. "Five thousand dollars!"

"Each?"

"For the entire posse. Now, go find him!"

Some men rushed out, leaving only the men who made their living from the turn of the cards. One called out, "Does this mean the guards are gone?"

"You're free to ride out. Or find Gillette. If you stay here drinking, know that the Silver Bucket is my saloon and you're buying my liquor."

The man asking touched the brim of his hat, smoothed his mustache and walked out. Asa knew he'd be astride his horse in ten minutes and out of Golden Junction in fifteen. Others followed him.

In a few minutes the Silver Bucket was empty save for the barkeep. He called out to Asa, "You keepin' me on?"

"If you want to stay, I'd appreciate it. How's it sound if I gave you twenty-five percent of the Silver Bucket as your share for running it?"

"Asa, you don't know him. He might steal you blind!" Wash sounded aggrieved.

"Let him. I'll still make more than I did before, which was nothing." He sank into a chair. His new manager came over with a bottle of champagne. Asa waved it away. "Give me some good bourbon, if you've got any."

"Comin' right up, Mr. Newcombe. And since you haven't asked, my name's Davey Larson. You won't need to worry none about what Mr. Reynolds said about me stealin'. I pour an honest drink, and I keep honest ledger books." He pulled out a bottle of fine bourbon from a special stock behind the bar.

Asa leaned back. This was the life he'd envisioned for himself ten years ago. He and his pa had talked about buying a saloon or a sporting house in New Orleans. That was what he had considered to be settling down then. What would his wife say if he told her he wanted to leave Meridian and come here to run the whole town?

He heard Rebecca's protests if he told her about the Silver Bucket and the King's Palace and how they would make a young fortune selling liquor. She wasn't a prohibitionist, but she drew the line at profiting off spirits.

Owning a whorehouse would never be acceptable. He'd have to give that to Miss Lorraine so he could deny having anything to do with it.

He knocked back a second drink. As it burned its way down to puddle in his belly, he sat bolt upright. He slammed the shot glass to the table so hard, discarded playing cards jumped.

"The posse's not going to find Gillette. He never left town."

"Why do you say that, Asa?" Miss Lorraine sat across from him. In spite of the dirt smudging her face and a large cut across her forehead, he thought she was one fine-looking woman. Not as beautiful as Molly Francis but handsome. And then he remembered what he had back in Meridian waiting for him. There was more than beauty there. There was love.

"You got a strange look," Desert Pete said. "You all right?"

"He'd need a pack animal for the sack of money. He stole my horse while I was on my way here, but the gelding's not going to be much use as a pack animal. He's too feisty."

"You don't think he'll worry about stealing what he needs, do you?" Wash scoffed at the notion Gillette couldn't get a second horse or mule.

"It'll be noticed right away. He wants to make a getaway with as little fuss as possible. The money will slow him down, unless he thinks to hide it."

"You reckon he's still in town hunting for a good spot to stash the money?"

"Then he'll ride like the wind to get away. When the fuss has died down, he'll creep back to Golden Junction and get the money. Gillette might think the town will be completely deserted in a few months."

"But it won't," Desert Pete said. "It'll be booming! There'll be a thousand people digging silver from the ground, refining it and every last miner getting rich!"

"He doesn't know that." Asa stood, replaced the spent rounds in his Peacemaker and asked Miss Lorraine, "Where's he most likely to go? You know the town better than any of us."

"Nobody'd look for him near the old rock crusher. Ore was brought down from up on the mountain for processing. When the gold mines closed, the crusher shut down, too. The owner never bothered to even strip out the machinery."

"I'd head back underground," Pete said.

"You know about the mines. He doesn't. You three

stay here. I'll check the rock crusher. If he's not there, I'll come straight back."

"Mr. Newcombe—Asa—let me come with you. Me and Wash." Miss Lorraine brandished her pistol. She looked fierce, but this wasn't her fight anymore. She had done what she could. It was up to him to finish it since Gillette had been his problem for so many years.

He pulled his pa's watch from his pocket and pushed the tip of his trigger finger through the hole. Asa returned the timepiece to his vest pocket and shook his head. When Miss Lorraine tried to block his way, he picked her up with hands around her trim waist, spun her about and deposited her behind him.

"Stay here. This is my fight."

She sputtered and protested, but Wash and Desert Pete stayed with her. Asa was glad to see that his new partner in the saloon, Davey, worked to stop her from inevitably getting hurt. He slipped into the street without further objections.

The sun sank over the far range. Long shadows preceded him as he walked slowly out of town to the rock crusher. He heard rats scurrying about in the ruined buildings. He also heard a horse. Working through the ruins, he found himself climbing a small mountain of gravel. His feet slipped, and keeping traction proved tiring, but he finally reached the top of a twenty-foot mound.

On the next mound over, a man knelt and dug like a badger. Gravel slid down the slopes as he hollowed out a spot to stash the canvas money bag.

There was a good fifty feet between them, from the top of one pile to the other. Asa doubted he could get

off the pile where he stood without causing a ruckus
He stood with the setting sun at his back.

"Gillette!" His voice rang out and echoed through
the deserted camp. "Laramie Frank Gillette!"

He felt some small satisfaction at the way his cal
startled the gambler. Gillette almost slid down the slope
of his gravel hill. He dug in his toes and flopped around
like a fish pulled onto the bank from his safe watery
home. "You!"

Asa made no effort at a fast draw. He pulled out hi:
Peacemaker, cocked, aimed and fired. The range wa:
beyond his marksmanship skills. Almost. He fired
again. By this time Gillette got to the top of his hil
and pulled his iron. He opened up. His target stoo(
outlined against the sun. He was also blinded by tha
same sun.

Asa fired his fourth round. His fifth. His bullet
missed by feet. He had one final round left. One of Gil
lette's rounds zinged by his ear. It had come close enoug
that he heard a lingering buzz in that ear. Considerin;
the prior five rounds he had fired gave him the range. H
fired the last round in his cylinder.

For a moment, he thought he had to reload and kee
firing. Then Gillette stood at attention. His pistc
slipped from his numbed fingers. He toppled forwar
and slid facedown the entire length of the slope. Whe
he reached the bottom, he didn't stir.

Asa took his time and reloaded. Only then did h
slide down the gravel slope and approach the felle
gambler. He rolled Gillette over. His bullet had h
dead center of the chest. About the same place the bu
let that had killed his pa had struck.

"Luck?" Asa considered it. Then he shook his heac

'Fate." He kicked at Gillette a final time to be sure the man was dead. He softly said, "Rest in peace now, Pa."

He pulled the bullet-hollowed watch from his pocket and dropped it on the dead gambler. Then he commenced to climb the gravel hill and retrieve a bag holding a half-million dollars in greenbacks.

CHAPTER TWENTY-NINE

Y OU TRUST US to do this?" Wash Reynolds shoo]
his head. "I don't think many folks will be willin
to let me boss them around."

"You're more than mayor," Asa said. "You're par
owner of the whole town." He sat back, stretched an
felt like he was on top of the world. The past few day
had gone swimmingly.

"I wish there was a way of thanking you for givin
me the mortgage on the Everest." Miss Lorraine pu
her hand on Asa's shoulder.

"You've got a flair for business. Keeping the book
for the Petered Out Mine will keep you busy, but if yo
want to keep the brothel open, well, that's your choice.
Asa saw how she was thinking hard on the offer.

"Pete can't run the mine by himself. He's too bus
prowling about and overseeing the actual mining. It'
take weeks to get the processing plant running. An
the town's seeing growth as word of the silver strik
gets around. By winter, there'll be two thousand peop]

ɪere again. Doing the mine's books and running the
ɪouse will be too big a chore. It'd be all right for me to
ɪublet the house and find one of the ladies to run it, I
ɪuppose." Miss Lorraine worked out how to run things
ɪust fine as Asa listened. She was the perfect choice.

"We should change the name to Silver Junction,"
ɪaid Wash. "Or maybe Newcombe Junction."

"Golden Junction is fine," Asa said. He felt good
ɪith having Wash, Miss Lorraine and Pete doing what
ɪhey did best. He had no interest in the day-to-day busi-
ɪess of running a boomtown. From the first estimates
Ɪiss Lorraine had shown him, he was going to be a
ɪillionaire without keeping everyone under his thumb
ɪhe way Big Ed Edwards had when he ran the town.

"Boss, all ready to go. You sure you don't want me
ɪnd some of the boys to ride with you?" Lou Gallant
ɪtood in the doorway. The sun caught the marshal's
ɪadge pinned on his vest.

Asa thought of Gallant as a wild card, but giving the
ɪould-be bank robber the chance to go straight and
ɪake honest money was a risk he'd take. Henry New-
ɪn Brown had done it. So had an improbable number
ɪf Dodge City marshals. Asa felt in his gut Lou Gal-
ɪnt would, too.

"He's right, Asa. That's a whale of a lot of money to
ɪe carrying around the countryside." Wash chewed his
ɪwer lip as he thought about a million stashed in the
ɪack of a buckboard and covered with a tarp.

"A guard will draw interest over what's in the wagon.
ɪ single driver won't even nudge folks' curiosity bump."

"So you say. You let us know the minute you get to
Ɪeridian." Miss Lorraine frowned. "I forgot. The tele-
ɪraph operator left Golden Junction three months back."

"There's a new key jockey coming in any day now. We'll be wired in to the rest of Colorado again before you get to Meridian," Asa's new marshal assured him.

"Before I get home," Asa said softly. He heaved to his feet, shook hands, let Miss Lorraine give him a peck on the cheek, then spoke quietly with Gallant. "You keep things from getting too rowdy. It wouldn't hurt any if families came to Golden Junction. Women want their children to be safe."

"No gunfights in the street, no, sir."

"Keep an eye on the bank, too. I left a half million for Wash to take care of redeeming the outstanding chips, making loans and starting businesses. And making a payroll," he hastily added. "You and your deputies need to be paid."

This kept Gallant on Asa's side, him and the few from Edwards' militia he had hired as deputies.

Asa's gelding neighed and tugged against the reins fastened to the rear of the buckboard. The mule that had brought him into Golden Junction waited patiently to begin pulling the wagon with its load of gambler and money. Old Abigail proved to be as dedicated as any animal he'd ever owned. The girls would love riding around on muleback once he got home.

Asa glanced back and saw Miss Lorraine in the doorway of the Silver Bucket. She smiled wanly, then turned and vanished into the saloon. He settled on the hard buckboard seat, snapped the reins and got the mule pulling northward.

The buildings moved past slowly, then lay behind. Asa kept his attention fixed on the road ahead. The more miles he put in every day, the sooner he rejoined his family. A glance over his shoulder at the lumps be-

1ind him in the wagon bed made him smile. Those might 1ave been bodies under the tarp. What the money did vas ensure the people of Meridian a future.

And there'd be money left over. Lots of it. The ma-ority of it. As he bounced and rattled along, he built vild dreams of how to use the remainder of his win-1ings. Never had he thought he'd be this rich. For that, 1e thanked Big Ed Edwards. All his days as a gambler 1long the river had been filled with promise of the "big ;ame." It had come, at least for the time. A hundred 1housand dollars had been a king's ransom back then. Vords failed him to describe what he had won.

If the silver mine produced anywhere near the assay 1e had done, the million dollars might be pocket change. Some of the mine owners in Virginia City and the Com-tock rivaled the railroad magnates in wealth.

Asa tried to imagine how his life would change be-ause he was filthy rich.

His daydreams evaporated when he saw the fallen :ree blocking the road. Where it had come from was a 1ystery since two large boulders framed the double ruts 1e followed. He tugged on the mule's reins and brought 1e buckboard to a halt. With two deft twists, he fas-:ned the reins around the brake and hopped down. He :sisted the urge to check his six-shooter. He had done 1at a dozen times before leaving Golden Junction. 'laying it all calm and collected now meant the differ-nce between life and death.

The sun beat down from almost directly overhead. 1hadows would not betray whoever had dragged the ead tree onto the road. Asa edged around to see if 1nyone waited behind the boulder to the left. No one. 1 quick move brought him face-to-face with the outlaw who had bedeviled him since they had ridden into Meridian from the Mosquito Pass depot.

"Riding with you into that jerkwater town way back when, I never thought we'd end up out here." The grizzled, bearded man sounded tired, and his clothing showed several bloody spots where Asa had wounded him. His gut had taken a knife. He moved forward on a leg turned gimpy from an ounce of lead Asa had put into it. The quickly disguised wince as he moved convinced Asa he had dealt a third wound to the man Desert Pete called "Little Wart."

"Did I wing you during the bank robbery? I need to improve my marksmanship. I intended to kill you."

"Shooting me in the back didn't work. See how quick you die facin' me!"

The short man went for his six-gun. Asa shoved his left arm out straight to the side at shoulder level and brought the spring-driven knife into his grip. The move commanded the outlaw's attention. His eyes followed the decoying motion of the gleaming knife blade. Asa slapped leather, got his Peacemaker out and fired. The range was short compared to the shootout with Frank Gillette. The round caught the man in the chest and knocked him back. A second shot to the gut sent him flopping to the ground.

Asa decided a third round wasn't needed. The outlaw wheezed. The first shot had punctured a lung. Pink foam bubbled out from the wound with every breath Little Wart took. Asa kicked the fallen six-shooter away and stared at the dying man.

"I hate you. You're nothing. You . . ." The coughing fit made it obvious he was torn up inside so bad, no doctor had the skill to patch him up. His eyes clouded over. He spit blood and twitched.

"What's your name? All I ever heard was Little Wart."

The outlaw tried to answer. Or maybe to curse Asa. Whatever his intent, words never escaped his foam-speckled lips. He died.

"And Meridian's not a jerkwater town. Not yet. Not until the railroad builds the spur. A water tower is something we'll need so they can haul back the coal to the main line."

He went to soothe his horse and Old Abigail, then hunted in the back of the wagon. A small spade let him dig a shallow grave for the nameless outlaw. Somehow, that seemed fitting to Asa. There was no reason for the man to be remembered, even for the short time a marker would stand over his grave before the elements claimed it. Using his toe, he pushed the bearded out-law into the grave. He landed facedown. Asa began shoveling in dirt, not caring if the man spent eternity staring up at the sky or downward at hell. A few stones laid out like a cross finished his work.

The mule made short shrift of dragging the tree away from the road. Asa clambered up to the top of one boulder and looked around for any other trouble. Little Wart had been left alone after Asa had killed so many in his gang. Whether he had worked for Gillette or been in cahoots with Edwards or worked as a road agent lured to Golden Junction by the huge pot was of no further concern.

Not seeing anyone ahead or dogging his back trail, Asa picked up the outlaw's fallen six-gun and tossed it into the footwell in case he needed a second gun. It took a few seconds to reload his own pistol; then he urged the mule to pull. The buckboard groaned and began its trip to Meridian once more.

CHAPTER THIRTY

SIDNEY EASTMAN FIXED his steel-colored eyes on Asa. Before, that had made Asa uncomfortable. Now he looked down on the world from a mountain of money. No matter how rich the vice president of the C and W Railroad was, Asa had more in the bank. Lots more. Even after the two-hundred-fifty-thousand-dollar payment to license and build the spur line.

"You are part of the negotiations now, Mr. Newcombe? I had thought Mayor Dutton wielded sole power in this matter."

Asa saw Oliver Dutton squirm. Dutton badly wanted full credit for saving Meridian. Asa was willing to give it to him, but he wanted to be sure the money went to exactly what was promised. Lawyers were the only creatures on the face of the earth slipperier than railroad executives.

"Can the line be built before winter sets in? From

the way the storms are already building over the mountains, the snow will be drifted ten feet deep before you know it."

"We are used to such weather, sir. The C and W has three snowplows mounted on the fronts of engines. It is quite a sight when they hit the high country and begin clearing track."

"I'm sure, but there has to be track for the engines to traverse. From what I understand, hearing civil engineers talk, you won't get half the track laid."

Eastman cleared his throat. Dutton found himself ignored entirely now. He sputtered and tried to inject himself back into the negotiations. Eastman pointedly ignored him. This made Asa feel more important. It also caused wariness. Eastman had no trouble ignoring the man who had brokered the deal in favor of another who controlled the money.

"A double crew will put down track at a rate more than twice as fast. You might find it difficult to build a proper depot here before the crew drives the last spike." Eastman's eyes narrowed just a tad. "Putting such additional workers on the spur, however, is likely beyond your financing capacity. It would take another hundred thousand dollars."

"That's not a problem," Dutton cut in. "We have the money. Don't we, Asa?"

Asa watched the surprise light up Eastman's face. He cleared his throat, took a leather-bound notebook from his coat pocket and began making notes.

"Is this so, Mr. Newcombe? Money is no object? I was led to believe you required additional time to raise the amount originally agreed upon."

"No object, yes, no object," the mayor cut in.

"I am pleased to hear that. Tell me, what's the source of this money stream?"

Before Dutton could speak, Asa said, "There's a considerable silver strike to the south, in Golden Junction. The principals financing the Meridian spur anticipate considerable cash flow from their share of the new mines."

"I'd heard Golden Junction was almost a ghost town. Haven't the mines played out?"

"The gold mines, not the silver mines. A huge strike," Dutton said. "We want to get this project started as soon as possible."

"As do all the officers of the C and W Railroad. We see this as a huge benefit. It will give us a foot up on our competition." Eastman scowled and hardened his expression. "You aren't dealing with another road, are you? This is exclusive to the C and W?"

"Oh, yes, Mr. Eastman. We aren't dealing with anyone else. Like you asked, we've kept it a secret," Dutton said obsequiously.

"There's considerable gossip around town, though. The entire population of Meridian is aware of our dealings." Eastman sounded accusatory.

"We don't have much contact with other towns. We're cut off and will be until the spur connects us with the Mosquito Pass depot." Asa maneuvered the talk back to business. Let Oliver Dutton run for reelection after the connecting line was secured.

"That's good, very good. Now, as to the coal mine, I saw no work done on opening the mine."

"The money has been allocated to bring in machinery. Without a train coming here, the equipment must be freighted overland. But it has been ordered."

"And paid for? Your benefactor from Golden Junction is footing the bill to open the coal mine? He must be a generous man."

Asa silenced Dutton with a discreet look. Giving details of where the money came from felt as if it tainted the deal. Better to let Eastman believe a secretive investor desired to pull strings from the shadows. That the investor sat across from the railroad vice president wasn't something he needed to know, even if everyone in Meridian knew. All Eastman had to do was casually inquire to get the full story of the apothecary shop owner winning the biggest poker game ever in the history of Colorado territory.

Asa wanted the man's signature on the line before that revelation.

"He is a rich man who'll own the coal mine."

"It would be useful if I spoke with him. I'd like to make a contract between the railroad and his coal mine. The C and W can ship all the coal dug up along our line and even sell it to settlers and other roads."

"You'd sell our coal to your competitors? That doesn't make any sense," Asa protested.

"It does if we make a big profit on every carload. Another hundred fifty thousand dollars and we can build coal yards for you and furnish the cars."

"That's unusual," Asa said. "We should be paid for the coal, not paying the C and W."

"We'll guarantee top price for every ton. This is money to be put into escrow against your future profits."

Asa tried to work through how this worked, but Dutton pushed him aside, thrust out his hand and shook Eastman's to seal the deal.

"A five-hundred-thousand-dollar payment is a huge

amount, but we can afford it." Dutton hissed to silence Asa. "We have done due diligence. The C and W is a solid company with a stellar reputation. Doing business with such a railroad will benefit us all."

"Here are the documents," Sidney Eastman said. He opened a case and pulled out thick sheaves of paper. "Let me enter the amount of money the town—or should I say city?—of Meridian will put up, change a few dates on completion of the spur line to guarantee connection before heavy winter and then add a few lines about the coal from your mine." He hummed to himself as he went through the dozens of pages of the contract.

"There," Eastman finally said. "All complete. And here's my signature as a managing vice president." He signed with a flourish, blotted the signature and passed the page across to Dutton.

"And here is the *mayor's* authorization, sir. A deal. Signed, sealed and delivered!" Dutton thrust out his chest until his buttons strained on his vest. "A proud moment."

"When will you have the cash? When I receive it, I'll be off to Mosquito Pass so I can telegraph the home office to begin construction immediately."

"It'll be waiting for you at the bank."

"Yes, of course, but when?" Eastman sounded peeved.

"Now. It's ready for you to take now."

Eastman's mouth opened and closed. He might have been a fish flopped up on a stream bank.

"A half million? Why, yes, this is the way to begin construction within the week!"

Eastman and Dutton left the office, talking deadlines and completion dates. Asa felt queasy, but that was natural dealing with so much money. Then he remembered he had not felt this way earning the money. Old habits and his old demeanor had returned at the poker table. Never did he get nervous like this with a deck of cards in his hands. He shrugged it off. He was used to winning money, not spending it.

He left the mayor's office to see how Rebecca fared. She had been sick while he was off in Golden Junction, but the two young girls had done well, taking care of their mother. Telling her the details of how the money saved Meridian would ease her mind.

He wondered why it didn't ease his.

CHAPTER THIRTY-ONE

A SA NEWCOMBE SHIFTED weight from foot to foot, waiting for the train from Denver to pull into the Mosquito Pass depot. A touch of autumn turned the air bracing, forcing him to turn up his collar. Tiny cold fingers still tickled his neck and caused goose bumps. For the hundredth time he drew out his pocket watch and stared at the dial.

"Train's runnin' late, Asa," the station agent said. He leaned against a hand dolly. Usually a calm man, he was on edge today.

"What's the delay about?" Asa snapped the watch's cover shut and tucked it into his pocket. He told himself patience was required. He had a shipment of new chemicals on this train, and there was a small outbreak of chills and fever among the men working to drive a shaft into Coal Mountain. The longer his crew was laid up, the longer it'd be until the C and W began paying for the coal.

"Where's the staging area?" He looked around. It hadn't occurred to him before but a lumberyard had to be placed near the tracks, along with storage for steel rails, railroad ties, explosives, equipment and all the other things a crew needed to lay track.

"Staging area? Don't know what you mean. Wait, there! Down the line. I see the exhaust plume from the locomotion. Finally!"

"What's got you all hot and bothered? Is there somebody on the train you want to suck up to?" Asa hoped it was Eastman or at least a track foreman. The few track foremen he had met who were responsible for the actual railroad construction had been tyrants. They faced the elements, hard rock, impassable stretches of mountain and all the supply problems of feeding their men and keeping them working with a constant flow of materiel.

"There is, indeed, Asa, there is indeed." The stationmaster put two fingers in his mouth and whistled, and three youngsters came running to him. "Mr. Pendergast don't like to see slackers. When the baggage car's door opens, you jump up and unload all his luggage right away. You got that, you scallywags? *All*. Leave behind even one teeny case, and I'll skin you alive." He stood straighter, then snapped, "Now! Don't dally!"

Asa had come to pick up his shipment but talking to the president of the C and W was a bonus. He had questions to ask about when construction of the spur was going to start. He'd gotten no satisfaction from the stationmaster, but the road president had to know. That might even be why he had come to Mosquito Pass.

The third car back was a fancy Pullman decked out with such luxury that Asa sighed just looking into the windows. The greatest European potentate had never seen such opulence. Gilt-edged statuary, fabulous woven hangings, an air of utter serenity permeating the entire railcar. Asa wondered what it had cost—and if he had enough money in the bank to buy a duplicate. He, Rebecca and their children might become Gypsies, traveling every mile of track west of the Mississippi.

His reverie broke when Luther Pendergast stepped down from the car. He spoke nonstop to two bespectacled men who recorded his every thought. Pendergast took a couple steps onto the depot platform, halted abruptly and came over to Asa.

"Sir, let me shake your hand!" The portly railroad president pumped Asa's hand as if it were on a pump handle and he was dying of thirst.

"Good to meet you, too, Mr. Pendergast."

"Call me Luther. Please. I hadn't expected such an august welcome committee." He looped his arm around Asa's shoulders and steered him toward the depot, where the stationmaster and his assistants already stood by piles of luggage.

"It's a coincidence, sir. I came to pick up a shipment from Denver. But it's good to see you." Asa paused. He had the feeling he had met Pendergast before and couldn't place the man. The world had spun by so fast during the past month it had left him woozy. The only tranquillity in it had been returning to Meridian and his family after the poker showdown.

"You don't recognize me, do you? Of course not. There's no reason for you to pick me out from a crowd of other gamblers."

Asa's mouth dropped open. He closed it before he

was accused of catching flies. "You were one of the
bettors at Golden Junction. The pin-striped suit."

Luther Pendergast laughed aloud. It welled up from
deep inside and rolled out, genuine and reassuring.
"You were busy winning the big prize. I came close to
being at the final table. Well, not that close. You cleaned
me out at faro, sir!"

"I'm sorry."

"Sorry? Don't say that. You should exult in your
victory. I had the time of my life."

"A million and a half is a lot of money."

"Pah," Pendergast said. "It's pocket change compared to the budget for the railroad. I spent more than
that on a house in Cheesman Park. I wanted to build in
the Belcaro District, but my wife insisted." He glanced
at the wedding ring on Asa's hand. "You know how that
is, I suspect."

"I never thought about that, but the half million for
the spur seems small." Asa grinned. "It might be a
small amount, but you came personally. When will
construction begin?"

"What are you talking about?" Pendergast's mood
changed. He had been jovial. Now he was confused,
wary.

"The spur line to Meridian. The one Meridian paid
for."

"Spur to where?"

"From here—Mosquito Pass depot—to Meridian."

"Whyever would I want to build such a line?"

"Mr. Eastman said construction would begin with a
double crew before it turned snowy."

"Who's that?"

"Sidney Eastman is a C and W vice president," Asa

said slowly as a pit formed in his stomach. "He took a half-million dollars of our money to begin construction."

"Son, I personally hire every vice president, and I don't know of any Sidney Eastman. Not on my road or any of my competitors. Even that scoundrel General Palmer, who hires foreigners, doesn't have anyone named Eastman working for him, unless he hired him after I left Denver yesterday evening."

Asa's stricken look caused the railroad magnate to fear for his health. They sat, and Asa spilled the entire story. Pendergast moved from sympathetic to outraged.

"This confidence man is besmirching the reputation of my company. This will not be tolerated." He turned and bellowed, "Edgar, get the dicks in the Denver yard on an express train. I want them here by tomorrow morning. There's a man passing himself off as a C and W executive I want brought to justice!"

Asa saw how the stationmaster blanched. "Brought to justice" had a different meaning when railroad detectives used it rather than law officers.

"Right away, Mr. Pendergast." Edgar ducked behind the counter. Seconds later the click-click of a telegraph key sent the message east to Denver.

"There's no spur being built?" Asa felt a cold knot form in his belly.

"Don't take this the wrong way, Asa, but there's nothing in Meridian to merit the cost. Even this coal mine you mentioned, while useful, is not worth the capital outlay."

"That's why Eastman had the town put up the money to lay the track."

"Your money, you mean? If he rooked you out of a half million, you still have a nicely large fortune. It's a crying shame you lost it, but be glad he didn't convince your town elders to run a solid-gold locomotive!" Pendergast laughed.

Asa smiled weakly. "If you'll excuse me, sir, I have to get back to my apothecary shop in Meridian. I have people needing treatment."

"You are a stellar young man, Asa. If you lose the rest of your winnings and ever need a job, look me up. There's always a job for ambitious men with the C and W."

Asa shook hands, but there was no thrill to it now. A half-million dollars stolen! All he had gone through to save Meridian was for naught. This theft assured the death of the town. Asa had some reluctance to moving his family to Golden Junction, but his fortunes lay there now.

Running an apothecary shop was a peaceful profession. Being the mogul running a silver-mining operation harkened back to the days he had been a riverboat gambler. He gathered his supplies, stepped up on his gelding and began the trip south to Meridian. The whole way he looked over his shoulder, as if Little Wart or Gillette or any of the others he had met and killed traveled the same trail.

And worst of all, the wind blowing through the tops of pine trees and through rocky ravines all sounded like demented laughter. Even after he had cleared out, Sidney Eastman mocked him.

CHAPTER THIRTY-TWO

SIDNEY EASTMAN HITCHED up his gun belt before entering the saloon. The sounds from inside buoyed him. He had hit it big. The original scheme had been to have the town raise five thousand dollars and steal it. That hadn't gone well because he had such poor henchmen, but fate had smiled on him when the rube had won the poker game. Never in his wildest imagination had he thought to ride off with the huge amount he had dangled in front of the greedy mayor to start the confidence game.

Every detail had added to the take. A half-million dollars! And now was the time to leverage that money into a real fortune. Where there were miners and fortunes in silver being pulled from the earth, there was opportunity. A half million in seed money could be leveraged into tens of millions in bogus mine deeds and other scams.

He pushed through the swinging doors and looked around. Poker tables were neatly lined up. To his left were three faro tables. The Brunswick bar looked brand-spanking-new, all polished and spick-and-span. He took a deep whiff. Most saloons stank. The sawdust on the floor had been replaced recently.

This was a first-class gin mill.

Two people crowded in behind him, herding him forward. He stood a few feet from a poker table with only one player, who sat with his back to the door. Eastman sneered. Even in a friendly place, sitting with your back to the door invited a killer to step up and cut loose with a round or two. Anyone that stupid knew nothing about odds and playing poker. He walked around the table, hooked his foot around a chair leg and pulled the chair over so he could sit.

"Deal me in."

The gambler across the table stared at the table, his hat blocking most of his face. He shoved the deck in Eastman's direction. "The ante is pretty steep. This is a high-stakes game."

"I got the money. No matter the stakes, I'm in." Eastman reached for the deck to shuffle. He froze.

"Keep your hand on the deck and away from your six-shooter." Asa Newcombe looked up. "It's good to know you've got a lot of money, especially since it's not yours."

Eastman tried to stand. A hand on either shoulder held him down. On his right side, a fancy-dressed black gambler grinned ear to ear. To his left, a man wearing a marshal's badge shook his head, cautioning Eastman not to move.

"Meet my friends. The man with the garish paisley

vest and striped pants is Washington Reynolds, mayor of this fine town. The other is Golden Junction's marshal, Lou Gallant."

"Are you ready for me to count the money and get it into the bank?" A middle-aged woman sidled up behind Asa. She clutched a ledger book. "The mine payroll's due this Friday, and I don't have time to waste."

"And this is the comptroller for the mine, for the saloon, for pretty close to every business in town since I own it all."

Asa reared back. He enjoyed watching Eastman squirm, but Miss Lorraine was right. Time pressed in. He had come directly to Golden Junction from Meridian after speaking with Pendergast. In all his years as a gambler, he had learned one thing: Greed knew no bounds.

Eastman had stolen enough money to keep him in clover for years, maybe for the rest of his life. As Asa had ridden back to Meridian after meeting Pendergast, Asa thought about that and knew Eastman had to swindle his way to even more money. Where better to do that than in a town splitting at the seams with a new silver strike?

Saying goodbye to Rebecca and his girls so soon after returning had rankled, but he rode fast and hard to get to Golden Junction. His friends greeted him but made it clear that they didn't need his help running any of the enterprises he owned. Asa appreciated that and went into the Silver Bucket to wait for Eastman. It had taken the crook only two more days to show up.

A smaller man showed up; he looked unlike the rest of the people crowded around the table, with dust covering his face and clothes. "Is this the varmint? Let me shoot him, Asa. You won't never be bothered by him again."

"And this is Desert Pete, the prospector who discovered the silver deposit under the town." Asa pushed Pete's pistol away. "Don't go shooting him. I don't care how Big Ed ran things before. As long as I own the town, the law will be enforced."

"Take him to the lockup, Mr. Newcombe?" Gallant slid his shackles out and clamped them on Eastman's wrists.

"When he tells me where he hid the money he stole back in Meridian."

"Look, Asa, this is all a misunderstanding. I'm—" Eastman tried to sound like an old friend. The fear tingeing his voice robbed it of any good-naturedness.

"You're a liar. I spoke with the C and W president. He'd never heard of you. Should I turn you over to Mr. Pendergast? He ordered a company of his railroad police out from Denver. They make up their own law and their own punishment. If Pendergast says you're guilty, well . . ." Asa shrugged.

"What do you want from me?"

"You're not stupid. The half million. It goes into the bank here in Golden Junction. Every last dime of it."

"I can get the railroad to build a line to Meridian. I know other railroad owners. General Palmer! He's a personal friend!" Eastman tried to stand. Both Wash and Gallant held him down, and Asa drew his Peacemaker and pointed it at the other man's chest.

"Return the money and stand trial back in Meridian. If you don't hand over the money you embezzled, there're quite a few men in town who can bring those C and W railroad dicks running. When I talked with

Pendergast, he was mighty interested in you claiming to be a vice president of his company."

"I buried it outside town. I— Don't give me over to the railroad bulls."

Asa looked at the marshal. Gallant grabbed Eastman's collar and lifted him bodily. Without another word, he shoved the shackled man out of the Silver Bucket. Asa saw three others join Gallant. This was the entire Golden Junction police force, but by general consent, there wasn't going to be any crime until the good citizens found out if the money had been recovered. Then the fights and shootings would begin again. But now? They were too entertained by the show unfolding.

Asa holstered his six-gun and looked over at the empty stage. The last performance there had been by Molly Francis.

"Wash, let's call that the Molly Francis Stage. Get a plaque and find some first-class acts."

"She'd like that, Asa." Wash settled into the chair Eastman had vacated. "There's an artist I heard of in Virginia City who can paint a picture of her for the curtains."

"Good. Do it." He stood to pull back a chair next to himself for Miss Lorraine before sitting back down again. "What's the good news from the railroad?"

Miss Lorraine cleared her throat, leafed through her ledger and opened it to a page filled with neat numbers and precise notes. She ran her finger down the column, then looked up.

"I contacted Mr. Pendergast and exchanged a few telegrams with his construction crew. The C and W president agreed that any railroad running a line to Golden

Junction could make a fortune as long as the silver mines are producing."

"A spur line from the Mosquito Pass depot?" Asa felt good about this.

"I pointed out that going through Meridian allowed the road to take on coal there. Another hundred miles to Golden Junction opened a new market. We need tons of supplies to feed the miners. Equipment moved in from Denver makes the operation even more profitable. And getting the silver to the Denver financial market is downright profitable for a railroad."

"They'll pay for the tracks?"

"Every penny."

Asa's mind raced. He finally had everything coming together.

"The half million we get back from Eastman? Put it into the bank. Use it to build around town. Make whatever goes up as fireproof as possible. I heard that Victor and Cripple Creek damned near burned down. What else?"

"Drinks all around to seal the deal?" Davey Larson held up a bottle of Grand Monopole champagne. Asa nodded to his bartender to start pouring. Everyone chattered away about the way the town would be resurrected. Asa knew it would, but his home would, too. Meridian. Where his family waited.

Asa Newcombe shook hands all around, let Miss Lorraine give him a peck on the cheek, then stepped out of his saloon into the bright autumn sun. If he hurried he could be back in Meridian in a couple days. He missed Rebecca and his girls. And he had reached a decision. Because of Wash and Desert Pete and Miss

Lorraine, everything in Golden Junction ran like a well-oiled watch and didn't need his personal attention.

He had an impossible amount of money to spend on a big new house, with servants to help Rebecca, built high on the hill overlooking Meridian. And he would still show up at the apothecary shop every morning at seven o'clock. He enjoyed helping the people and curing their aches and pains. This wasn't any kind of life for a gambler, but Asa Newcombe knew it suited him just fine.

Ready to find
your next great read?

Let us help.

Visit prh.com/nextread